The Honey Wall

The
Honey
Wall

*Karen
Latuchie*

W. W. NORTON & COMPANY

NEW YORK   LONDON

For information about permission to reproduce selections from this book,
write to Permissions, W. W. Norton & Company, Inc., 500 Fifth Avenue,
New York, NY 10110

Manufacturing by The Haddon Craftsmen, Inc.
Book design by Lovedog Studio
Production manager: Amanda Morrison

LIBRARY OF CONGRESS CATALOGING-IN-PUBLICATION DATA
Latuchie, Karen.
The honey wall / Karen Latuchie.—1st ed.
p. cm.
ISBN 0-393-05837-9
1. Women—Pennsylvania—Fiction. 2. Identity (Psychology)—Fiction.
3. Unmarried couples—Fiction. 4. Childlessness—Fiction.
5. Pennsylvania—Fiction. 6. Adultery—Fiction. I. Title.
PS3612.A935 H65 2004
813'.6—dc22

2003022549

W. W. Norton & Company, Inc.
500 Fifth Avenue, New York, N.Y. 10110
www.wwnorton.com

W. W. Norton & Company Ltd.
Castle House, 75/76 Wells Street, London W1T 3QT

1 2 3 4 5 6 7 8 9 0

For Barry
boundless gratitude and love

The Honey Wall

Part One

1994

HOW MANY WORDS did Eskimos have for snow? Nina
couldn't remember. Fifty? A hundred? Big flakes. Small flakes.
Wet. Dry. Falling straight down. Coming at you sideways. She
thought that after all those years in Vermont she would have
gained a more subtle grasp of the substance, though even if she
had, it probably wouldn't have done her any good here, in
Pennsylvania. What would Eskimos call snow that would not
melt? Snow that was still two, maybe three feet deep in the second week of March where she and Tony had been led to believe
they would find milder winters.

"Jesus," she moaned, stopping in her tracks, lolling her head
back, her face to the sky. She pictured her tracks receding behind
her, boot-shaped white shadows in the white field. Or they were
coming toward her, as if she hadn't made them herself, as if they

were the sign of an invisible presence. As if anything could be invisible in this endless, staggering brightness.

"This is really enough," she said, her voice low but full of impatience, just in case that was all it took. Just in case someone could actually hear her and reply, 'Is it? Okay. All you had to do was say so,' and the snow would be gone, the river fast and high, spring green showing in damp fields, robins, crocuses, a sun that made its warmth felt.

Snow was a possibility every day for the next three days.

It's beautiful, Nina forced herself to think, and then forced herself to notice the surface of the snow, blown smooth, each crystal defined in a dazzling blue glitter. Frantic trails left by mice in the moments before they were lifted off the ground by hawks whose wings left patterns like feathers in the snow. The brilliant monotony of the flat floodplain flooded in this way. The thin crust of ice crackling under her steps. Her feet disappearing into a foot of dry, powdery snow which rested on top of another one or two feet of compacted, unbreachable stuff, each step bringing up a small spray of otherwise undisturbed flakes. Every movement, the slightest change in the broad stillness, immense. She wasn't blind to any of it.

She was finally nearing what had been and would be again the river's moving edge and what she had trekked down here to see. Great slabs of ice pushed up out of the river by the river itself during a thaw two months earlier. The water had been shallow enough in early winter to freeze quickly and thoroughly, and the thaw had caused it to break into huge pieces, room-sized pieces, small houses, cars, boat-sized slabs of ice heaved onto the banks before the open water froze again and stayed solid.

She'd come down here about a month before when there'd been a foot less snow and the slabs were uncovered, their layered insides revealed in their edges. Strange, glass-like, green-hued, made by time and temperature, stacked crazily on top and against each other, forming river-length ranges of river solidified into small jagged peaks. A kind of northern wilderness look, misplaced in this decidedly mid-Atlantic setting. But now she discovered that the last month's snow had hidden and softened the edges of the ice. What had been fascinating was shrouded, insulated. She thought about how long it would take for the slabs to return to their river-form, and, turning slowly where she stood, about all it was going to take before anything would be revealed below this unmarked slate of white.

Her eyes were beginning to tire from the brightness. She closed them for a minute but her lids seemed imprinted with a lingering impression of light from the inside, and an unrelenting brilliance from the outside. It made her feel slightly off-balance, as if the light had weight and volition, was pushing and pulling at her. She opened her eyes and quickly moved her gaze to the bottom of the line of trees that snaked up the hillside, using the vertical certainty of the trunks to steady herself. She was suddenly yearning for the warmth of her house, which, just half an hour ago, had felt stifling enough to send her out into the twenty-three-degree afternoon. She began to retrace her steps, making her boot prints double-sided, coming and going at once, and then broke a new path toward the trees.

Halfway up the hill Bill's cabin came into view, first the roof and then the rest of it, slowly building down until the foundation planted it just where Nina should've expected to see it, though she hadn't. She'd forgotten where these trees would lead her: just across the road from her own house but needing to pass close by the cabin to get there. She'd taken the long way down to the river, past the general store to the public access track, just so she could avoid seeing Bill, and now, unless she wanted to go back to the river and around—an extra twenty minutes, at least, of trudging—she'd certainly catch his attention. She was feeling too strangely about the story he'd told her over dinner last night, his voice filling the small room for an hour, and then another, her own muted by what she was hearing, by surprise and fascination, or prurience. She didn't want to see him again just yet, didn't know how to fit everything she now knew about him into a neighbors' everyday exchange.

The snow had drifted unevenly on the hill: her feet sank and then they didn't; she was up to her knees or her boots were hardly covered. She had to catch herself from stumbling and slowed her pace, giving herself the time she needed to find each step's footing. Her eyes settled on the dark wood siding of the cabin, finding some distant relief from the snow's glare, but the longer she let her gaze linger there, the more she felt as if she could look through the wall to see herself the night before, entering the cabin, struck immediately by the sense that her presence, her weight and volume, would necessarily displace some of the clutter that covered almost every surface in the room. Only the small wooden table where they would eat was clear, and a little counter space around the stove where Bill was cooking deer steaks and potatoes. In contrast, the walls, smoke-yellowed and stained, were practically empty: a five-gun rack holding two hunting rifles on one wall; a small, ornate crucifix low on another; a photograph from the late 1940s or early '50s—a woman and two men, their arms around each other, easy smiles on their faces—over the wooden table where Nina sat while Bill cooked.

She'd been surprised by the meal, had expected the taste of the steak to somehow reflect the state of the cabin, Bill's tattered appearance, his smoker's cough, the unhealthy cast to his skin. Oily and overcooked, tough and gamy was what she'd prepared herself for, taking a deep, preparatory swallow of the wine she'd brought, and instead tasted garlic and tomato in the first mouthful of tender meat, and then rosemary, none of which she'd smelled inside the tobacco-thick atmosphere of the cabin. Bill had been amused at her surprise, and surprised himself by enjoying the wine, having been a beer and whiskey man all his life, he said. It loosened their tongues evenly for a while: she explained the New York City to Vermont to Pennsylvania route her life had taken so far, her life with Tony; Bill talked about oil rigs in Oklahoma and Texas, Venezuela, and Saudi Arabia. When the conversation fell into a lull, Nina turned to the photograph over the table, intending to ask Bill about it, and suddenly recognized him in one of the young men.

"That's you, isn't it?" Bill had looked quickly at her and nodded. "Who are the other two?"

"My brother Joe," he said slowly, almost as if he were surprised to know. He shot a glance at the photograph. "And Eva."

"Eva who owns this farm?" Bill's cabin was part of the farm, the empty farmhouse part of his responsibility as caretaker.

"None other," he said.

"I didn't realize you'd known her so long." Nina leaned toward the photograph, trying to see the timeworn woman she'd met once a few months ago in the youthful beauty captured by the camera.

"Sure," he said. He turned his head to take in the photograph. "We go way back."

Nina hadn't spent a great deal of time with Bill, but enough, she'd thought, to be sure that his gruffness extended seamlessly from exterior to interior. Yet, with his eyes on the photograph, his face had a wistful look that seemed so deeply ingrained in his skin, Nina wondered how she hadn't noticed it before.

"Yeah," he said, dropping his gaze to his plate, stabbing the last piece of deer meat with his fork. When he looked up at Nina, every trace of the wistfulness was gone. "Joe brought her home on Thanksgiving, in '48. Married her six months later."

"Really? That's so odd. She told me so much about herself the day we met"—more than I would have been comfortable telling a complete stranger, Nina remembered thinking—"but she didn't tell me she'd been married to your brother."

Bill put down his fork. "It's not so odd," he said, looking Nina full in the face.

His eyes looked weak: they were rheumy, the whites almost the same yellow as the cabin walls, but the intensity of their gaze at that moment felt almost solid to Nina, as if his sight had become touch in order to find what it couldn't immediately see. And after a long moment, Nina assumed it had found whatever it had been looking for: his lips lifted into a one-sided smile of satisfaction. "No," he said, leaning back, folding his arms across his chest. "There's a good reason for it actually."

Nina had reached the top of the hill now and stopped to catch her breath. What had Bill seen in her face, she wondered for the tenth time that day, what had she neglected to hide, what had she not even known was there that had made him so certain he could tell her his story?

There were only about a hundred feet between her and the cabin and the farmhouse now, and beyond them, another fifty feet across the road to her own house. Clouds had moved in again. Bill might go to his back door to study them for the likelihood of snow, and if he did he'd also have a clear view across the deer-printed field to where Nina stood, her dark parka clearly marking her an intruder on the white landscape. She imagined she might look like a component of a black and white photograph, high contrast, but its meaning murky. The sky would appear this exact shade of gray. If snow fell now, it might be mistaken for the grain of the film. Nina saw herself stilled in time, on paper, hung haphazardly on a wall. Fifty years from now, someone telling the story behind the image, trying to hold someone else's interest.

She started across the field. It was slow going: the snow had drifted evenly but deeper than on the hill; the deer paths ran in directions that weren't helpful to her. Bill would have plenty of time to see her before she got to the road; but she would have plenty of time to think of how to say hello without meaning anything else. Halfway across the field, snow began to fall, faint against the paleness of the sky. Soft. Billowing. Delicate. Dry. And for all that, just more of it.

*   *   *   *

Nina was startled out of sleep. She banged the top of the clock but the alarm went on ringing. Not the alarm. The phone. Side of the bed. The floor. She knocked the handset off its cradle. The ringing stopped. She got the handset up on the pillow, leaned her ear and mouth toward it, got her arms back under the warmth of the blankets.

"Yeah," she said, her voice something between a croak and a whisper. Tony was laughing on the other end.

"I woke you up, babe. I'm sorry." He couldn't quite hide his amusement.

"What time is it?"

"It's after two. I woke you, didn't I?"

"Yeah," she said, leaving off the 'what do you think?' she was thinking. "What's going on?"

"Nothing." She heard him draw on a cigarette, which meant he was with people who were smokers, the only circumstance he lit up in these days. "I was just thinking about you. Missing you."

"Where are you?"

"Jack's." That would mean a spur-of-the-moment dinner had been prepared for eight or ten. Lots of food and drink, quality lagging slightly behind quantity. There'd be some students, a few other artists, Jack's current girlfriend, and probably a few prospective collectors who would have brought the only bottles of better-than-average wine. Either everybody would know each other already, or, given the mix of ages, finances, and expectations, they would be passionate about each other—adoring or abhorring—before the end of the night. "You should be here. We were figuring it out. It's almost two years since you and Jack last saw each other."

That was fine with Nina; and she was sure it was all right with Jack. "Well, maybe next time you go down," she said.

"He sends his love." Nina doubted it. Tony liked to make nice sometimes. And anyway, she could hear the booze in his voice. He was a strong drinker: if his tongue was at all slippery she knew he was already drunk. "But I send more," he added.

"Good thing," Nina said softly. With her wakefulness increasing against her will, she began to wonder what had happened to make Tony miss her so suddenly at two in the morning. He hadn't called in three days and now in the middle of the night from an apartment full of people.

She heard a burst of laughter behind him, several female voices and Jack's. "Who's there?" she asked.

"Mostly people you don't know," Tony said, but he began to describe them anyway.

Nina tuned most of the details out and let Tony's voice become background to her own thinking. It wasn't unusual for him to go three or four days without calling when he was in the city: he was teaching, the school had given him studio space, he made no secret that he was enjoying the social life that was there for him to step into. But she had called him a few days ago and when he hadn't called back, which he was usually quick to do, her mind had wandered toward an old explanation of what was going on, never quite reaching it until this minute when her thoughts suddenly pushed their way past her reluctance to have them and coalesced: there might be someone keeping him occupied. Maybe he'd had his eye on her for a while—a student, a colleague, someone he'd gotten to know in the neighborhood—and she was there at Jack's tonight. Maybe she had already made it clear to Tony that she found him attractive too, handing him the conquest—Nina didn't think he'd ever had to work for it—which would have made it no less compelling to him. Maybe he'd spent the night flirting with her playfully, or maybe he'd already touched her with just the right combination of tentativeness and demand, and kissed her. He could be deciding now whether or not to sleep with her, hoping that hearing Nina's voice, saying he loved her—he'd be telling the truth, Nina understood that—would prompt him to think twice, a third time, as often as was necessary to keep him from this other woman. Making Nina in some way responsible for his decision.

Nina heard music over the phone. Someone would be pretending to know how to tango. She could picture the light in Jack's apartment: low, but augmented by whatever was coming in through the wall of windows; the Empire State Building visible at an angle, but close enough that it seemed to add its glow sometimes. Nina's eyes were open, but only darkness reached them. Tony's voice wound down. He took another drag of his cigarette. "What are you smoking?" she asked, ignoring everything he'd said.

"What else?" His voice was as soft as hers, but there was a hint of impatience in it. If he'd called her to help keep himself from another woman, he'd probably hoped for something other than a question about his cigarette brand. She had no idea what he meant her to say; she wasn't sure she would have said it even if she'd known what it was.

"What time are you planning to get here on Saturday?" she asked, her voice uninflected.

"Are you angry at me Nina?" he said, his voice suggesting that if she were, there could be no good reason for it, her name acting as a catchall for everything he might be feeling: impatience, annoyance, perhaps his own convoluted anger.

"Tony, I'm half asleep. You're having a party. I'm half asleep."

There was a buzzing silence in the phone for a minute. "Sorry," he said, but Nina imagined he was sorry now only that he'd called.

"So when are you coming home?"

He sighed audibly. "Midafternoon. I've got a crit in the morning."

She could hear him thinking. "Be kind," she said.

"What do you mean?" His voice snapped just a little. Maybe he was still looking for help.

"Your student," she said. "The crit. Don't clobber her."

He said nothing. Another drag on his cigarette, a quick exhale. He would crush it out now. "It's a him. And you wouldn't worry about him if you spent more than five minutes looking at his paintings." His voice was clear again, full of too much liquor and nothing else. "But I promise I'll clobber him kindly. Okay?"

Nina imagined that he'd made some decision about the woman. She closed her eyes and there seemed to be less solid darkness around her then. She couldn't think of anything to say.

"I'm gonna go," Tony said finally. "I just wanted to hear your voice. Go back to sleep."

"I'll see you Saturday."

"Dream about me." Tony had said this to her for the first time nineteen years before, the first night they spent apart after they'd begun to see each other. It had become habit over the years, as if he were afraid that if he didn't say it, didn't urge her to keep them connected on some level when they were going to be in different beds, they might never get back to the same one.

"I'll see what I can do," Nina said quietly. It was clearly not the response he'd hoped to hear: he hung up, gently, but without saying goodbye. She leaned over the edge of the bed and dropped the handset, bull's-eye, onto its cradle. She readjusted the pillows and blankets, turned on to her right side, her left; pulled the pillows out from under her head and lay flat on her back. She was not going to get back to sleep easily. It wasn't simply that Tony might be making the first tantalizing moves toward sex with someone not herself. It was that he felt he had to make a pre-confession. Do it or not, she thought, feel guilty or don't, but leave me out of the process.

She didn't want to conjure up the image of Tony with another woman, but it was there before she could think about it, as if it had entered her head on the ribbon of Tony's voice, punishment for not having given him whatever it was he'd hoped to get from her. The image of him sitting on the edge of a bed, pulling her, whoever she was, toward him, unzipping her pants or lifting her blouse, something to expose skin to his tongue, all thought of Nina expunged from his mind with that first taste.

Sex had become a two-day theme, she thought, and she was nothing but a voyeur. First it was Bill's story, which she was finding impossible to get out of her head. Why hadn't she stopped him when she saw where the story was going? Why hadn't she said then what she was thinking now: that it was too personal, too intimate, that Eva certainly wouldn't have wanted Nina to know those things about her, her marriage, her daughter, Lilly. Nina saw herself at his table, in a trance of listening, attentive to everything but the hesitation she should have been feeling.

And now Tony. She would try at least to imagine him discovering that tonight's woman hadn't actually been trying to seduce him; or that he hadn't been able to come and the woman, rather than creative, had been infuriatingly understanding.

1950

EVA MISSED THE COUNTRYSIDE. In Alsace before the war, her family had had a sheep farm among gentle hills that ran along a river valley. After the Nazis invaded, her father lost the farm and they became exiles, first from their home, then their town, ending up near Marseilles for the duration of the war. She never made the details clear. As long as people understood that her family had not been Nazi sympathizers or Vichy supporters, then that was all they needed to know. That was certainly all Joe needed to know. Eva was so beautiful, he couldn't say for sure that even if she had been a Nazi he would've been able to keep away from her. She wore her coal-black hair like Veronica Lake; and her dark, intense eyes could bore into his, though only when he wasn't keeping his eyes on her body: it curved in all the right places, moved in all the right ways. She had that twisty accent— though she probably spoke better English than anyone in

Overton—and the more-German-than-French sound of it didn't go over well just after the war. But instead of making her shy, it seemed to make her bolder. She dared you to assume anything at all about her. If you did, she'd find a way to put you in your place while she was adjusting your notions. And if you didn't, she showed her gratitude with a brisk warmth that made friendship easy. In Joe's case, the warmth grew less brisk, more languorous, as if she were slowly opening a door to him, and he jumped at the invitation. In 1948, he brought her home for Thanksgiving and she fell in love with Overton. She insisted she didn't like ultimatums, but she'd resorted to one before Christmas arrived: she wouldn't marry Joe if he was planning to stay in Philadelphia, where they'd met, or any other city for that matter. By the time of their wedding in May of '49, he'd cashed in his GI bill and put a down payment on the old Lewis farm on Riveredge Road.

Eva had made a strong first impression on Bill at Thanksgiving. She was an immediate presence in the house in a way that seemed to him even his mother and two sisters weren't. Partly it had been the way she looked: eye-catching if a little too glamorous in a well-fitted dark green dress with a vee-neck that gave just a hint of what it concealed. And partly it was the way she sounded: her accent ringing off the plain walls of the living room as if some exotic bird had gotten happily trapped inside them. But it was also that she made herself at home. If Joe had told her it was a dour house, she paid him no mind. She asked questions of everyone, commented on the house, the yard, as much of the town as she'd seen on the drive in. She raised her voice or lowered it to a whisper for dramatic effect; she laughed loud, touched the shoulder or arm nearest her to make a point. She insisted on helping in the kitchen, and at the dinner table she didn't hide her appetite, or her pleasure in eating. Bill could see his sisters exchanging surprised and disapproving glances when Eva asked for just a little more of those delicious yams after everyone else had finished eating. And his mother seemed to be dabbing the corners of her mouth with the napkin much more than she usually did, her surprise masquerading as manners. Bill didn't do much talking, but he was having a good time, watching discomfort spread around the table like a contagious bout of hiccups. He'd never seen his father look so nonplussed, and he could imagine the old man wondering how in hell he was going to have himself a peaceful holiday dinner ever again with this foreign woman in the family. Whoever could make his father squirm was all right with Bill, so even though he felt a little intimidated by Eva, he was able to tell Joe that he'd liked her right off the bat.

But he had mixed feelings when they came to Overton to marry and settle. Joe was seven years older and Bill had always looked up to him, thought of him as a guide through their family life. The two sisters had come along between the boys, but neither of the brothers had ever been close to them. There was an unspoken division in the family: the girls were the mother's to raise, the boys were the father's. Years ago Joe had told Bill that when Bill was about three, Joe had overheard their mother telling a friend that she'd decided not to get too attached to her youngest since she suspected her husband would eventually tell her not to baby him so much, just as he had with Joseph. It explained a lot to Bill at the time: his mother wasn't neglectful of him, but neither was she particularly loving. Bill had difficulty feeling much besides fear of his father, who was prone to outbursts of anger, cruel humor, or dismissive silence, and he figured his mother must have felt the same way. But he could never feel more than pity for her in her mute, weak response to her husband's harshness. And in his sisters he could see only a dull reflection of their mother. That left Joe for Bill to admire and rely on to mediate with their father and, eventually, to map out a path away from him and Overton. That's what Joe's move to Philadelphia had seemed like to Bill: the first eventual step. Bill was nineteen at the time, still living with his parents and working construction with his father, but he was already imagining how to save up a little money and get himself to Philly, to sleep on his brother's couch while he looked for a job. That's when, he thought, his life would really start, out of this house, away from these people. But if Joe couldn't really get away, what hope was there for Bill? He didn't blame Eva for forcing his brother to come back, but he didn't not blame her either.

When Eva and Joe returned from their honeymoon at Lake George, Bill kept his distance, thinking that it was the best way to hide his disappointment and ambivalence. But Eva was relentless. After Bill had refused several dinner invitations, she cornered him one morning at the general store and, with a smile on her face, told him she wouldn't take no for an answer and if he didn't show up by six-thirty that evening with his hands washed and his hunger huge and ready to be satisfied, she'd find him and drag him by his ear and treat him as if he really were the child he was acting like.

"Can't say no to that, Billy," the owner of the store said after Eva had left. Bill's face turned red inside out, but at six-thirty he knocked on the door of the old Lewis farm.

"Well, if it isn't my shy brother-in-law finally showing his pretty face," Eva said, holding the door open for him. He stepped inside, feeling wooden and speechless. There were lush aromas coming from the kitchen, but Eva showed no signs of the fatigue and annoyance his mother often wore while she cooked. Eva didn't even have an apron on; and she was wearing slacks.

"Here. This is for you," he said abruptly, handing her the jar of strawberry preserves his mother had insisted he bring.

"Thank you, Bill. I didn't know you were handy in the kitchen." She moved behind him to close the door.

"Well, I'm not . . . really . . . I . . . It was my mother . . . I don't—"

"I was kidding." She put her hand on his arm and moved around in front of him again. He felt circled in, but her hand was gentle, and didn't demand anything except that he feel at ease.

"What's going on out there?" It was Joe calling from the kitchen.

Eva raised her eyebrows in mock annoyance. "Come," she said. "He's already sitting. And waiting. And pretending to be king."

The evening surprised Bill on all counts. He'd been worried that he wouldn't like Eva's cooking, but he happily ate everything. The stew had a richness of flavors he wasn't used to, and the noodles had a deliciously extravagant amount of butter on them. The coffee was dark and strong and the apple pie—which Eva called a tart—was still warm from the oven. She made the conversation come to life in the same way she had at Thanksgiving, but on this night she focused her attention on Bill. She asked him about his job, about how he'd done at school, how he liked living at home, where he wanted to go when he left, what he liked to do in his spare time, who his friends were, his girlfriends. He felt uneasy at first, not used to talking so much about himself, and he thought Joe would run out of patience or interest or hear something he hadn't known before and make something or other of it. But Joe concentrated either on the food or on Eva. He seemed satisfied just to watch her, though Bill thought he noticed the satisfaction on Joe's face slowly transform into a look that would require satisfying in other ways. There was that air all around them during the meal, filled with the promise of what was going to take place between Eva and Joe once Bill had left. He felt like a voyeur just admitting to himself that he felt it, but neither Eva nor Joe made any attempt to camouflage it, and at times Bill felt they were doing what they could to make it obvious: certain glances, touches, shared laughter. And was he imagining that their legs were intertwined under the table?

That night Bill began to sense that there were other freedoms besides leaving a place, and his subsequent dinners with Eva and Joe made him certain that this was true. He felt freer when he was with them, something of their spirit—or was it just Eva's?—rubbing off on him. Soon he didn't have to be asked to dinner, he would call on the phone and see if there was room for him this night or that, room inside that thick, promising air. He began spending time on the weekends at the farm too: there was a lot of work to be done both inside and out and the newlyweds didn't have enough money to hire help. Bill was willing to do what they needed done if it meant he could be out of his parents' house and let in on the fact that there were secrets he was adult enough, man enough, to uncover and understand.

Bill liked Eva more and more, liked the fact that even as he got to know her, she continued to be like no woman he'd met before: opinionated, funny, physically strong. And bold in ways he didn't think women usually were. "We're going to make love now, little brother," she said to him on a Saturday night, pulling Joe from his chair on the porch and leading him inside the house. Joe didn't even look back to see how Bill had reacted, as if it were the most natural thing in the world for a person's sister-in-law to say something like that. "Don't you listen," she called over her shoulder from inside the house. After a while he heard the bedsprings moving and Eva's voice—could you call that kind of moaning and sighing a person's voice?—growing louder and louder. He pretended not to listen, but he thought his blush could probably light up the porch.

Eva liked to make him blush. On the day they finished work on the sheep barn, she asked the brothers to hold the ladder so she could bang a nail over the inside of the main door and hang up the picture of her barn back in Alsace. She fussed about getting the nail centered.

"Eva, you think the sheep are going to care?" Joe asked, winking at Bill.

"I care," she said, pulling the nail out again.

"You're a strange woman, Eva."

"That's not what you said last night," she said and gave the nail a solid whack with the hammer. "Or this morning, for that matter." She laughed a low, smooth laugh, not looking down at Joe, who was smiling up at her, up the back of her legs. Or at Bill, who kept his head low as his cheeks heated up.

That summer was no warmer than usual, not particularly different than the summer before or the one before that. But for

Bill it seemed to stretch out, as if the days had new hours, and the weeks new days. Toward the end of August, when he wasn't needed on his father's construction crew for a few weeks, Bill began to spend all his time at the farm. It felt more like a home to him now than his parents' house, and of course he preferred Eva and Joe's company to the rest of his family. And he had always loved this farm. One of the Lewis clan of ten had been his best friend for some years when they were kids, and the farm had been a limitless playground, as it was now in a way. Though now he was also able to appreciate it for its other values as well: forty-five acres, twenty of them fronting the river, the best place in the county to grow feed corn. The rest of the acreage rose out of the floodplain in a broad, gently sloping hill, so from the back porch of the house, there was a long and wide unob-structed view of an easy bend in the river, and the old steel bridge just downstream. Beyond that, the water itself was obscured, but you could see in the cut of the valley where the river turned sharply to the west. Sometimes in the evening the fields were lit by fireflies, or filled with a soft haze that turned moonlight amber. And in the morning the mist rose up off the river as if the valley were slowly exhaling. Bill had never noticed that it was a beautiful piece of land before, and maybe that had to do with being twenty instead of ten, but even so he had Joe and Eva to thank for giving him the chance to really feel the dif-ference a decade can make between a boy and a man.

A solid two weeks of Indian summer drew the warmth into October. But as if to keep some balance in nature's book, there was no smooth segue to the cold: seventy degrees one after-noon, a blowing rain that night, and all the furnaces coming to life the next morning. The first snow fell in the first week of

November and lingered on the ground in a thin cover until the next storm two weeks later, and by Thanksgiving, it looked like Christmas outside. All outdoor construction came to a halt, and Bill went back to helping Joe and Eva pretty much full-time, on the inside of the house now. Day by day, he felt less like the "little brother" and more like an accomplice in an elaborate game of house in which he wasn't exactly either a brother or an in-law, and he certainly wasn't son or husband or father. But given the day and the time of day, he could be a little bit of one or the other, or a combination of some or all of them. He felt like a kind of hybrid, like a new strain of corn they might try to sell you at Taylor's, even though the characteristics couldn't yet be precisely described. Often, if he was too tired to make it back to his parents' house, or the roads had iced up, or he'd had a little too much beer and schnapps, or he couldn't find a reason, but knew he wanted one and that was all the reason he needed, he would sleep on the cot in front of the living room fireplace. Sometimes he was woken by the sound of the river freezing. He knew exactly what made such sound: long barges of thin ice formed in the dropping temperatures after nightfall being pushed by the open current into the thicker ice already in place along the bank. If he hadn't known, he might have thought he was hearing metal on metal, a struggle between machines, and then a violent kind of giving up.

They worked through the cold months, Eva using a saw or hammer or wrench with as much energy as the brothers and with growing expertise. She joked that by April she wouldn't need a man except for one thing and Bill had grown so comfortable that he was the one to put a sly lilt in his voice and ask: "What thing would that be Eva?"

"The thing you wouldn't be asking me about if you were doing something about it yourself," she said.

Eva was intent on getting Bill a girl, inviting this or that one to Saturday night dinner at the farm, prodding him under the table with her foot if he wasn't talking enough or talking too directly to Joe or herself. But these were girls Bill had known all his life, gone to school with, spied on, gotten into mischief with, even kissed and touched. He couldn't stop Eva from trying to match him up, but if he kept up his end of the conversation around the dinner table it was mostly to avoid her kick to his shin. He'd decided even before he met Eva that there was no girl in Overton for him. And knowing Eva had just made him more certain of it. Not because she was the one he wanted, but because she was different enough from the girls he knew to stand for everything he hadn't seen or done yet but intended to, which included girls, or women, if he could manage it.

By mid-March much of the snow cover was gone. On a Sunday at dawn, the river valley had filled with the deep groaning and scraping of the ice breaking up and in the afternoon Bill joined a crowd of people on the bridge watching the ice pile up and explode into collapse, pile up again and collapse as the liquid river came back to life, flowing into spring.

When he got back to the farm later that afternoon, a shift in the atmosphere seemed to have occurred in the house as well. He sensed it as he opened the front door. It was as if he'd walked into the last reverberation of an echoing voice: no actual sound left, just the small push of air as the sound wave took up its last space. And by the time he'd closed the door behind him, the raised voices of Eva and Joe coming from the kitchen in the back of the house were loud and comprehensible. He hadn't

heard them arguing like this before: their voices giving off a
fierce heat, making an intimate sound, more revealing somehow
than anything Bill had heard when they'd made love. He knew
he should go back out, take a drive, do something to give them
the privacy the sound of their voices demanded, but he couldn't
get himself to move.

"I wouldn't have asked for any of it if you'd told me that the
money was getting low," Eva shouted in response to something
Bill hadn't heard.

"I'm trying to take care of you, Eva—"

"I don't need to be taken care of, Joe," she cut in. "You think
I can't do without things when it's necessary? Did you already
forget what was happening to me before you ever thought about
fighting the war?"

"No, Eva. I didn't forget. But you're not there anymore. I
should be making the hard decisions now. For both of us."

"Oh Joseph, please. You make me feel like I'm talking to a
boy. You think this is taking care of me? Handling things badly?
Not telling me that the money, *our* money, is running out? You
want me to see what a big, generous, strong man you are, and
now you're going to be away so much you could be a little, weak,
squeaky man and I wouldn't know the difference."

Before Bill had a chance to move, Eva was coming down the
hall toward the front of the house. She saw him immediately and
kept her eyes on him but said nothing. He wanted to apologize
for being there, for having overheard, for being careless enough
to let her find out he'd overheard, for something, anything, to
take the anger and indignation—and what was that other note,
fear?—out of her voice. But her gaze silenced him: it was stern
and unapproachable, and it seemed to be telling him that he

might play in their life, but he wasn't really part of it; that he was no more than "little brother"; that he could do nothing now. He stood where he was without moving a muscle until she had gone upstairs and he heard the bedroom door close. He took his boots off slowly and quietly, hung his coat and hat on one of the hooks by the door, and went to the kitchen. Joe was staring out the back door smoking a cigarette. It didn't seem at all odd that he hadn't heard Bill come in. Bill poured himself a cup of coffee and turned to offer Joe a cup, but he was already halfway out the door.

Where there had been the heat of argument on the day the river broke, for the next few days there was an icy silence, as if indoors and out had exchanged weathers. Bill felt invisible and uneasy, just as he often did at his parents' house. And Joe and Eva suddenly seemed much older to him, more akin to his parents than himself. But even more unsettling was how much Joe looked like their father in the silence: sullen and mean around the eyes, his mouth pinched around the cigarettes he was lighting up one after another; just like their father did when he was angry, as if the cigarette would stop up words that might be uncontrollable otherwise. At meals, Eva directed all her words toward Bill, but they were perfunctory and expressionless and, he could tell, only meant to make Joe feel excluded. He decided it was time to spend a few days with cousins in the next county who he hadn't seen in a while, and when he got back to the farm, Joe and Eva were talking again. But they were more civil than affectionate with each other and at the dinner table, Bill felt a little like a kid trying to be invisible in the presence of adults.

While they were driving into town the next day, Joe insisted on telling Bill what the argument had been about: the money Joe and

Eva had planned to buy the sheep with was pretty much gone. Eva blamed Joe, but he'd only been trying to do what she wanted: fix the barn just so, the house a certain way, get the place ready for geese and hens, and the apple trees she wanted. Bill listened, but he suspected that there were other drains on the money Joe wasn't talking about. A buddy of Joe's in Philly had given him a taste for poker with serious stakes, and there'd been a weekly game up in Wellspring for years. But Bill wasn't really interested in the details: the sound of the voices he'd heard from the vestibule the day of the argument, the fierceness of them, still lingered in his head: as if the previous months had never occurred, as if the pleasure Eva and Joe had taken in each other had risen up out of nothing and subsided into nothing, meant nothing. And he couldn't get out of his mind the look in Eva's eyes when she'd seen him in the vestibule, putting him in his place, making him deserve the same anger she was feeling toward Joe. All of that would have been enough to dampen his curiosity about what had happened between them, but there was this other thing again too: the similarity in Joe to their father. The disdainful edge to his voice, as if Eva wasn't only wrong, but idiotic to think what she did, because it was impossible that he could be wrong. Their father never admitted he was wrong either, even when the consequences of a mistake had landed at his feet; never apologized; made sure their mother carried the blame for most problems and mistakes. The same edge that was in Joe's voice now, sawing away at the space inside the car. Bill had stopped hearing the content of Joe's sentences; only the sound, the tone of voice reached him. But when Joe said he'd taken a job on a crew in New Jersey, Bill's attention was grabbed. He'd be away during the week, Joe said, earning extra money doing night watch on-site.

Houses were going up by the dozens in Jersey and Joe'd be making good money, which was what they needed most now. And he'd be home on weekends. He knew it would be hard on both of them but he didn't have a choice: he had to get money. And yet Eva was still angry as a hornet, Joe said; he couldn't understand it, couldn't understand how she could be so damn angry at him when they were both responsible.

Joe pulled a cigarette from a pack on the dashboard, his eyes twitching from the road to his brother's face and back. "What's the matter?" he asked, holding the cigarette in his teeth as he maneuvered a match to strike. "You're looking at me just like Eva did."

"Well, what about her?" Bill asked, and thought: What about how you seemed to love each other last week? What about the fact that you suddenly resemble the old man? "I mean, what is she going to do?" It was all he could get himself to say.

"She'll be fine." Joe threw the matches back on the dashboard. "Just like she likes to tell me over and over again. She's handled harder things in her life. She'll get used to this." He flicked his hand, cutting the conversation short.

1994

NINA DIDN'T ENCOUNTER Bill when she walked across the snow field past his cabin. But two days later, late in the afternoon, he knocked on her door and presented her with a bag of kale he'd just picked from his cold frame. She had no time to consider her discomfort: she just managed to squeak out an invitation before needing to step aside and make way for him. He hadn't been in this house for fifteen years, he said, not since the Swifts moved out. He was taking in everything he could, his neck craning while he stamped the snow off his boots onto the rug just inside the door. Nina helped him off with his coat and looped it over one of the wall hooks. The smell of his cabin—cigarette smoke, old cooking, over-used air—rose up out of the fabric. Everything she'd been breathing the night he told her his story, and when he'd finished, everything she had pulled into her lungs suddenly, taking a full breath for the first time in an hour, maybe longer. The thickness of odors, and with it something like the lingering substance of Bill's words, as if they'd been hovering over the table, waiting, like parasites, for the proper host. She'd stood up quickly, accidentally banging her chair against the wall, wanting to shake herself loose from her posture of listening, the table, the added weight of his words inside her. He had refused her offer of help with the dishes, so she'd watched him, expecting, in vain it turned out, that something about him—his stooped back, slow gait, maybe his old man's thin-skinned scalp—would tap the sympathy in her that might have undercut her growing uneasiness with the fact that he'd revealed so much to her, little more than a stranger to him. A little later, he'd helped her on with her coat, thanked her for her company, and as she'd walked across the road to her house, she thought she could smell the cabin, the odors caught inside her nose, her lungs. And here they were again—odor, sensation, atmosphere—as overpowering to her as they were unnoticed to Bill.

"What the hell's this?"

Nina jumped at the sound of Bill's voice, her hands letting go the grip they'd tightened on the coat. She followed him into the dining room where what she'd been working on sat in the middle of the table.

"It's a contraption." Bill looked at her quizzically. "A toy," she said. "I guess." She never knew how to explain them.

Bill was peering at it closely. He touched the small coiled tower gingerly. It wobbled. "What's it do?" He clasped his hands behind his back.

"Nothing yet." She turned the structure around so that what would be its front was facing them. The whole thing wobbled and shimmied, but it hung together. She bent down to point. "When it's done, you'll release a little ball at the top of the coil, and when it gets to the bottom it'll depress this platform, which will open this hinge." She looked up at Bill's still puzzled-looking face. She straightened up. "It's a Rube Goldberg kind of thing. In the end, there'll be a small ball that goes through this hoop."

Bill nodded intently. Nina reminded herself that here was a man who had built oil rigs. She felt like a kid at show and tell with a somewhat tolerant teacher.

"I was just about to have some wine," she said, reclaiming some adulthood. "Would you like a glass?"

"I wouldn't argue with a beer if you have it."

Bill looked with suspicion at the bottle Nina handed him—Saranac Black and Tan—but mumbled "Not bad," after his first quick taste. They sat in the living room.

"So you made that thing? The toy?"

"Yeah. I've been building them for years."

"What do you do with them?"

"There's a store back in Vermont not far from where we lived that sells them for me."

"Is that right?" He took a drink of the beer, looking around the room. Nina didn't think the sparseness would appeal to him, though the clutter she was letting accumulate in Tony's absence might make him feel at home. "Well, the place certainly looks different than when the Swifts were here." Nina smiled her appreciation of his tact, though she wasn't sure he noticed. He was craning his neck again, looking toward the back of the house. She obliged his curiosity with a tour, downstairs and up. Bill carried his beer and nodded at each room, commenting on what had been, conjuring a past in which Nina was an intruder.

She started downstairs but he didn't follow her until he'd finished talking into the last of the bedrooms.

He peeked back at the contraption before joining her in the living room.

"Didn't you tell me you were a car mechanic?" he asked, lowering himself slowly onto the couch.

"I was. But I lost interest when cars started to be about electronics. I'm still good with the older ones, but I'm useless on the new ones."

"Old ones like that Spitfire your husband whips around in, huh?"

"Yeah, I take care of the Spitfire." Did it matter that Bill had gotten Tony wrong? Probably not. "Tony's not my husband," she said anyway.

"Oh. I thought you said you were married a long time."

"We've been together a long time, but never married."

"How long is a long time?" He seemed to expect her to give him an answer that would prove she was a little naive, a tyro at this life he had much more experience in.

"Nineteen years."

Bill nodded his head slowly, his eyebrows shifting upward. "Cradle-robbing," he said, his gaze slipping down from her face to her body.

"I was twenty-three. Old enough." The bite of her voice pulled his eyes back to her face.

"Was he your professor?" The sound of a leer was just perceptible in his words.

"No." She would keep the bite in her voice. "We met at a party."

"Nineteen years ago."

"Uh-huh."

"That makes you forty-two."

"That's right."

"I wouldn't have believed it."

"That's very kind of you to say. Thanks."

"Not kind at all." He took a last drink of beer and pushed himself up. "You'll have to tell me that story over our next dinner," he said and winked.

"Which story?"

"About you and Tony meeting."

"I just did," Nina said slowly.

Bill was at the door. "When's that not-husband of yours coming home?" He took his coat off the hook and swung it around his back, grunting to get his arms into it. Nina smelled the cabin again. She coughed involuntarily.

"Saturday," she said.

"Maybe I can get him to tell me the story." A sly smile on his face. "Thanks for your beer."

"You're welcome. Thanks for the kale."

"Fry it up in some oil and garlic," he said, going down the front porch stairs. "It's good for you." He walked slowly to the end of the driveway, stopped to light a cigarette, and continued across the road. Nina watched him until he disappeared around the corner of his cabin. She wondered what he thought he would hear in her and Tony's story, imagined his disappointment in how plain and straightforward it actually was: A run-down apartment on the Upper West Side of Manhattan in December of 1975. A typical Saturday night gathering: a mass of people crammed into a place where there was enough dope of one kind or another to get at least twice as many people high. In fact, half of her memories of the night were just elaborations on sketchy, drug-infused recollections which no one else could possibly care about. Even Tony's interest in the details of that night was limited.

Bill had been out of sight for some time and there she was, still standing at the door, lost in the thoughts he had suggested she think. She walked back toward the dining room, picturing Bill standing over her contraption with his hands held behind his back, either respectful or mocking. She couldn't decide which. Would he stand over her too, if she told the story he wanted to hear? His look the barometer of her success at satisfying his curiosity, as he probably believed he had hers with his story. She didn't imagine he'd care about the details that interested her: the way the light from an overhead fixture in the living room of that apartment, the room with the most people packed into it, spilled over everybody's heads onto the collective shelf of shoulders, most of the light caught there, but a few rivulets dripping down to a clavicle or the front of a torso, and nothing getting past the hips, the darkness at the floor creeping up at least that far. That she could see this effect because she'd been deposited on the one couch in the room by the movement of the crowd, spun slowly out of it by an imperceptible centrifugal force. That the voices had been a huge din, but the music, something Motown or Stax—this detail forever unclear—had been even louder. That a television was on in one corner, its sound turned off, *Fellini's Satyricon* unfolding across its black and white screen. She thought, for starters, Bill would be more interested to hear how she had made sure Tony saw her when they'd approached each other in the long hallway that led to the living room. She'd had her hair gathered in one hand, but as Tony approached her—her attention grabbed, his eyes not yet on her—she let go, knowing her hair would spread slowly from its twist and fan out around her face, fall halfway down her back, the color, chestnut and red in equal measure, catching his eye, seducing it to linger, to move to her face, wildly delicate inside the frame of hair, and into her own eyes, the green there seeming to deepen even as they narrowed in intent—or so some other man had once narrated to her about herself. Tony had been leaving, but he turned then and followed her back into the massed bodies.

She imagined she would have to concentrate on the seduction to keep Bill's interest. Move through the next hour, get to the moment when, still nameless to each other, Tony had muscled them a small circle of space at the center of the crowd, and ignoring the music that was playing—still probably Motown or Stax—invited her into a close, slow dance, which she accepted by putting her left hand on the back of his neck and spreading her fingers down inside his collar. He put his right hand on her back just at the top of her pants, under her shirt. His left and her right hands were clasped and pulled close and, though minutes before they'd been separated by a roomful of people, there was no space between them now. They put their lips to each others' ears and their cheeks touched in between. Names were finally exchanged, the soft heat of their faces, the instantaneous yearning for more.

Nina quickly felt swathed in Tony's body which seemed to be observing hers, discovering everything, every part of him somehow touching her, more than one sense in his touch. She thought of what other people might see if they were looking, what her body looked like moving together with Tony's, the stark intimacy they had found. The thought of other eyes on them made the intimacy more intense for seeming less private, and so tantalizing that something Nina wasn't even aware of having held back, let go. She felt Tony's hand move slowly then, farther around her back, his thigh move between hers. He opened the palm of her hand and moved his lips across it, a caress never quite fulfilling the promise of the kiss it finally didn't need.

She would tell Bill what Tony had told her later that night. That her fingers had found the most sensitive part of his neck. That the skin on the small of her back was so fine it made him anxious to know all of her skin. That at some point he felt the last measure of hesitancy leave her body, leaving it somehow smoother against his, and he'd let his hand move slowly then, farther around her back, until he imagined himself encircling her completely, spinning out the filaments of a cocoon, and at the last second, the last silk floating toward its mark, sliding inside it with her. That the difference between their dance and stillness gradually became imperceptible, dance no longer an excuse for their embrace which finally signified nothing but their desire to be embracing. That they had spent that night and the next day making love, staying high, unsatiated, brilliant with each other's bodies. That sometime in those twenty-four-plus hours she began to feel, not altogether comfortably, that more than their bodies were involved, that their lives were beginning to intertwine, already showing the complicated intensity of a stubborn knot.

"Sounds like us."

Nina spun around from the table. She could've sworn that that was Bill's voice. But of course—"Of course," she said out loud—it had been in her head. No one was there. Not Bill, and not Tony, who had actually said those words years ago, when he'd overheard her complaining about a knot she couldn't undo in a twist of wire she'd been using in one of the contraptions. Fucking knot, she'd said. Sounds like us, Tony had said.

She sat down at the table. Her sudden movement before had knocked the contraption down, and the hoop, which she hadn't put permanently into place, was knocked off. Maybe she'd leave it off. Break the whole thing down even more. Start again, make it a perfect small replica of an oil rig. Collapsing.

She didn't have to tell Bill anything.

*   *   *   *

Nina woke up Saturday morning with her head full of Tony: angry about his phone call four days before, anxious to have him home already, unable to pin down which feeling was stronger. He'd been gone for almost two weeks: a long time to be apart, though she imagined that the time hadn't felt as long to him as it had to her, for all kinds of reasons. She threw the covers off and got out of bed. The sight of him coming through the door later that afternoon would push her one way or the other. In the meantime, she needed to take care of the house.

Downstairs, in the kitchen, she lingered over a cup of coffee. Clutter made Tony crazy, and she was a wizard at creating it, especially when she was working on a contraption. She liked having all of her supplies around her: small appliances to be stripped for parts, and all manner of found objects, anything that might function to make a small piece of engineering amusing, everything out of the containers so she could see what there was. In Vermont, each of them had had an outbuilding to use:

Tony for his studio, and Nina for her shop, as she insisted on calling it; but here, the one barn was given over to Tony. Nina used the largest of the three bedrooms as a work space, but it felt tiny in comparison to the shop, and her supplies were stashed all over the house, orderly only because there was no alternative. When Tony was away, she spread out and let the house attain at least some of her shop's comfortable chaos, but she always got to this point: Tony's imminent arrival taking the comfort out of the equation. And today she thought it would be wise to create a more neutral ground than this mess would appear to be. Better to not give him something to read into before she knew what she wanted him to read.

She took a final sip of coffee and turned to the sink which was brimming with dirty dishes. She ran the water but her hands immediately felt slow and clumsy. She did not want to be doing this. She did not want to move back upstairs to her cramped room with its great view of Tony's roomy studio. They'd rushed to winterize it just after they'd moved in, but he'd hardly used it since, having found more to keep him in the city than he'd anticipated. She let a fistful of silverware drop noisily into the sink. She could hardly remember why she'd agreed to make the move to Pennsylvania. It had been a great idea for Tony—he'd be teaching fewer classes at Cooper Union than at Cannen, have more time for his own work, have the kind of constant connection to New York that he'd been missing more and more. The move was going to be good for his career, and he'd be getting a better salary, but he'd nonetheless seemed to understand Nina's reluctance. She'd been surprised eighteen years before to find herself loving the country, but her feelings hadn't wavered since. She'd passed almost her entire adult life in Vermont; it was part of the way she thought of herself in the world now. So they hadn't jumped to the decision, and Tony had even suggested that if, in the end, Nina felt she couldn't make the move, he would rent a small place in the city, and they'd find a way to afford it.

"On the other hand," he'd said one evening in her shop, "I'll go mad without you." Nina had said nothing for a minute while she took in his smile, sly and sweet. The look in his eyes told her he liked the sound of the eighteen-year-old echo he knew she would hear in the words, as if they could telescope those years down to an instant between two declarations of the same heart. As if they could enter her in the same way they had eighteen years ago when they'd become part of the reason she'd decided to try to make a life with him, even though it had meant leaving the city, her friends, the only life she'd ever known, the only one she could imagine for herself then. Now his words only reminded her that what each of them was capable of doing for and to the other was nothing like what they'd imagined eighteen years before.

"You go mad with me," she said finally.

He leaned toward her. "One madness over another," he said, and kissed her at the corner of her lips. "I'm going to start dinner," and he walked out of the shop, leaving the door open behind him. Nina felt as if his kiss had bolted her to the seat; she sat perfectly still. She became aware of the peepers, their sound making its way up from the pond, growing in complexity as it grew in volume. Usually, she could hear a kind of music inside the cacophony of that sound, but just now it was a wash: high and ringing, frantic. She put down the wire cutter she realized she'd been gripping tightly the whole time Tony had been there.

She took her time closing up the shop and walked toward the house. She could feel the gentle brand of Tony's lips at the corner of her mouth. She wondered if evening light in Pennsylvania would take on this same azure blue in the moments before true darkness. As she neared the porch, the sound of the peepers began to fade, and what was left was the music of it. Real madness, she decided, would be she and Tony having separate homes again, now, after so much time and so much else.

But six months after the move, Nina wondered if they hadn't set up separate homes anyway. This corner of Pennsylvania had been the compromise: only two hours to New York, yet just as deeply, if differently, rural as Vermont. But all the time Tony was spending in the city, the reasons for it: he might just as well have moved in with Jack, given how often he crashed there. She turned her back on the sink, her hands dripping soap on the floor. The living and dining rooms with all their mess were visible from where she stood. She turned off the water, dried her hands, threaded the dish towel through the refrigerator handle. She slapped the kitchen light off and moved to the dining room table: stuff, and a seemingly endless supply of it; all hers; all out of place; all waiting to be ordered, packed, and stowed. She grabbed a pen and a piece of paper and wrote in large, block letters: WELCOME HOME OUT WALKING BACK SOON, and hung it where Tony would see it when he came in the door.

She walked only a couple of miles downriver and back but she walked slowly, keeping her attention close on the river: on the formations of the ice, the herringbone of deer prints across its width in certain spots, the muskrat scrabbling around a small patch of open water. She hadn't seen open water since mid-January, but she refused to let herself feel hopeful about winter's end. She stopped frequently to listen to what finally amounted to silence: a brief gust of wind, dry branches crackling quickly against each other, a jet she couldn't see, a car on the road behind her, but mostly no sound at all, the air as still and empty as it was frigid. And, in any case, none of it, sight nor sound, was enough to keep her mind off Tony. Approaching the house, seeing his car in the driveway shrouded in the quickly fading daylight, she thought how it could almost have been a continuation of her thinking, a conjuring, her unbreakable train of thought having managed somehow to transport him up out of his own reality and deposit him in hers. She liked the image: Tony finding himself in the center of the house, not at all sure how he got there, or even where *there* was for the first few confused moments, but aware of some pull on him, growing stronger and closer. And he would look out the front door and see her cresting the last small hill to the house and realize where he was and wonder at the power that had gotten him there, humbled to such an extent that he would apologize immediately and profusely, for everything, including those things he couldn't pinpoint but knew he needed to make amends for anyway.

The image worked to amuse Nina for an instant but then she caught sight of smoke coming from the studio chimney: Tony had already made his way out of their shared world—nothing compelling enough to keep him in the house to wait for her— and into his own. She went into the house and saw her note to him amended: WELCOME BACK YOURSELF. OUT ~~WALK-ING~~ PAINTING. COME BACK THERE SOON. He'd clearly had no sense of the agitation and annoyance that had pushed her out of the house earlier. The brevity of the note, which she'd intended to hint at her state of mind, had apparently communicated nothing—besides its possibilities for co-opting—and, she had to figure, neither had the chaotic state of the house. Tony had dropped his bag in the middle of the dining room table, next to the contraption, amid the clutter of her supplies. Maybe he'd been taking a look at the toy and been so delighted by it that he failed to notice what would have otherwise made him crazy; or maybe he'd just swept through the house from the front to the back door, too inside his own head to notice what she'd intended him to see, some idea about a painting so involving that he failed to notice that she'd left the house in fuck-you condition.

She went out the back door and followed the path through the snow toward the studio. From a distance she could see through the window that Tony was sitting at his worktable, his back to her and bent over what she assumed was one of his notebooks, since the position of his head told her he was writing not drawing. He had pulled one of the standing lamps to his side, creating a narrow pool of light to sit in. With the window framing him, and the darkness solidifying around it from the outside, he seemed to be the subject of a painting, of one of his own if Nina let her eyes blur, dissolving edges and image and abstracting his figure. A painting like many of his in which the colors had been laid down in such a way that white seemed to shed light off the canvas so it could turn back and illuminate the whole thing from a distance. She never understood how he did what he did with paint, no matter how many times he thought he'd explained it; she couldn't see what it was he saw when he was working, she couldn't understand how he saw, why one color or line or juxtaposition was right and not any other. She could only see that it was right. Years ago she'd sit in his studio and watch him work: he didn't mind, and at first she thought it was because he liked having her there. But she quickly came to understand that he stopped being aware of her altogether once she'd settled into a chair or onto the floor. She wasn't there for him then; nothing was except the canvas, and as the painting progressed he seemed to grow more and more attached to it, less and less part of the world around him. She learned to wait for him to want to show her a finished or almost finished painting, when he would stand back from the canvas while she looked, and she could approach it, enter it in her own way, without having to make her way past him, or understand how to go through him. Without being invisible to him. But this vision of him, now, through the window, inside the frame of light inside the frame of the window's rectangle, the painter and the painting as inseparable as possible, put her at that old distance. As much as Tony might have thought he wanted her to join him in the studio, she knew she'd be an intrusion. She turned and went back into the house, and carried boxes of her stuff to the closet upstairs in her workroom. Looking out the window she could see the studio: Tony bent over his notebook, a glow of light encasing him, the window encasing the scene, and night the final encasement.

1950

A FEW DAYS after hearing Joe's side of his argument with
Eva, Bill found himself alone with her in the kitchen after a
particularly tense breakfast. Joe had announced that he'd
decided to leave a day early for the new job, so he could get settled into the trailer before the week started. Eva had said nothing in response, and then nothing for the rest of the meal. Now
she began talking as she cleared the table. Bill was finishing a
cup of coffee.

"That brother of yours can't seem to learn the first thing
about being married. He thinks it's all about the bedroom." She
spoke softly, walking between the table and the sink. Bill kept his
eyes on the back of her head or on her mouth, whichever was
facing him. "Once we get the sheep, he expects I'm going to run
the farm myself while he's off living in a trailer with his good-
for-nothing friends doing God knows what." Back and forth,

table to sink. Back of her head. Her mouth. She said something in French; or maybe it was German. "You never find out about a person soon enough."

"He asked me if I wanted to go in on the farm," Bill said quickly, and realized just as quickly that far from changing the subject he had added to it. Eva was at the sink. She had two cups in her hand and put them down deliberately and gently. When she turned to Bill her face was composed but her eyes looked darker than usual.

"And what did you say?" she asked slowly.

"I said I'd have to think about it.

"You would."

Bill nodded. He couldn't look at her. He felt again as he had hearing them argue. "But he asked me if I'd at least stay on while he's in New Jersey so he doesn't have to worry about you."

"So you can take care of me while he's not here. Was that it?"

"Something like that, yeah." He looked up at Eva. She hadn't moved. He rushed his gaze back to his cup. "I said I would but only if that's what you wanted."

Eva was silent for a moment. Out of the corner of his eye, Bill could see her nodding slowly. "Sure," she said finally, flatly. "We don't want Joe to worry."   ·

Bill kept out of the way in the last few days before Joe left. At his parents' he was sharply aware of his mother—how she moved, the sound of her voice, the look in her eyes—and how different she was from Eva. If Joe and their father seemed more and more alike, the same man divided over two generations, the women they'd chosen couldn't have been more different. Yet the effect was turning out to be the same—Joe's dismissiveness with Eva just a variation of the kind he'd learned from their father, and then practiced and perfected on their mother. And Bill had been no better with her, he had to admit it. He hadn't been dismissive like Joe and his father, but perhaps he'd been dismissive in his own way. There had been no sympathy in his pity for her, no impulse to help or to understand. There still wasn't. Now his pity just made him want to run. And it was past time for him to go anyway. So when Joe suggested he move into the cabin on the farm, Bill agreed without a second thought. Joe wanted to avoid the question of propriety that might arise if Bill stayed in the main house. Bill was unconcerned with Joe's reasoning; he cleaned the cabin out in a day and moved himself in the next morning.

A month went by: Joe home on weekends and Eva, as far as Bill could tell, seeming to make peace with Joe's comings and goings. Their playfulness with each other had come back, though Bill sensed an edge to it that hadn't been there before. But he didn't pay it much mind, preoccupied as he was with his own life now. He'd settled into the cabin, and had been immediately pleased to think of its cramped, close two rooms as his. No one to answer to, nothing but evidence of himself wherever he looked, the radio on late into the night, no one to count his beers. The main house wasn't visible except from the side window and he kept that shade down. Looking out the door in the morning, cigarette lit even before the coffee was made, he let himself believe he was looking at his own spread, tasting what that would feel like. He was feeling more expansive and unfettered than he had ever imagined possible.

Spring barreled past the moment when everything looks most bare and forlorn, when the snow is gone and the woods are brown and flattened, the deer skinny and ravenous. This year the world was already green under the last of the snow and it seemed to burst up and push the snow out of its way. Green everywhere, the brilliant exaggerated green of spring, unsullied and sweet, just as Bill had begun to imagine the flesh on certain parts of a woman's body might feel. At night, when the green was hidden, the lushness of sound took its place: the trills and croakings of peepers, and the immense, musical static of the falls below the bridge. Moths came to the windows, ants swarmed under the sink, and in the first real warmth of the mornings, gnats went into orbit around his head. Bill took notice of everything, amazed at the difference his new vantage point was making in the way he was seeing and hearing things he thought he already knew inside out.

But other things eluded him. He noticed only the most obvious changes in Eva's behavior: that she'd stopped teasing him about girls and sex. And he put that off to Joe's absence, thinking that some of her boldness depended on her husband's proximity. But he didn't notice, at least not at first, that the warmth and playfulness Eva directed toward him now was acted out against a background of something more hidden and still in her, something waiting. And maybe he wasn't meant to notice until he did, maybe Eva planned it that way, knew when he would lift his head out of his self-absorption and was preparing for that moment. Maybe that was the waiting in her. Or maybe she planned nothing, imagined nothing until she noticed Bill looking beyond himself wondering what was different which gave her the idea that something could be. Because one day something was different. One day, unlike the day before it, Bill thought that Eva's words often seemed carefully chosen rather than merely spoken. He didn't understand her choices: the words made sense, but made some other meaning as well, something he strained to hear but could never quite make out. Sometimes she seemed on the verge of saying something that never actually got spoken, and when that happened, the silence seemed to fill with all the possibilities of what she might have said. Bill couldn't really imagine what that would be, but he felt as if he understood it anyway, though how that was possible he couldn't say. Nor could he say how it was that sometimes when he and Eva were together—driving to town, turning over the gardens, talking through the wall separating room from room where they were working on different parts of the floor—he felt at the same time both younger and older than he was, in years and experience, and the feeling was charged with mystery and excitement he also didn't understand.

There was nothing he could pinpoint that drew a line between one day and the next, and yet suddenly it was that next day, and he went to bed wondering why he felt agitated, anxious to get into and out of sleep and on to the morning. An unerasable line drawn between those days and these, and he couldn't see how Eva had drawn it, though certainly she had. And on this side of the line, on a warm day in April, she called to him from the top of the stairs. What did he hear in her voice that made him run up from the basement? Something like fear but not exactly that. Concern was more like it, maybe. She was startled by something, but was she pleased as well? He was instantly a little anxious, and curious, and moving fast. She was back in her bedroom by the time he got to the second floor and he could see her standing with her ear pressed against the wall near the bed's headboard. She waved him over, and then again when he hesitated, and even from the middle of the room, he could hear the hum, a monotone chorus that seemed to divide the room in two: where it could be heard and couldn't, where Eva was and wasn't. He moved slowly across the room, the sound growing in delicate increments, Eva taking up more and more of his sight. When he was within reach, she took his arm and pulled him the last few inches. He laid his ear flat against the wall and it was met by a vibration, the hum grown huge and physical.

"I think it's bees," Eva said, her voice low and throaty, resembling the sound it was referring to. "I was changing the linens"—just the bottom sheet so far, Bill noticed—"and I heard a noise I couldn't make out at first and then I realized it was coming from behind the wall."

They stood motionless, ears pressed against the wall, their faces a foot apart. Bill tried to keep his gaze cast down, but when his effort slipped and he glanced up quickly, he saw Eva's gaze directed at him. It was possible, he thought, that she was not deliberately trying to catch his glance, that in her concentration on the sound in the wall she was focused past him toward the sound itself. But when he said, "It's got to be a gigantic hive," needing to say something at that instant, anything, Eva nodded in agreement and her eyes stayed locked on his, looking at, not through him, and it was clear she was agreeing to something else as well, for both of them.

She's going to kiss me, he thought. He felt deliriously helpless and though he could detect no inclination in himself to adjust that feeling, an image of Joe sprang to mind as Eva began to move along the wall toward him. Joe, she's going to kiss me. Joe? As if his brother could answer or interrupt or understand. But then Eva was kissing him and he thought, Jesus. She parted his lips with her tongue and leaned against him. Mother of God, he thought. When she pulled him down onto the clean bottom sheet on the bed where his brother would be sleeping again in just four days, he thought: Jesus, Mary, and Joseph. But that was the last time he thought his brother's name that afternoon.

Before Eva seduced him, Bill would have said that he wasn't exactly a virgin and he wasn't exactly not a virgin: it all depended on how you measured those things. After they had sex the first time, he concluded that in fact he had been a virgin. Responding to Eva's invitation the second day, he wondered what he had become. There was a word for women like that—would he have used the word, he wondered, if Eva had done this with someone else?—but for himself, he couldn't come up with much more than son-of-a-bitch and he thought he could live with that for now.

"The bees have started in," she whispered across the back of his neck on the third afternoon. "Let's join them."

They hardly spoke to each other at all when they weren't having sex, and when they were, it was mostly Eva, urging Bill to do one thing or another, telling him how this or that felt, asking how he was being made to feel. He felt foolish even thinking of answering her, and hoped his unplanned exclamations would speak for themselves. Hoped after the fact: while they were together he wouldn't have been able to put two coherent thoughts in the right order even if he'd wanted to, and the only thing he wanted then was more of what was happening then. The silence between them at other times seemed made of anticipation, more tense and sustainable for not being spoken. His body moved through it as it moved through her hands when they were together, every nerve put on blissful alert. He took the charged silence to the cabin at night, and only three words, 'this is easy,' formed inside of it as he fell asleep, declaring what some part of him believed would be most convincing. It worked.

On the fourth afternoon, Eva pulled him up to the wall in the bedroom. "They've gotten louder in their honey wall, no?" She pulled him to her and they made love standing against the wall, one of her legs slung around his hip, the sound of the bees around them like the feel of honey itself.

The fifth afternoon was a Friday, warmer than any day they'd had that week. Eva called Bill from the yard, her voice carrying the same combination of concern and startled pleasure that he'd heard four days before, but not since. What would it mean this time? He ran outside and into the sound of the bees: amplified and multiplied as if he were with them inside the wall. The air seemed to be made of the sound. It seemed impossible that he wouldn't have heard it from inside the house, impossible that the whole town wasn't hearing it. The air was that thick with the sound. And with the bees as well. Hundreds, maybe thousands of them emerging from a narrow space where the furnace chimney didn't quite meet the house wall. The bees had found a loose clapboard there, an entry to the inside of the wall, the perfect place for their hive. Lulling sound effects for everything that went on in the bedroom. But here, outside, the sound was less lulling, carried as it was by these tiny, darting, stingered bodies. A patch of clapboard, maybe two feet square, the staging area for exit and entry from the hive, was black and molten with the bees. Countless more were airborne, spiraling above the hive in a twenty-foot column, a tornado of insects that produced a storm of sound instead of wind. Others were scattering in erratic patterns of flight that looked like anger or desperation. And Eva standing in the yard, staring up into the heart of the activity.

"Isn't it amazing?" she said, her voice barely audible above the hum.

Bill walked gently up behind her and took hold of her shirt. "Yeah. But we should probably go inside." He tugged, but she held her ground. "Eva, bees can be nasty when they get like this. We should go inside."

"Do you think all these bees live in the wall?" She sounded hypnotized.

"Seems so." He took her arm and pulled gently. "Eva, come on."

She relented a little, but only enough to lean back against him. Her head was braced now by his shoulder. "There's probably a hundred pounds of honey in there."

Her voice was near his ear. He shifted his body just slightly, enough to feel her full length against him. Their breathing seemed to synchronize, their bodies moving together in that tiny undulation, motionless in comparison to what was going on around them, but enough movement so that Bill felt as if some of Eva's amazement were pulsing out of her and into him. "I wouldn't be surprised," he said. He followed her gaze back up. It was amazing, there was no denying that. He'd never seen or heard anything like it. He followed the column of bees to its top—it might be thirty feet above the house now, forty—and then back down to the pool of bees on the clapboard, watched them darting in and out of the crevice behind the chimney, imagining them crawling in and out of a tiny crack under a board, order somewhere in the chaos, into and out of the chambers of the hive where the queen had grown impossibly large giving birth, and the honeycomb, built in tiny hexagonal tubes, growing like a wall itself, inside the wall of the house, making a cushion of the wall where he had stood with Eva, their ears pressed against the wall, their bodies pressed together pressed against the wall. He felt Eva's back against his chest and imagined the wall taking on her shape, the honeycomb responding to the pressure of his body against hers. A bed of honey.

The column of bees was beginning to break up, there were more and more flying in other patterns as if they'd been shot from the group into an endless ricochet. Bill grabbed both of Eva's arms and pulled her toward the door. "I think we should get inside Eva. Just till they calm down." Though she didn't turn around, he felt her give in. But it was only when she turned to kiss him once they were in the vestibule that he understood she'd given in to her own desire. She pushed him gently onto a low step of the staircase and straddled him, her skirt pulled up (she'd worn a skirt today, for the first time he could remember all week), her blouse unbuttoned, his fly open, he feeling hypnotized, a kind of delirium and disbelief laced into it. Was this real? Was she sitting on him here, was he really inside her? She moaned softly and leaned back from him. Her shirt fell open and he moved his hand from her waist up her torso and inside her bra. Her nipple was hard and thick between his fingers. This was real. Just as real, as undeniable, as the sound of the bees which he could still hear even through the closed door, and through which he also heard a new sound:

a car pulling up in the driveway. The car that he instantly knew to be Joe's even before he could see it, even though Joe wasn't expected for several hours. And of course it was him: Bill could see him now through the narrow window on the side of the front door. Stepping out of the car, leaning into the back to pull out his duffel bag (dirty laundry, rubbers, a bottle of whiskey maybe), turning suddenly to look up, Bill assumed, at the bees.

"Oh my God," he whispered because he couldn't find any more of his voice. He grabbed Eva's shoulders. "It's Joe."

She must have known before he said it, she must have heard the car just as clearly as he had, but even as he locked her shoulders between his hands, her hips kept moving against him.

"Eva, for God's sake. It's Joe," he said, more brusquely this time, beginning to push her off him. He could see Joe, still gazing up at the bees. Eva found her footing and stood up. Joe turned toward the house. Bill could see him face-on now: his brother moving toward the front door where he would find *his* brother and wife. Eva was still standing in front of him with her blouse open, her eyes half shut, and he'd be damned if there wasn't a smile on her face.

"Jesus, Eva!" His voice was a whispered screech. "He'll catch us. Get the hell away from the door!" He grabbed her arm and pulled but she pulled away, the smile disappearing from her face, her eyes opening wide and filling not with fear but with excitement, she took off down the hall toward the kitchen. Struggling with his pants—close the belt, close the fly, both seemed impossible—he followed her with the sound of the front door opening, the sound of the bees behind it, the sound of Joe's rushed entrance—was he getting away from the bees or had he seen something through the window?—that put his gaze directly on Bill's back, hurrying after Eva's back into the kitchen.

Or at least that's what Bill assumed, though Joe said nothing, just called hello from the vestibule, hung up his coat slowly enough so that Bill had time to get himself seated at the kitchen table, and Eva to arrange herself around the stove and coffee pot with what Bill thought was amazing calm, and say they were "in here" in an equally amazingly neutral voice, with just seconds to spare before Joe was at the kitchen door.

"Surprise, you two," he said with what Bill thought pretty muted enthusiasm. He walked across the room to Eva, put his arm around her waist, and kissed her just to the side of her mouth so her lips met nothing. She pulled his head back to her and kissed him full on the lips, quick and hard and followed by a glance that was so sharp it seemed to crack the air around it.

"Hey, little brother," he said to Bill, tousling his hair, something Bill couldn't remember Joe having done to him for ten years at least. He sat down across from Bill. "I'd love a cup of coffee, if you've got it, Eva. Maybe Billy wants some too." Joe had stopped calling him Billy years ago as well.

"No thanks," Bill said, keeping his eyes on Joe, as if he might make a sudden, dangerous move. "I was just getting ready to go back to work."

"No, sit for a minute," Joe said, taking the cup Eva had brought him, looking up at her, so Bill couldn't see what might be in his eyes now. "Tell me what you two've been up to."

Eva sat opposite Joe and told him about the bees. Joe drank his coffee noisily, nodding once in a while, saying, "Is that so?"

his voice edgy and challenging, and Eva countering with her own icy, "Yes, that is so." Glaring at each other past Bill, around him, through him. He was back to being invisible. But he could still see, and what he saw was that Joe knew what had happened. It was in his expression: smug and angry and gathering strength of a certain kind. And Bill could see that Eva was making no attempt even to pretend that she didn't realize Joe knew. She was telling him about the swarm, but not about the sound in the bedroom wall. Her voice became breathy describing the bees emerging from the hive, the sound they made, and, to Bill's surprise, the way he had "rescued" her. She turned her eyes toward him then: it was a brief glance, but it had in it the same demand for silence that he'd seen in her eyes after her fight with Joe. And suddenly, and without any doubt at all—as if these were the words she'd just said to Joe—Bill knew that she had known Joe was coming home early today, known it all week; that everything that had happened between them during the week was part of a plan she'd cooked up. Maybe she'd even managed to wrangle the bees into a swarm. He wouldn't put it past her now.

"I've been meaning to thank you, Billy, for looking after my bride," Joe said, still not looking at him. "I knew I could count on you."

Bill pushed his chair back and stood slowly. They both looked at him. He looked at a spot on the table between them. "I'm gonna finish up that fence."

"You do that, little brother," Joe said, a stiff smile stretching his lips. "Me and Eva have a little conjugal business to tend to."

Eva gave a short laugh, but there was no real argument in the sound, or in the look she moved back to Joe.

Outside, Bill walked past the fence and through the fields to the river's edge. He imagined Joe and Eva going up to their bedroom and Eva pretending to hear the sound of the bees in the wall for the first time. She'd pull Joe to the wall to hear it and they'd have sex with the sound of the bees behind them. And Joe would guess that he was following his brother's footsteps back into his own, and Eva would know he knew and she would wrap a leg around his waist so she could have him deep inside herself, helpless in that way, and at that moment, Bill guessed, she would have gotten what she wanted.

Bill finished the repair on the fence that afternoon, and then refused Eva's invitation to dinner. "I'm sure you want some time alone with Joe," he said, the sound of his voice slightly unfamiliar to him. Did it sound hurt or certain of itself, or both? He didn't mind the sound in any case, since it seemed to take Eva by surprise.

He found things to do most of the weekend that kept him away from the farm, but on Sunday morning Joe came to the cabin, came in without knocking, stood in the doorway, one hand still on the doorknob.

"I want you out of here before I get back next weekend," he said quietly, stepped back outside and closed the door after him. Bill's gaze stayed for some time where Joe had been, facing down Joe's afterimage, the only way he was ever going to be able to get out of the cabin.

He kept clear of Eva all week, making sure he was outside when she was in and vice versa. She made one attempt to talk to him, to explain, she said, but he turned away before her second sentence was finished and she didn't try again. He thought she was probably relieved that he hadn't given her a chance to speak.

Or maybe not: maybe she would've enjoyed prolonging the lie. In any case, by the following weekend, he'd cleared his stuff out of the cabin. A friend of a friend was working down in Oklahoma in the oil fields, making a good living, and that's where Bill went.

1975

WHEN THE PHONE RANG, Nina wasn't sure she'd actually been asleep. The glowing clock hands showed that Tony had left her just about an hour ago.

"Who is it?" she bleated into the mouthpiece.

"I got the job, Nina." It was Tony, some combination of high, wired, and exultant.

"At Cannen?"

"Yes." He drew the *s* into a fuse about to blow. "They are, they say, tremendously pleased to offer me the position."

"That's great, Tony. Congratulations—"

"Forget that," he burst in on her words. "Now you've got to come with me." He'd been trying to get her to make a decision even before he knew if he had the job.

"What I've got to do, Tony, is get up in three hours to go to work. I'm wrecked. Can we talk about this tomorrow?"

"What's to talk about?"

"I don't know if this is what I want to do—"

"So you don't know. So maybe this is it. You and me living in Vermont. Together."

"Yeah, exactly. In Vermont."

"You'll love Vermont."

"I love the city."

"Only because you've never lived in Vermont."

"Neither have you."

"Yeah, but—"

"What am I going to do in a town with a population of ten and a half?"

"You can do anything there that you're doing here. People need mechanics just as much in Cannen as they do in Spanish Harlem."

"Tony."

"Nina," he said, matching her tone with his. "Okay. I don't know what you're going to do. But you'll figure it out. And while you're doing that we'll be together. I want you to be there. It'll be perfect."

"That's asking a lot—"

"Nina. I do not want to go without you. That's all there is to it for me. I'll go mad without you. Nina."

His voice had slowed and lowered so that it had landed on her name in a plaintive note, yearning, unsure. Some part of her heard it and wanted to say yes right then, and go. Without thinking about it. Just let his wanting convince her. Just be irrationally enthusiastic, thoughtless. Let her desire for him, his for her, be the only factors. Forget the niggling thoughts, the numbers: the ten years between them, the mere seven months they'd been

together, the idea of following a man to the life he'd decided on
for himself when she was only twenty-three. She wished she
could hear only: I'll go mad without you.

"Where would we live?" she asked, not sure if she was capitu-
lating or restating her doubtfulness, but she could practically
hear Tony's face break into a smile.

"They've offered me a cottage on campus," he said, trying to
pretend he wasn't feeling victorious already. "Low rent, convenient, handyman takes care of the upkeep."

"Other faculty as neighbors, right?"

"I don't know. I guess—"

"Oh, you see?" She felt herself get another foothold on
doubt. "I spent my entire childhood and adolescence avoiding
all the faculty types that came blowing through our apartment. I
don't want to move in with these people now."

"Come on, Nina. It's me you're moving in with."

"I've got to think about it Tony."

"I'm coming over," he said, and she could hear him heave
himself out of a chair.

"You just left."

"I'm coming."

"I've got to get up in a couple hours—" But she was talking
into a dead line.

She let the phone fall to the pillow by her ear. She filled the
silence on the other end of the line imagining Tony gathering
himself to leave his apartment. Keys, wallet, cigarettes swept up
off tabletops. A beer from the refrigerator, kitchen light off. He
decides against the beer; kitchen light on, refrigerator opened
and slammed shut. Light off. Matches in the third pocket he
tries. The bare bulb lamp is still on: he stops to look at the

painting-in-progress it illuminates, sees what he couldn't see before, sees where he went wrong. Stares, lights a cigarette, remembering what he's thinking so he can go back to it later. Unlocks the front door, finds the police-lock pole, misses the floor-catch on the first try (well, he's tired, high, excited). Thinks of his downstairs neighbor, the skittish light sleeper. Gets the lock in place with quieter clatter. He's out the door, his keys shoot the bolts, his footsteps recede down the stairs. He's leaping, taking them two at a time. The apartment is silent, still, the painting brilliant in the sphere of light, and mistaken (she'll have to take his word for it). She stands off to the side, staring at the painting, which is of her in an abstract, ill-defined way. She wonders how he sees to begin a painting, how he sees. But there's no time, the alarm is going off—

Nina came awake suddenly to the disconnect signal in the phone. She hung it up and turned onto her back. The ceiling was cut with a pattern of streaks and blocks of pale light, night on the street entering around the window shades and tempering whatever darkness her bedroom might have contained, which was darkness enough for her. This was how she liked darkness to be. This was what her bedrooms had always looked like at two in the morning ever since she could remember that time of morning: shades of gray, darker where there was a piece of furniture, a picture on the wall; the pattern of light on the ceiling put into motion when cars passed outside. An easy progression for the eyes from this to a lamp turned on. She liked being able to see the world she was lying in. Now Tony wanted her to live in dark Vermont. Would it matter that he was with her in bed every night if she couldn't make him out?

"There's electricity in Vermont," Tony said about twenty-five minutes later, after he'd let himself into her apartment, gotten into bed with her, and listened to the description of what had gone on in her head just before he'd arrived. "We can get a night-light."

"That's very funny."

He nodded his head. "I know. I'm sorry. I'm not really trying to bulldoze the things that're bothering you." He had his hand on her cheek, his thumb resting on her lips, a finger set on either side of her ear. All the skin he could touch.

"I'll never make love to you again if you don't make the move with me," he said not long after, when he was already inside her. If she'd thought there was any chance he was serious, she would have agreed to Vermont immediately.

*　*　*　*

Nina and Tony were given one of the four faculty cottages on campus at Cannen: it was called Sophia and the others had equally proper names, the origin of which no one seemed to know. All the cottages were set back from their cul-de-sac and there were trees and shrubs to provide a sense of privacy. But the truth was, if Nina had wanted to keep tabs on her neighbors, she'd have had no problem. Or so one of them had proved to her on the second morning she was there.

"Hello?" When the voice came through the screen door Nina realized that she'd heard, but not registered, footsteps nearing the kitchen. She returned the greeting with the same question embedded in it, and went to the door. Tony had briefly described some of the neighbors to her, as if he'd observed them in the L-frame of his thumb and index finger to see if they were canvas-worthy. And here was one of them: tall, long, dark-haired, thin-faced, tomboy attractive, just as he had said, and offering one of her "arrow-like" hands to Nina now. "I'm Diane Gunther," she said. "I'm in Erin," pointing behind her to the cottage on the far side of the circle.

Nina introduced herself, but Diane already knew her name, had known when she would arrive. The woman was friendly and energetic, probably a little older than Tony. A faculty spouse. Nina looked her up and down and tried to imagine herself as a Diane Gunther.

"I brought a little welcome eats. Made it myself this morning," Diane said, holding up a foil-covered plate, her eyebrows raised in some expectation Nina couldn't understand until she realized that the screen door was still shut between them.

"Sorry." She fumbled with the latch, and when she pushed the door open the wind caught it and it slapped Diane in the side. "Sorry," she said again, wincing with discomfort at her clumsiness.

Diane waved her apology away. "The wind's a bitch today." She glanced around the room and Nina was suddenly aware of the immense chaos she seemed to have created rather than controlled by beginning to unpack a few hours ago. "I could see you were in the middle of it and thought you might like a little refreshment." Nina wondered what else she'd seen from the window of Erin. "But if this is a bad time, I can just leave these—"

"No," Nina said, taking a deep breath. "Come on in. Please." Nina stepped back and Diane stepped into the room. She held up a thermos. "I brought a little something to drink too," her eyebrows rising again. Nina felt somehow prompted by their movement, and then thankful for their prompt, and rushed to clear enough space on the table for the plate and thermos.

She cleared the boxes off a couple of chairs and, inviting Diane to sit, sat down herself. Diane settled into the other chair and, removing the foil from the plate, revealed a perfect cake, chocolate icing smoothly swirled into perfect peaks and valleys. Nina couldn't take her eyes off of it; no one she'd ever known could have baked a cake like this. "Think you can locate some dishes and a knife?" Diane asked with a laugh.

Nina popped out of her seat. "Oh sure, sorry." She winced again, hoping that it looked like a smile on the outside, and turned to the boxes behind her, not at all sure which one might yield dishes.

"This is really nice of you," Nina said from inside the box she was unloading; she'd seen plates at the bottom.

"It's no problem," Diane said. "Don't bother with glasses. I brought paper." Nina pulled her head up. "A house with kids is a house with paper cups."

Earth mother, Nina thought. She felt prompted again, this time by something in Diane's voice, and asked about the children as she deposited the plates on the table. Diane proceeded to give her the "vital statistics" of the Gunther family, more than Nina actually listened to as she searched for forks and a knife. Diane seemed content to talk to Nina's back, and Nina smiled over her shoulder once in a while to show she was listening. Finally, she uncovered a knife and some forks, and sat down.

"Do you have any?" Diane asked, cutting the cake. It had three perfect white layers.

"I'm sorry." Nina popped up again. "What else do we need?"

"No," Diane laughed, waving Nina back into her seat. Nina sat, feeling like a remote-control doll. Stand, search, sit, say sorry, say thanks, say oh how very nice. "I meant kids," Diane said, handing a cup across the table. Nina's arm reached, her hand grabbed. "It's ice tea with just a touch of Cointreau for flavor." Diane winked and took a sip, rolling her eyes in pleasure.

Nina took a long drink, glad to find that there was more than just a touch of the liquor in the tea. "Tony's got a son," she said as evenly as she could, "but he lives with his mother. In Boston." Seven-year-old Jay was the cause of deep uncertainty, and not a little discomfort, for her. She didn't know how Tony wanted her to fit into the child's life, or how, or if, she wanted to herself. And it was not a subject she was comfortable talking about, especially, she was discovering, with strangers.

Diane asked a few questions, but she must have felt Nina's guardedness because she moved away from the subject, smoothly segueing into a description of the other children and parents in the cul-de-sac: an English professor with former-student wife and rambunctious three-year-old; and the psychology professor, her medical-writer husband, and their two children, ten and twelve-going-on-twenty.

"There's plenty to know about all of them, which you probably won't be able to avoid knowing sooner or later," Diane said, putting her fork down. "Can I bum a cigarette?"

Nina pushed the pack toward her. "Why do you say that?" She put her fork down as well, though she'd barely touched the cake.

Diane lit up, her face showing the pleasure of someone who hadn't smoked in a long time. "Well," she said, exhaling luxuriously, "it's a small place. Hard to keep a secret."

"I guess that's good to know," Nina said, laughing uneasily.

Diane leaned forward and reached across the table to lay her hand softly on Nina's arm. "I'm saying too much. Forget it. It's just the old hand in me, the seven-year veteran. It's really a lovely place to be. Good people. Quirky, but good." Nina smiled and nodded. "And very welcoming, very warm," Diane said, vehemently grinding out her cigarette. "You're going to feel at home in no time." Nina was still nodding her head and Diane started to nod in time with her. "You don't believe a word I'm saying," she said with a smile.

Nina matched Diane's smile with her own, stilled her head. "I'm sorry," she said, without wincing this time. "It's just that my parents both teach at Columbia—"

"No kidding," Diane said, her interest immediate and clear even in these two words. "What do they teach?"

"My mother teaches mathematics and my father teaches engineering—"

Diane's laugh cut her off. "No wonder you fell in love with an artist."

Nina laughed with her but she felt as if she were hearing someone else's laughter. The conversation seemed to be getting away from her again. "Maybe," she said, nodding her head slowly. "I sure didn't expect him to become an academic."

"You make it sound like an arms dealer or something," Diane said, pouring herself more tea, toning down her laughter in response to something in Nina's voice.

"Well. No." Nina felt very young suddenly. She averted her

gaze from Diane's. "I just thought I was done with academia after high school, when I left home."

"But I imagine that this will seem awfully different to you than—"

"Yeah, but that's only part of it." Now her voice sounded young too, as if she might be on the verge of a tantrum. And when she lifted her gaze to Diane's, the patience and acceptance she saw there only made her feel more reticent about explaining herself. "It's just that I've never lived outside the city," she said, evening out her voice. "So everything feels really strange right now."

"Well, that makes perfect sense," Diane said, standing up. She was smiling sympathetically. "I hate to sound like an awful cliché, but I'm sure you'll get used to it with time. And if you need help with any of it, including the unpacking, just let me know. All right?"

Nina nodded, wondering if she'd seemed to want Diane to go, wondering if she did.

Diane pushed the thermos toward her. "Have another drink anyway," she said in a slightly conspiratorial voice. She swept her eyes across the room as she moved toward the door. "It's good to meet you, Nina. Come by anytime." She pushed the screen door open with her back and stepped outside.

Nina stood up and held the door. "Thanks for the cake."

"You're very welcome," Diane said and went down the steps, waving behind her. "Don't forget. Anytime."

Nina watched Diane make her way between the cottages. She didn't seem to need to look where she was going: it was as if her feet and the hidden mechanism of her balance had memorized the contours of the lawns, the cracks and holes in the pavement. When she stooped to pick up a toy at the edge of her own lawn, her body made an effortless reach without ever coming to a stop. There was knowledge of place and custom inside the way Diane moved, and Nina thought of herself, earlier that morning, trying to negotiate the maze of boxes in the house, lugging and pushing, every movement dull and ungraceful, unknowing in the most basic way. When she'd gotten off the bus from New York two days ago, she'd stumbled on the bottom step and was saved from falling only by the quick hand of the driver, who then passed her off to Tony. It had seemed funny to her then, her first step in Vermont a kind of tumble into Tony's arms. But in hindsight, it seemed more ominous, as if settling in Vermont would require that, beginning with walking, she relearn everything elemental.

She turned back into the kitchen, and her eyes filled with the mess of boxes and haphazardly unpacked things strewn across counters, the evidence of indecision and lethargy—she hadn't even come to the simplest decisions that morning: where to put the pots and pans, which drawer to use for silverware. She sat at the table, lit a cigarette, drank the last of the ice tea in her cup, and then filled it from the thermos, glad for the Cointreau. Her conversation with Diane seemed to be swirling around the kitchen in pieces: she couldn't pull it together, couldn't tell if, in the end, she'd said anything she might wish she hadn't, revealed too much, trusted too soon. Or maybe she needed to apologize for having insulted Diane's husband by ruing the fact that Tony was becoming an academic. And it was possible that Tony wouldn't have wanted her to talk about Jay; or that Diane had picked up on her discomfort with the subject, which was definitely more than Nina needed to give away at that moment.

Nina took another cigarette out of the pack. She had to remind herself of her own tendency to look too closely at conversations. "Looking it into a frenzy" was how a friend had described it. That's what she was doing now: looking so hard that her conversation with Diane was bound to start to spark and shift and break apart under the pressure of her inner gaze. She lit the cigarette she had in her hand and then saw the one she'd left burning in the ashtray. Crushing it out, she reminded herself that this was just day two: second day in a new home, a new community, Vermont. Second day of living with Tony. Of course it was going to be difficult. She looked around the room again. Once all their things were settled into place, then she could begin to do the work of settling in herself. First one thing and then the other, if she could just think of it that way, tackle it that way, she'd be okay. She rested her cigarette in the ashtray and turned her chair so she could unload the open box behind her.

It was the box where she'd found the plates before, and now she took out the rest of them, tearing off the newspapers she'd folded around them on the other end of the move, relishing the sound of the ripping paper: progress. She stacked the dishes carefully on the counter. They'd been a wedding gift to her grandparents in 1925. Nina's mother had planned to give them to her when she got married, but when Nina announced that she was moving with Tony, her mother said it was about as close to marriage as she could hope for from her daughter. And it was hard for Nina to imagine that getting married would have been any more momentous or upending than this. She was setting up a life with Tony, combining hers with his, and even more than that: placing hers inside his, for now anyway, but maybe for longer than she imagined. She couldn't predict how quickly she'd be able to find a job, find the people who would become friends, get used to not being in the city.

She unwrapped the last dish from the box, broke the box down, and leaned it behind the door. That was going to be the hardest thing, she thought: getting used to the quiet and inactivity here. She lifted the dishes into a cabinet, expecting some satisfaction in the effort, but getting none. The room seemed no less crowded and chaotic. This was going to take forever. She let herself drop into a chair, and took another drink of tea, doubting now that the Cointreau would have any effect. If she were in the city now, she could have stepped outside her door and hooked into the movement of the crowds and traffic, into the soundtrack of voices and noise, into the sight of shifting surfaces, accidental tableaux, easily losing herself to all of it.

She got up from the table and stepped outside. She could hardly believe herself here, on the steps of a cottage called Sophia, for God's sake. A gust of wind lifted her ponytail off her back and she was aware of a sound she hadn't noticed before: like water, waves breaking through the upper branches of the pine trees that surrounded the cul-de-sac like a deeply inverted moat. She leaned her head back and watched the branches undulate, each gust making a new shape of them, and under the gusts, the more sustained blow, moving the trunks of the trees in a deep sway. The movement was mesmerizing: Nina couldn't take her eyes from it, not even when she began to sense that the sway of the trees was growing erratic, each tree moving according to its own heft, uncoordinated with any of the others, uncontrolled, the possibility of trunks colliding growing by the minute. The trees could snap into pieces, she thought, crash onto a roof, breach walls—simple roof and walls, one layer against the elements, oncoming crises, these trees. In the city there'd been locked doors behind other locked doors, walls buffered by halls, other apartments, other buildings. Wind came through windows, moved shades, dust, pieces of paper. The trees might bend, a branch might be broken, but she'd always looked down from her windows onto the tops of whatever trees lined the streets she'd lived on in New York; never up along neck-bending heights like these, looking up at them from the bases of trunks that seemed nowhere near thick enough to support such height, up at them while they dipped and creaked, their decades of survival no guarantee against a wind with just enough power to be too much for them.

Nina got herself into the house quickly. She closed the door solidly behind her. When the latch caught she imagined the house being sealed, sound and oxygen sucked out of it in the process, the outside denied, but not protected against. She had to make an effort to take a deep breath. She felt her discomfort move from mind to body, her body begging to outrun her feelings. She spotted the keys to the Spitfire on the table, grabbed them, and went out again.

She steadied her foot on the accelerator as lightly as she could until she was through the campus gate where the grounds edged into a quiet back road that skirted the town. She drove fast now and at the road's end gave choice over to chance: a left turn would have put her behind another car, a right gave her a clear road. The Spitfire was low to the pavement and her body began to give up its agitation to the vibrations of the engine and the road. The top was down and whatever the wind had seemed before, now it was a familiar element of driving, controlled by the speed she used to get through it. She untied her hair and it was a relief to feel it lift around her head.

She found her way onto roads whose long curves seemed made for speed, and she didn't notice that the houses were growing fewer and farther between, or that cow fields were giving way to woods. But then she had to jam on her brakes to avoid hitting something streaking across the road. A squirrel? Raccoon? Who knew what she might encounter out here, her heart racing now that the car was stopped. She looked around, seeing nothing but towering trees, the road on an incline, open sky in the distance. The gusts reached into the car again, and they seemed even harder here, wherever here was. She wouldn't have been able to retrace her route if her life depended on it. Even the map would be no help if she couldn't find something that might be on it. She drove toward the open sky, the road leveled out and there was a place to pull over. She got out of the car and saw below her the valley she hadn't realized she'd been driving up out of. She could see the campus: a cluster of white buildings, like the village of Cannen itself, but on a smaller scale. And a few miles east of the campus, the village with its church steeples and commons; roads leading out of it along the track of a narrow river and disappearing into the hills. There were cows grazing, white spots against green; and red barns, white farmhouses here and there. She let her eyes move slowly across the valley and then back again, trying to convince herself that it was a scene of peace, not lifelessness. Her heart continued to race and her lungs felt incapable of accommodating deep breaths. She swept the valley with her eyes again and again, her body beginning to follow the rhythm of her gaze. Slowly back and forth until the valley became a wash of color, nothing more than distance and depth. She could learn to call it home or she could leave it; neither alternative seemed possible. She pulled air into her lungs, as deeply as it would go, and held it in case it could open something else inside her too, space for something other than this agitation.

She closed her eyes and let the breath out, the sound of her exhalation folding into the watery sound in the trees which was enfolded by the sound of a gust of wind grabbing the upper branches. Nina thought she could feel it come down along the trunks and move up behind her, pushing her off balance. She opened her eyes to steady herself and saw how close she was to the edge of a steep fall of rock and stubby trees. She stepped back quickly and that feeling, the need to be moving out ahead of herself, was waiting for her where her feet landed, rushing up through her.

She got in the car, approximated her place on the map, and started, fast, for the campus. Were these the same roads she'd come on? The curves seemed tighter, unbanked, slippery though the pavement was dry. The Spitfire's steering had too much give, the brakes were spongy. She wished she'd tied her hair back, or put the top up. She pushed the car faster. It suddenly seemed very important that she get back to the cottage before Tony. What would he think if she raced in the door checking behind herself where nothing apparent would explain her behavior, and told him tales of threatening trees and sentient wind? What else could he think then but, at the very least, that he'd been mistaken about her strength or confidence, or sanity? She would get back before he did and he would find her in the kitchen, getting the unpacking done, eager to get on with other things, with this life which her face would show was nothing less or different than a welcome adventure.

Which is what Tony thought he saw when he got home in the late afternoon: Nina looking tired but composed, the kitchen almost cleared of boxes, Coltrane coming from the living room where she'd set up the stereo, dug out some of the records. He walked her to the bedroom with one arm around her from behind, gathered her hair to one side, and kissed her on the back of her neck. He felt her shudder and kissed her again, and then again, pulling her shirt aside to make a path for his lips along the contour of her shoulder.

Nina kept her own lips tight, trying to stop the tears his touch had triggered, her body shuddering with the effort. She leaned back against him when they got to the edge of the bed, so he wouldn't stop kissing her, wouldn't see the tears, which she managed finally to turn back, and turned herself in his arms to find his mouth with hers. She didn't summon the memory, but it was there all at once: herself in the clearing off that deserted road, alone, removed, rocking like a child who gets comfort from nothing else, staring down onto the tops of houses whose roofs were vulnerable to falling trees; onto the top of this house, this roof, in whose underside she noticed a long, delicate crack just before she closed her eyes on it from the bed below.

Tony had already started dinner by the time Nina got up. She'd fallen asleep after they made love: the finally, perfectly mindless physicality of the sex overwhelming the emotional exhaustion of the day, making her forget what she wasn't telling him, and then forget everything but the feel of his hand on the inside of her thigh as sleep overwhelmed even that feeling.

She put on the kimono he'd gotten her for her birthday. It was made of a slightly coarse cotton woven into a simple pattern of black, brown, and white. According to the man who sold it to Tony, it was a Japanese farmer's kimono made in the 1930s, but he'd assured Tony that all kimonos, no matter the material, were cut to hang beautifully from the human body, and he'd been right. As Tony described it, the straight, simple lines of the cloth offset the complex, curving lines of Nina's body. Especially since the kimono hung open in the front, revealing a column of flesh it was never meant to reveal—the farmer would have worn it over other clothes—but the thought of which had convinced Tony to buy it.

No man Nina had been with before Tony had watched her the way he did, looked at her with such obvious pleasure in the simple act of looking. He loved what he saw, he told her: her body moving, at rest, aware of him or not. It was enough sometimes, he said, to let his eyes have all the pleasure. He made countless sketches of her: clothed and naked, caught at random and manipulated into exact poses. She liked having his eyes on her, or imagining them there when they weren't. It sharpened her own eye for him as well. She'd never been very particular about men's bodies: sinuous arms, the curve of a neck into straight shoulders, demanding eyes, a gently muscled back—any one aspect of a man's body could grab her attention. But there were many more than one aspect of Tony to admire, and to want. "The package," she remembered saying to her closest friend, Chris, "is very good." She could almost believe that the power of their attraction to each other, the brashness of it, the intense pleasures in satisfying it, could be sufficiently strong glue to keep them together if everything else failed.

"She walks," Tony said as she came into the kitchen. She smelled garlic and onions cooking. He was slicing mushrooms. She put her arms around his waist from behind, her kimono opening wide, her breasts pressing against his bare back. "Nice kimono," he said.

"Yeah, but all the buttons are missing." She kissed his back and moved around his side. "What're you making?"

"Spaghetti. Tomato sauce. Simple." He'd moved on to zucchini, slicing quickly, evenly, one hand just ahead of the knife blade wielded by the other.

"I don't know how you do that," Nina said, reaching for the bottle of wine Tony had opened.

"I'll teach you."

"Forget it. Then I'd have to cook." She opened the cabinet where she thought she'd put glasses: it was full of plates. She'd rushed to unpack the boxes that afternoon before Tony had gotten home, hardly taking note of where she was putting anything.

"You can be my *sous chef.*"

"Your what?" Two more cabinets before she found a glass.

"My *sous chef.* My second. My under cook."

"Your under cook." She poured for herself and filled his glass. "Sort of along the lines of your underwear?"

"Sort of." He threw the zucchini in the pan with the garlic and onions, stirring with one hand, gently grabbing the collar of the kimono with the other and pulling Nina to a kiss. "You want to make a salad?"

"Sure." She opened the refrigerator. "Did you see this cake?"

"Yeah. I was going to ask you about it." He was opening a can of tomatoes.

"Diane Gunther brought it over this morning. She made it herself." Nina moved bottles and packages around looking for lettuce. Tony had stocked the refrigerator before she arrived. "And she brought a thermos of ice tea with Cointreau."

"Not bad for the welcome wagon." Tomatoes into the pot. "What'd you think of her?"

"She seems nice." Nina closed the refrigerator with her foot, her hands full of what would go in the salad. "It was a little weird though."

"Why?"

"Well, she said she could see I was unpacking and thought I could use some refreshment. Like she'd been spying on me or something." Tony was leaning back against the counter now, watching Nina, a glass of wine like an extension of his hand hanging at his side. "I mean, she can see into our kitchen window."

"Nina, in the city you were practically living in *Rear Window*." Her apartment had backed onto a courtyard where everyone was exposed to everyone else's eyes and ears.

"Yeah. But nobody brought me cake."

Tony laughed quietly and shook his head. Nina was glad he found it funny; it reassured her that she was managing so far to hide any sign of the turmoil she'd felt earlier in the day.

"She seemed pretty cool to me," Tony said as he walked into the living room. He put on the other side of the Coltrane album that had been on when he'd gotten home. When they'd met, Tony had been amazed at Nina's record collection, as heavily weighted toward jazz as his.

"No, she's really nice," Nina called after him, hoping her voice sounded nonchalant. "It's just, you know, everything's a little weird. I mean, I'm making a salad in the kitchen of a house named Sophia as if it's perfectly natural."

Tony came back into the kitchen. He slid his hand inside the kimono and around her waist and moved her into a slow dance. He was always ready to dance. "Well, it's true," he said. "Nothing you do in the kitchen is anywhere near perfectly natural."

"Yeah yeah yeah." She pushed him away. He swung the kimono wide open before turning back to the stove.

They let the music take the place of talking for a while. Nina went back to preparing the salad. A little weird: that would be all she would say about the day. It was odd and disturbing to be so unforthcoming with Tony. They had quickly gotten into the habit of telling each other everything. In the first weeks they were together, they had recounted their lives, each story, any bit of information or recalled impression, another fraction of self revealed, each minute revelation an instance of unexpected trust. Except for Chris, Nina had never told anyone as much as she told Tony. It had never occurred to her that anyone else would be interested in knowing her so well, wouldn't be bored or disappointed, would care about the details that mattered to her. But the way Tony listened, and the questions he asked, the depth of self he revealed in return, gave her the impetus to keep telling. And she even surprised herself sometimes: hearing things she was articulating for the first time. Tony never seemed surprised, just interested or concerned or delighted.

He'd asked her once what she hoped her life would be like in five or ten years and she told him that years ago she'd decided that a simple life would be good. He'd laughed and said, "With that mind? Are you crazy?"

"I'm not interested in a life of the mind," she'd said dismissively. That had been what she was getting away from when she'd left her parents' home—all the surfaces of her family's life cool and smooth, thought out and through, theory always getting more consideration than actuality. No one yelling in any form of anger or joy. Everything Nina did and didn't do on her own functioned as antidote and buffer against the rigorous thoughtfulness of home. When she was seventeen and her mother told her that she didn't like the person Nina had become, Nina was triumphant.

"It's not the same thing," Tony had said. "Your mind's not like theirs." Nina already trusted him completely by that time, but that didn't mean she thought he couldn't be wrong about her. Today, for example, she thought: she had lived deep inside her mind, was still there, couldn't drag herself out of it, her thinking in a perpetual circle around her uneasiness.

"So what about you?" Nina asked, putting things back in the refrigerator. The salad was done. "How weird was your day?" She thought her voice sounded pushed out, exaggerated and false. She was surprised that Tony didn't react to it, that she was so capable of hiding herself from him. She felt herself collapsing a little, just as she had when he had walked her to the bed before. She sat at the table behind him, and lit a cigarette.

"Weird enough," he said, laughing. He put the spaghetti in the pot. "There's all this committee stuff I've got to figure out. A lot of *Sturm* and *Drang*. Lots of personality, capital P." He mixed a salad dressing while he talked. "But the students seem good. It's hard to say what they're all up to yet, but they're serious. Some interesting portfolios. Toss," he said, putting the bowl in front of her. "You all right?"

"Yeah, I'm fine." She mixed the salad and got up to find plates and silverware. Tony directed her to the right cabinets. How was it that he knew these things better than she did?

He put the bottle of wine on the table. Nina could feel his arm move close to her face, but it seemed to be much farther away. He brought the spaghetti to the table and sat two feet from her, but she felt as if she would have to lean with her whole body to touch him. Or that her leaning would only measure, not bridge, the distance she had put between them by hiding herself. That her touch wouldn't be solid enough for him to feel in any case.

He poured them both more wine. He leaned toward her and ran his finger from the bottom of her throat down between her breasts. "I love this kimono," he said, and leaned back, keeping his eyes on her face. "If I knew what peaked meant, I'd say you look a little of it. Dig in, babe." She ate just enough to look as though she were enjoying the meal, and Tony seemed convinced.

•　•　•　•

The wind died back to normal after another day, but it had pulled autumn in behind it two weeks before the calendar insisted it would arrive. Too quickly for Nina, something else to give up: the long, easy transition between summer and fall that she was used to in the city. She liked to think that any cold air arriving there in September or October was tempered by the summer-stored heat in concrete and pavement, buildings, even the skin of crowds, leaching slowly out and back up into the atmosphere. But that notion had no place here. Whatever heat had accumulated in the soil over the summer—the only place she could see where it might have—seemed to have been sucked up out of the ground by the two-day wind and scattered. In the course of her first five days in Cannen, Nina put socks on for the first time since the middle of April, closed half the windows in the cottage, and started thinking of coffee not just as a hit of caffeine, but as a source of warmth. She wasn't ready to hunker down like this; she didn't feel like herself in the cottage and the cottage didn't feel like home.

After the push through the kitchen boxes, Nina had lost momentum. Tony thought she should wait until they could do the unpacking together, spread the job out over as many weekends as it took. He'd been surprised that she'd done the kitchen in a day, that she'd been content to spend a day like that. Nina was tempted at that moment to tell him about her drive, but she held back. She had no distance from what she'd felt that day, no way to describe it calmly, no way to present it the way she assumed Tony would want to hear it: as introductory jitters, a temporary glitch in surety, self-possession, anything he'd said he was drawn to in her when they first met. All of those things seemed in short supply now for Nina. In an instant—any instant, there was no pattern—she could be completely overwhelmed by a feeling that she was unrecognizable to herself, somehow sealed in the house; or by the restlessness and agitation that made her need to move. And despite the frenzy of that first drive, she turned to the car when these feelings took over again. It seemed the only alternative, though she thought enough now to open a map and keep it on the seat beside her: if she stopped, she wanted to be sure she was stepping out of the car onto a convergence of points that she could plot, that had a

context, clear routes of escape. She felt much calmer on the
road now, felt muscles in her neck and hands relax, her lungs
deepen. Finally, after a few days, she made a decision to split her
days, give herself the mornings to do whatever unpacking she
could manage, and then get herself onto the road before the
restlessness might hit. If she could avoid even the onset of all
that commotion from now on, the fact that it had ever occurred
might come to seem part of a distant, isolated past, the one she
began to imagine receding behind her every time she got the car
onto a road where she could push it faster than was legal, faster
than was probably safe. She kept the top down despite the
increasing cold: it was the one way she defied the change in seasons. She wore a hat, scarves, gloves, a warm jacket, but there
was always the electric edge of cold on her face, keeping her
alert, her driving sharp. The map stayed open on the seat beside
her, but she used it less and less, remembering to trust her sense
of direction once she'd learned the basics of the area.

She was all right in these moments, the movement carrying
her above the stream of her thoughts, her uneasiness, her questions and doubts. Her mind gave up the habit of over-thinking
to the press of seeing and hearing, the sensations of wind and
temperature and speed. But each time she returned to the campus, she felt muscled back into its particular world, as if adjustments were being made in her without her involvement:
sensation to thought, movement to stillness, openness to con-
traction, all the drive's sensual details stripped away as the car
moved slowly now through a cavern of overhanging trees and
past the false town commons of the campus center. She passed
students and faculty whose looks seemed to scrape at her further. At the cottage door she felt herself shaped by undoing, the

right form to fit inside the cottage where all her thinking was waiting to be firmly taken up again.

Instead of talking to Tony, Nina confided everything to Chris in long phone calls to New York that she knew would add up to a ridiculously high phone bill, something, at the moment, she couldn't get herself to care about. It was essential for her to talk to Chris: an experience only felt complete to Nina when she knew Chris had it in her head as well. They'd been confiding in each other for almost their entire lives: they were three years old when their mothers put them in the same playground sandbox. Learning to talk had meant learning to talk to each other. Later, they made up their own words for the important things and ideas in their six- and seven- and eight-year-old lives, their own names for people who crossed their path, a way of communicating their secrets without the need of whispering, which caused their parents, siblings, and teachers great consternation, and solidified an intimacy that would move with them into and then beyond adolescence. There was almost nothing now that had happened to one that the other didn't know about. For Nina there was great comfort in that, though she could no more explain the comfort than remember her life before Chris was part of it. She was the sibling Nina had never felt she had in her brother, six years older and so different from her that they never found a way to talk to each other with any depth. Chris's voice, on the other hand, entered Nina like a drug, its kick a calming one, the dense fabric of their friendship clear to Nina in every one of Chris's words, even the ones she repeated annoyingly at the end of each phone conversation they had now: "You should be telling Tony all this."

But Nina wasn't. She was telling him enough so that he knew she was spending a lot of time in the Spitfire, but she let him think she was merely satisfying her curiosity about Cannen's surroundings. He knew she was feeling out of place, but she pretended to wear the feeling with a kind of pride: she wasn't easily labeled, she needed time to make her own way. He knew she was lonely for her friends, but of course she was, he was too; it was just a matter of time. She didn't want to need to be taken care of, to need with so little definition, to see the scope of her need by watching Tony try to answer it. Instead, all her need of him became physical, satisfied not just when they made love, but in the sight of his skin, the warm breath of his voice from close behind her, the sense of his eyes wandering her body. Satisfied and fueled at the same time. Her skin sparked under his most off-hand touch, the softness of which was perfect in itself for an instant and then reminded her how much more there was to want. In the mornings she tried to memorize as much of him as she could, everything she knew about his body, everything she might have just discovered, every sensation he raised in her, every one of her senses alive to his sensations as well. But none of it was enough to occupy the house with her once he had left.

With Tony gone, whether for a couple of hours or the entire afternoon, Nina became aware again of how tenuously she occupied the cottage herself. The more of their things she unpacked and settled into place, the more displaced she felt: each box emptied, broken down, carried to the trash was one less connection to her life in the city, which nonetheless continued to feel like her life. Without Tony to focus on inside these walls, they seemed to thicken with all the other lives that had been lived there, as if they could corral her, take her imprint, and turn her particularities into similarities to someone or more than one someone else.

Each day Nina reminded herself that only so much time had passed: nine days was nothing given all the changes she was making, ten days, eleven. But rounding the end of her second week, the count began to lose its power of small comfort. She spent more time on the phone: with Chris; with her sister-in-law in lieu of her brother, who was perpetually hospital-bound in the second year of his residency; with Ernie, the owner of the makeshift garage where she'd worked, who shouted, "*Es nuestra muchacha!*" past the mouthpiece of his phone to summon Izzy or Ruben, whoever was there, to bemoan her absence, and to rhapsodize about her car-smarts, the way she looked in her coveralls, the sound of her mangled Spanish. She called her old roommate Laurie and listened to the details of a delay on the subway or a weird conversation overheard at the corner bodega as if she were being told important secrets, anything she heard over the phone more vivid to her than everything her own eyes and ears were taking in at that moment, whatever that moment was.

Nina introduced herself to the other people living in the cul-de-sac when she encountered them on her way to and from the car. They seemed nice enough, though she thought they'd all have more in common with her parents than with her, and their names and the names of their children went in and out of her head without pausing.

She used the cake plate and thermos needing to be returned to force herself to knock on Diane's door one morning. Diane was welcoming and easy, and kindly brushed aside Nina's apologies for being so long in returning her visit. Nina thought Diane could probably sense that her apology functioned mostly as something to say, but it didn't seem to matter. She thought Diane might be easy to talk to: she had that kind of patient eagerness to hear. And there was something about her that made Nina think of what Chris might look like in twenty years or so. But she found herself answering Diane's questions with a false lightness—everything's coming together, things were a little hairy when you came over but I'm doing okay now, I think I'm going to really like living up here—that strained every muscle in her face, and some in her hands which were doing their best to express an enthusiasm Nina was afraid her voice might not be conveying. Diane said she was happy to hear that Nina was starting to feel more comfortable, but her eyes showed her concern. For one instant Nina was caught by the understanding in Diane's gaze. Her thoughts began to find an order appropriate to being spoken, her throat to prepare a timbre to voice the truth. But in the next instant Nina thought she might be mistaken about Diane's gaze, that what it showed might be impatience or pity, boredom, noninterest, her sense of psychological superiority. It was only because Chris wasn't here, she realized, that she was even thinking of confiding in Diane. She wanted Chris's face in front of her, the comfort of her gaze, not Diane's, no matter what was in it.

She walked slowly back to her cottage. Following the curve of the curb, she saw what everyone else saw from their front yards: the other houses at various angles, into certain windows of the other houses, down the street to the small rear wing of the science building, the clock tower of the Commons, the summit of Mount Equinox in the distance. Finally, she sat on her own front steps. It seemed to her that the view from Sophia was the most limited: the front of Diane's cottage, the woods behind it and along the road, the full curve of the cul-de-sac, which led her mind's eye back to herself, turning it inward.

She had gone to Mount Equinox a few days before, paid the price and driven the snaky road up its nearly four thousand feet. It had been a Wednesday, just after noon, and she had been almost alone at the summit. There was little besides her body for the wind to make its way around. The fall colors in the trees made swaths of red and yellow along the mountainsides and down into the valleys, which would have been breathtaking if she hadn't been short of it already. What she was looking at was so open and so beautiful, empty and crushing. She felt alive to the emptiness, as if she had to move into it, fill it, learn it. None of it made sense to her. She drove down the mountain too fast, too hard on her breaks, smelled them burning. She downshifted to second gear from third, but she hated the complaint of the straining engine. When the switchbacks lengthened, she slid the car into neutral and let gravity pull it headlong. She wanted to feel what it would feel like to give up control of the car. Thinking about that afternoon now, chilled by her own reckless-ness, she thought about how she had never before been so sepa-rated from the people who tied her to her world, and who, often just with the simple fact of their presence, kept her reeled in when she most needed it. The phone calls with them now, their letters, were like a net cast toward her, silken and bracing at the same time. But it didn't always hit its mark: she would feel it land tantalizingly close, its comfort clear but just out of reach, the voice at the other end of the line growing slightly disembodied, the handwriting in the letter more difficult to decipher than it

had been in the instant before, the net cast again as a scrim, separating her from what she needed to see and hear.

She could always see and hear Tony clearly, but she didn't
always trust the clarity. She was too anxious to give over, to disappear into him. He had become a place to her, home in a way
no structure could be. He was where she felt calmest; where she
could shut out everything else, including herself. She yearned for
the moments when there seemed to be nothing separating them,
not skin, not air, not the space where their perception of each
other occurred, not the fact that he could help her only in this
way, not all the things she wasn't telling him.

1967

BILL'S FATHER BEGAN to die long before he told anyone. He kept the doctor's report of cancer and the prognosis of six months to a year to himself, brushing off his wife's concern as a petty annoyance, the change in his appearance as age and the effects of having an annoying wife. He smoked as long as he could, which was almost up to the moment of his collapse. When the call about his father finally tracked Bill down in Saudi Arabia, he was being rotated off that job anyway. Otherwise, he wasn't sure he would've gone back to Overton then or ever.

He'd been gone for almost seventeen years by that time, and though he'd kept in touch intermittently with his parents and his sisters, he hadn't felt the need to attend weddings (both sisters), or funerals (one set of grandparents, an uncle, a newborn niece, a great-aunt), and certainly no occasion more minor. He hadn't tried to be in touch with Joe, and he heard from Eva only in the form of birth announcements: Lilly in 1951, Joseph, Jr., in 1953, Ray in 1956. By the time he'd heard that Joe had left Eva in the tenth year of their marriage, he had left his own marriage after ten years and three kids. He knew Joe's second wife was a woman from Wellspring, and that they had two children. But that was all he knew: not the names of their kids, not exactly where they lived.

He couldn't imagine that he and Joe would find a way to talk to each other: they'd be strangers now even if nothing had happened between them in the past. So he delayed his arrival in Overton until a few days after the funeral. It wasn't hard to explain: even his mother, who'd never been farther afield than Philadelphia, knew that Saudi Arabia took some getting to and from.

He spent the days he delayed with a friend from the first Oklahoma fields he'd worked in who was living in Queens now, not far from Kennedy Airport. He helped Bill spend some of the money he came back from the desert loaded with: a neighborhood bar, a high-stakes poker game, a used car Bill paid for with five new hundred-dollar bills. His friend said he could get him a date while he was in town, but Bill declined. Something about his father's death made him feel constrained in that way; as if controlling that urge in himself made a show of respect.

Once he got to Overton he needed all the control he could muster just to get himself through the front door of his parents' house, and then to keep himself from turning around immediately. His father had kept the outside of the house meticulous: it looked as if it had been painted within the last year; the shrubs around the foundation were shaped and trimmed; the fence around the vegetable garden was taut, the gate on a strong hook.

The screen door didn't squeak or slam when he stepped through it. But the gentle sound of its closing felt as large as if a steel gate had come down behind him: the house was rotting inside its well-tended skin. A wave of revulsion washed over him: how could anyone live here? In the living room, where he stood, the shades were mostly drawn, but even in the dim light he could see the sofa and chairs layered with years of grime. His father's mostly: home from work each evening coated with the fine refuse of his job, mindless of his own expectation that his wife would keep a clean house. Colors had faded or been rubbed into a lifeless wash; the rug was worn to the backing in more places than not. The walls showed their true color around crooked pictures, though even that color looked dirty, as if the pictures hadn't been straightened in years. The curtains were frayed along the edges. There seemed to be a terrible delicacy to everything: table legs might snap, floorboards give way, the ceiling crumble. But even more unsettling than the sight of the room was the smell: the familiar pall of cigarette smoke mixed with the sickly sweet air freshener his mother had always used against it. And something new as well: as if his father's years of coughing had left a residual odor of sick, overworked breath. When his mother walked into the living room from the back of the house, Bill saw an old woman, stooped and dry, her face pinched and hidden, and he knew he was smelling her as well: her aging flesh, and what he imagined as a different kind of stale exhalation, her halting sigh of relief in being both unburdened and undone by her husband's death.

Bill felt so little for her that he could hardly bend his head toward her kiss, which, in any case, communicated no more affection for him than he was feeling for her. He followed her into the kitchen where the raised shades didn't so much allow brightness to enter the room as they placed the room under the scrutiny of the light. Nothing had changed in the years he'd been gone except that everything—the floor, the sink, the refrigerator and stove, the napkin holder on the table—had become a drearier, more depressing version of itself. Like his mother had. Maybe like he had too.

She'd prepared dinner for them from the casseroles she'd gotten from neighbors after her husband's death. Bill had no taste for fancy foods, but these dishes were inedible. His mother ate two mouthfuls and put her hand on the table, holding the fork in her fist, like a child might.

"So, tell me about yourself Billy," she said, looking in the direction of his face, her eyes never actually focusing on him, just as he imagined she wouldn't focus on what he might say in reply to her question. And what could he tell her? That he'd made lots of money and blown most of it on one thing or another. That he'd married Rose because he'd gotten her pregnant and then regretted it for ten years, through the birth of each of his kids. That he hardly ever saw his kids because of work, but that he'd taken whatever work came his way because he didn't care enough to be around for them?

"I'm fine, Ma," he said, taking a last forkful of an unidentifiable casserole. "What about yourself?" He thought that if he got her to talk, he could unfocus, not be so undeniably where he was: in that room, with her, facing maybe two weeks of this. "How're you holding up?"

Slowly she recounted the progress of the disease through Bill's father once he'd entered the hospital: the details of his dying body, of the efforts made to keep him out of pain, and their failure. She described picking clothes out for the funeral, for herself and her dead husband. The viewing at Hansen's, the church service, the turnout at the cemetery, the burial, the kindness of neighbors. Bill found it impossible to turn his mind from her words. Instead, he was fascinated by how devoid of feeling they were; how they described neither grief nor release, nothing but appearance, affect. Like all the conversations that had taken place around this table when he lived here: all the hollowed-out, angry, mindless conversations. He pushed the memories aside wondering if there was a beer in the refrigerator, got up to find that there wasn't, sat down again, his mother never interrupting her droning recitation.

When she finally stopped, she sat for a minute staring at the table, waiting, it seemed to Bill, for the sound of her voice telling the tale of her husband's death to dissipate completely before she went on to something else. After a long moment, she looked up. "How long will you stay, Billy?"

"I can stay a couple of weeks," he said, lighting a cigarette as if to remind her that it would be two weeks of habits she might not care for. "If you need me." Bill actually had five weeks before he needed to be in Texas, but he'd be damned if he'd spend it all here, sleeping in the same bed he'd slept in as a kid.

"We'll see," she said, pushing herself out of the seat. "I'll make you some coffee."

It was late June, but the temperature had dropped through the evening. Over the years Bill had become much more comfortable in heat than he was in cold, but he opened the bedroom window wide when he went to sleep: the room was so close and musty he thought he would choke otherwise. Only a few crickets sounded as he was falling asleep. He thought it must have been a cool spring, and wondered when the river ice had finally broken up. He would've liked to have seen that again. No place he'd lived since he'd left had ice that wasn't made in a freezer.

Bill drank coffee with his mother in the morning, ate the cold toast she put in front of him ("I've been up for two hours already," she said), declined the congealed eggs, and discovered that he was on his last cigarette, which gave him an excuse to get out of the house.

"Be careful on the road, Billy," his mother said. She was at the kitchen sink with her back to him, and he thought if she turned around she'd be surprised to see that she wasn't talking to the young Billy, who wouldn't have listened to her anyway. "Cars drive a lot faster these days."

Than when? he thought. His life had obviously stopped for her when he left seventeen years before. "I'll be back in a little while Ma."

"I want you to see your father's grave," she yelled to him as he reached the front door. She'd said it twice during breakfast as well, but this time some otherwise depleted lung power came to her aid, and though her voice cracked, her determination carried clearly from the kitchen.

Bill let the sound of his feet on the front steps be his answer for now. There'd be plenty of time to go to the cemetery if he was going to be here two weeks; if he lasted two weeks. And what did she think he would see in a mound of dirt covering a not-yet-settled grave? He suddenly couldn't remember for the life of him why he had decided to come back here.

The quarter mile he walked to the general store looked almost exactly as it had seventeen years before. The Skylars were taking in guests now, but except for the sign ("Overton Inn: Rest and

Relaxation on the River"), the property looked the same. A boulder had been placed at the foot of the flagpole on the tiny triangle of grass that served as the town square; a plaque had been attached to the boulder, and Bill could see that Overton had been declared a Historic District. It didn't say who had made the declaration, but he thought it described the town perfectly: history, and nothing but history, grinding the place and its people into dust, a little more each day. He imagined that nothing new had come to this town since Eva, and as far as he could tell from the little he'd heard about her over the years, even she had succumbed to the weight of Overton's history: she'd Americanized and Overtonized herself, fitting in with all the people who couldn't hold a candle to her when she'd first arrived.

Despite a new owner, the general store also looked like it always had: boxes of matches sitting next to cans of sauerkraut; work gloves by the beans. The same cans of beans, for all Bill knew, that had been there the day he left town. The new owner even looked like the old. It was like seeing the symptoms of a disease that kept things and people immobilized, not new or young, but unchanging in every other way. Bill thought that if he hung around too long he might get infected, might be overtaken by the twenty-year-old he was before he got out into the world, as if that person still existed in some ghostly, amorphous form just waiting to return to his body and force him to take up what he'd left behind so suddenly seventeen years before.

There were three other men in the store, all of them talking with the owner, whose name Bill picked out of the conversation as he walked to the post office at the back of the building. He sent the monthly money order to Rose, and though the woman behind the counter looked at him strangely, he assumed it was because she didn't know who he was, not because she did. He was hoping that was it: he didn't want to have to explain himself too often, wanted to get back out of the town before being pulled too far in.

When Bill went back up front, the three men were still at the counter, but he could tell that their conversation had changed. Their voices seemed more studied, declamatory, each of their words less related to those being spoken by the others. And though they were standing exactly where they had been when Bill had first come through the store, their postures were different, angled just slightly away from the counter, their attention thrown out of the corner of their eyes toward the wall of magazines opposite where they stood, and in front of which stood a girl, her back to them as she dragged her finger over the racks. She had on blue jeans and a gray sweatshirt that had the Penn State emblem on it. Her hair was jet-black and tied back in a tight ponytail. Bill couldn't tell what her age was but he guessed by the attitudes of the men in the store that she was old enough. And old enough, he could see, to be aware of being looked at. She kept shifting her weight from one leg to the other, pressing the curve of her bottom against the denim of her pants seat. She had one hand on her hip, and under its grasp, Bill could see the curve of her waist descending into the hip. He could see what the other men saw, what pulled their attention toward her, maybe even against their wills. Grown men, maybe with daughters of their own who were this girl's age, or would be soon, who would be the trigger for this kind of guarded reaction in other men who would be made uneasy by what they were feeling. Bill, on the other hand, had three mama's-boy sons. He only wondered if they'd ever pull out of her shadow long enough to see that there were girls like this to think about.

The girl turned suddenly: she'd found the magazine she was looking for. But Bill had the distinct impression that she'd also felt his eyes on her, the unfamiliar attention of a new observer, because as she turned she swept her gaze across his and he was startled by the way her eyes seemed to know they were catching him out. And by the way he seemed to know those eyes. But her gaze was so quick to move on that he immediately doubted what he thought he saw there, and then she was focused on the three men at the counter who shuffled just out of her way, wanting and not wanting to be touched by her.

When Bill heard the door swing open and his name being called, he had to wrench his sight off the girl to see who the voice belonged to. The man coming toward him was familiar, but not familiar enough to have a name.

"Bill, how you doing?" he said in a loud, friendly voice, holding his hand out. Bill shook it, smiled, said fine, fine, how about yourself, while he nodded his head and hoped some knowledge of the man might shake loose. "Frank. Frank Lewis," the man said, his hands held out as if to give himself a frame.

"Frank. Of course. Sorry," Bill said, realizing why he hadn't recognized him: seventeen years had doubled Frank Lewis's weight, pushed out much of his hair. He'd been a kid when Bill had left town, one of the younger siblings of the Lewis clan. He was a man now, gone soft and red in the face. "I'm still catching up to myself here. Just got off the plane from Saudi Arabia a few days ago," Bill said, trying to explain his forgetting in other ways.

"Well, I knew you were going to be around. Your sister

Maggie told me you were coming in after the funeral. So I've been on the lookout."

They were both nodding now, hands moving into their pockets, their feet squaring off, assuming the posture of conversation. Bill slipped into it more easily than he'd expected himself to. "Sorry to hear about your father," Frank said.

"Yeah. Thanks."

"How's your mother doing? She seemed pretty good after the funeral."

"I think she'll be all right." Now that they were talking, he could look away from Frank, and he was looking for the girl. She was no longer in the store, but over Frank's shoulder, he could see her walking slowly down the center of the road, flipping through the magazine.

Bill missed a few of the things that Frank said, but it didn't seem to matter much. The conversation wound slowly around itself, leading nowhere in particular.

"Why don't you come up to the Stoneridge tonight?" Frank said out of a short silence. "See some of your old friends."

"Maybe I'll do that," Bill replied, nodding again. "Get me out of the house." He slapped Frank lightly on the shoulder. "Yeah, maybe I'll see you tonight then."

Bill bought cigarettes and walked the quarter mile back to the house. He had that girl on his mind: walking down the center of the road like all the world would naturally make room for her. Hips doing a slow rock. She was probably sixteen or seventeen, but obviously nothing like the girls he'd known at that age. He thought of his friend's offer to get him a date while he waited out his extra days in New York. Now he wished he'd taken him up on it.

The day passed slowly. Bill's mother took a long time explaining the details of his father's will. She read through every sentence, the party of this part and that part, as if she were exhibiting some special knowledge by being able to read the language of lawyers. He stopped listening after it became clear that he was barely involved: Joe had power of attorney where "the estate" was concerned (Bill glanced around him when his mother read those words, stifling a laugh and wondering if some lawyer had intended a cruel joke) and he didn't imagine there'd be much of anything left after his mother died, or that he'd want to have to deal with his brother in order to get it, however much it might be.

His mother gave no indication of knowing what had gone wrong between him and Joe, but she knew that enough of something had happened so that she shouldn't expect them to be in the same house together. She'd spoken about his sisters wanting to see him and when they might come over; aunts and uncles, cousins, but no mention of Joe and his family in that regard. Bill wondered what Joe had told her, what he'd told their sisters, his wife. He gave Joe credit anyway for not turning the family against him, but he was still at a disadvantage not knowing what they thought they knew. And maybe that was enough for Joe, to know that Bill would be wondering.

Maggie visited that afternoon with her kids, ten-year-old Kenny and thirteen-year-old Tim. She was about forty-one now, Bill realized, and he thought she looked it. She had that before-her-time middle-aged look that he'd seen women take on after they'd had what they wanted to be their last child. Everything about her said, 'no more sex, if you don't mind.' Just like Rose. Until after he'd left her. Then she went back to dressing and acting the way she had when he'd first met her, and fallen for her.

Kenny and Tim seemed confused that they had an uncle they'd never met, and their grandmother's shrill admonition to shake their uncle's hand like little men didn't do much to endear Bill to them. Nor did he make much effort on his own behalf.

"How're your boys, Bill?" Maggie asked when an uncomfortable lull cut into the conversation.

"They're fine," he said, but no more, not wanting to have to explain anything about his marriage. And Maggie didn't pursue it.

Her husband showed up a little while later. He was a schoolteacher, a decent guy, Bill thought, but they had nothing in common and Bill had grown tired of even thinking about making conversation. He stayed quiet through much of dinner while Maggie recounted the details of the funeral that Bill had already heard from his mother. As soon as he could, he made a quick excuse, pushing his chair back from the table with enough force to rattle some of the plates. Everyone looked a little surprised but he figured no one would raise a word of protest and no one did.

Bill took the drive to the Stoneridge slowly. The deer would be foraging for food, as liable to step in front of a fast-moving car as not. He remembered when he was a boy, walking along this road with Joe sometimes on an evening like this, scouting out the deer they might be hunting together come the next winter, trying in halfhearted ways to get the animals used to humans so they'd be easier to target. Bill hit the accelerator. It seemed like every inch of this town could push up some memory that might take him over, make him feel as though he belonged here now just because he once had. Well, the day had never come when he and Joe hunted together. Bill was too young, too inexperienced, would take too much tending in the woods; Joe always had an excuse. Bill just had to follow each memory far enough and maybe he could avoid the pull of memory altogether. He pushed the car faster still.

"Let these deer fend for themselves," he said, his voice garbled in the noise of the wind rushing in and out of the window.

There was only one other car in the Stoneridge parking lot when Bill arrived. He hadn't realized how early it was, but that was okay: he'd have a couple of drinks by himself, which he realized was what he really wanted once he'd opened the door and saw the place empty except for a man at the far end of the bar. Solitude, anonymity, enough booze to get him to an easy sleep. Bill had only been here once or twice years ago—it had been the watering hole for his father and his cronies—so there was hardly a trace of memory embedded in the place for him. He sat, nodded to the other drinker, and ordered a beer and a shot. His first taste since a few hours before he'd arrived at his mother's house yesterday, and it went down like silk. He ordered another shot and downed that too before taking a drink of the beer. Maybe he'd get out of there before anyone he knew came in. What was he supposed to say to people after seventeen years? They'd all been kids, himself included, when he left: in their late teens and early twenties, but kids all the same. He could hardly remember himself then. The circumstances of his life, yes, but himself inside of them hardly at all. And he'd spent most of the first year in Oklahoma forcefully putting his past away. Long hours working: backbreaking, mind-numbing, dirty, humiliating until he became adept. Staring into faces of men he saw every day but couldn't know, into the flat sameness of the plains, the sky, the blue eyes of women. He tried only to date women with blue eyes. One look into a dark pair of eyes, no matter what invitation or challenge he saw there, and he turned away. He hadn't wanted to be reminded of Eva, though he was certain that there was not another pair of dark eyes with the intensity of hers, the promise and knowledge. The connivance. He figured every woman's eyes held some of that, since they all seemed to have that ability built in. But Eva's ability was especially fine-tuned. Maybe the only thing she hadn't known she was doing was teaching him to be suspicious, which, as it turned out, kept him out of trouble with a lot of other women.

Except with Rose. He hadn't seen clearly enough with her. She'd been sexy and brash and blue-eyed. She'd grown up around the oil fields, her father a wildcatter, her two brothers riggers. She liked the smell of oil and the money it brought in. She liked to spend the first part of a Saturday night at a bar with Bill, flirting with every other man who looked her way, and the rest of the night convincing Bill that she flirted only to get him jealous and just hot enough under the collar to make him hot. And then she was pregnant. They got married, William, Jr., was born, they were a family, and Rose suddenly wanting family things—their own house with a nice kitchen, a station wagon because certainly Billy wouldn't be the only child—rather than the things she'd wanted from him when there was no child, when she wanted him without fail every Saturday night into Sunday morning. So he started taking jobs that kept him away from home for a few days at a time. That made a difference for a while: she'd be glad to see him when he got back and be like her old self once the baby had been put to sleep. But that would wear off after a week or so, and instead of asking how long he'd be staying like she had earlier in the week, she'd be asking him when he thought they might be able to put a down payment on a house.

He used that as his excuse. The only way he was going to get money for the down was by working: overtime, twelve-hour shifts, and as he became more experienced, on the Gulf rigs where the pay was higher, the conditions more dangerous, the shifts measured in days and not hours, and then, finally, in weeks. He was so blindly hungry for Rose when he got home, he didn't realize for a long time how angry she was, or how pregnant. Eighteen months after their second son, John, was born, made even more hungry for Rose by the taste of other women, he didn't realize at first that their third child, the first one to be brought home to their own house, might not be his.

Bill was aware of his name being called, but it took the slap to his back to bring him up out of the past. And when he raised his eyes, the bar was growing populated. Frank Lewis was sitting next to him.

"Where were you?" Frank asked, laughing. "I called your name half a dozen times before you heard me."

"Just where I shouldn't be," Bill said. "Wrong place. Wrong woman."

"Speaking of which," Frank said. He ordered a beer. "What did you think of your niece?"

Bill assumed he was talking about his sister Jean's daughter. "I haven't seen Jean's family yet," he said.

"No, I mean Lilly. Joe and Eva's girl."

"I never met her. Born after I left." Frank had begun to laugh quietly, as if he were just getting an inside joke, but Bill had no idea what it might be. He went on: "And I don't think Eva's going to come 'round with her kids to meet the uncle they've probably never heard of, brother to the father they don't see. Wasn't a very friendly divorce according to my mother."

Frank's laughter had slowed down while Bill was talking. One last chuckle came out like a belch. "You're not kidding, are you?"

Bill lit a cigarette, snapped his lighter shut. "About what?"

"You didn't know that was Lilly."

"Who?"

"The girl in the store today. That was Lilly. I figured you were talking to her before I got there."

Bill suddenly realized that Frank was talking about the girl at the magazine rack. She was his niece, probably conceived in some fit of jealousy or heat that Eva had used him to generate with Joe. "How would I know that was Lilly?" Bill ordered another round, trying to keep his voice nonchalant.

"Well, I figured you must've seen pictures over the years." Bill shook his head no. Frank raised his eyebrows in surprise. "Well, then because she's a dead ringer for Eva."

Bill pushed his empty glass to the back of the counter. The bartender put a full one in front of him. He'd lost count of how many he'd had already, but his mind was working with inescapable clarity. Lilly's image pulled instantly into focus: turning from the magazine rack, catching his glance. He'd been right: he did know those eyes, it was just that they were in a different face than he remembered them in.

"I guess I didn't see the resemblance," Bill said, hoping they could leave it at that. He didn't want to discuss what he'd thought of the girl he hadn't known was his niece. Or the way his mind was easily slipping back into those same thoughts now even though he knew.

"Well, that would make you the only man around here who doesn't," Frank said, his voice huskier than normal. "And nobody's sorry to have two of the same kind to look at." He gave Bill a sidelong, conspiratorial glance, which Bill saw but ignored. He was thinking instead about Frank admiring Eva over the years, which, clearly, he had. Wanting her, probably. Dividing that wanting into two when Lilly got old enough. And not just Frank; maybe most of the men in this bar.

"What did you mean about her being a wrong kind of woman?" Bill asked. A wrong kind of woman like Eva? How much could Frank know about Eva unless she had made herself known to him, to other men as well? Other men than Bill. The thing that he had never considered before.

"Well, she's got some of Eva's spunk, if you know what I mean."

"No, Frank, I don't."

"Well, I just mean that Eva was always a little different than the other women around here."

"That makes her a wrong kind of woman?"

"Well, different then, like I said. A little more adventurous maybe. Not the kind any of us would have thought of marrying really. Not until Joe showed us the way."

"And you think Lilly is like that? More adventurous, not the kind you'd want to marry."

"Look, I don't mean any disrespect to your family, Bill. But you've got to admit, Lilly has a different kind of maturity than most girls her age."

"I guess I didn't see that either," Bill said. He'd been staring at Frank, but he turned his head now toward the bartender who was standing with his arms folded, nodding at the one-sided conversation someone was having with him. That's the way Bill wished he'd kept it with Frank.

"Well, I'll say it again," Frank said, ignoring, or maybe just ignorant of the checked anger Bill's voice had held. "You're the only man in that store who didn't." He patted Bill on the back as if he were dealing with a cranky child.

Bill wanted to swat Frank's hand off, to do more than just swat at him. Because, of course, he had noticed everything about Lilly, and he hated that Frank could know what he felt. And he hated being stirred by this girl, the offspring of that time he'd tried so hard to forget, or hate, or both.

Another hand slapped his back and he turned to find Rick Beecher. They'd been good friends once; Rick was the only person who had known that Bill left Overton because of a falling out with Joe. And though Bill had never told him what had caused the rift, he remembered how good it had felt then to tell even that much of the truth to someone.

"Man, it's good to see you," Bill said as Rick took the stool next to him. He hadn't said that to anyone else since arriving in Overton, hadn't come even close to the feeling. And truthfully, he couldn't say for sure that he felt it about Rick because he still felt a bond of friendship after seventeen years, or just because he was relieved to have a reason to turn away from Frank and the other men who had joined him.

Bill and Rick caught each other up on their lives in a determinedly undetailed way. Neither of them was anxious to recite his past, and realizing that, they were able to relax with each other. The conversation made its way to Bill's father's death and the funeral, which Rick had attended: he seemed much more thoughtful about it than either Bill's mother or sister. His voice was quiet compared to the rest of the men around them. He had always been soft-spoken, but Bill suspected that the death of his son in a diving accident at the river three years before—which his mother had told him about in a letter just after it happened—had quieted him even more.

"I was really sorry to hear about your boy." Bill had thought about sending a condolence card at the time, but never got around to it. Now he couldn't even remember the kid's name.

"Thanks Billy." Rick looked down into his drink, nodded his head slowly. They were silent for a couple of minutes. "You think about all the times you went off the bridge yourself, and you can almost imagine what it was like for him to go under." He squeezed his eyes shut and Bill patted him on the shoulder. Rick looked up, a slight smile of thanks on his lips. "I don't know if you knew it, but he was a little slow." Bill hadn't known. He'd only learned that Rick even had a son when he'd heard about his death. "Not retarded. But a little slower than the other kids. None of them were really mean to him. But they were kids. And Wayne didn't usually get when they meant things as a joke. He figured if he did whatever they did, they'd accept him." He took a drink and lit a cigarette before going on. "We couldn't always watch him, but every spring I sat him down and told him to keep away from that bridge, even when the other kids went there to dive. He couldn't even swim except for the doggie paddle. And he didn't know enough to know when the river might be dangerous."

Bill was quiet, grateful to not be answering questions about himself. And Rick seemed to need to talk.

"But Wayne really loved your niece," Rick said. He didn't see the surprise in Bill's face. "He talked about Lilly all the time.

How pretty she was, and how nice she was to him. He would've done anything to get in good with her."

"What do you mean?"

"Well, we figured he probably just tagged along with her. And she was too nice to tell him to stay away."

"You mean she was with him when he jumped?" Everything about Bill showed his surprise now—his posture, his face, the clutch of his hands, one around his glass, the other on the edge of the bar.

"Your mother didn't tell you?"

"She only told me that Wayne had died jumping off the bridge. Not that Lilly had anything to do with it."

"She didn't have anything to do with it, Bill," he said, putting his hand up.

Bill was looking Rick straight in the eye, but he had stopped being able to see how much pain it still caused Rick to talk about his son's death. Bill was only concerned now with knowing the whole story; Lilly's involvement had sparked his interest. "She was there?" He could hear that his voice was perhaps too insistent.

Rick was hesitating. Bill forced softness into his voice. "I'm sorry, Rick. We don't have to talk about it." Rick took a deep breath. "It's just strange," Bill went on, still pushing a little, "that my mother didn't say anything."

"I'm sure she just didn't think it was important since you didn't even know Lilly. And it was nobody's fault. Really."

Bill said nothing, sensing that Rick would talk about it without any prompting.

Rick finished his drink and ordered another. He adjusted his body on the stool, and placed his forearms on the bar. He folded his hands around his glass, and began talking. He told Bill how

Wayne and then Lilly had jumped, how a woman from the other side of the river had seen them, pulled Lilly out of the water, called the police. He told Bill exactly where Wayne's body had been found. He described what it was like to identify the lifeless body of his own son; to bury that body next to the generations of the family whose deaths in old age had made the sense Wayne's hadn't. He told Bill how his wife had stopped going to church after the funeral, saying to him one evening, "Now you can talk to me about not believing in God." How her sadness hadn't lifted yet; how he had to be less sad for both of them, and for their other two kids; how he lied in order to be able to do that: he was as sad as his wife was, and he didn't think the sadness would ever lift.

Rick talked without a break until he came to the end of the story. Bill didn't know what to do for a man who seemed about to cry. "I can't imagine what it must have been like, Rick." It was all he could think to say.

"Yeah," Rick said, turning his glass in his hands. He hadn't so much as sipped at it since he'd started talking. "I guess no one can imagine it even if you've got kids of your own. It's something your mind won't let you think unless it absolutely has to."

But Bill hadn't been thinking of his own kids. He was responding to the terrible sadness he saw in Rick—that was what he couldn't imagine. Even at his worst, just after Joe had told him to leave and he'd decided to take his brother's demand to its extreme: to leave Overton, then Pennsylvania, then the Northeast, and eventually the country. Even then, as sad as he had had a right to feel—leaving everything he'd ever known, all his friends, everyone in the world who knew him—he'd been able to turn it into something else. He wasn't really sure what to call it: determination maybe; sheer will; simple cussedness. Whatever it had been, it had gotten him through a tough, lonely, uncertain time. He wished he could give Rick the secret to that transformation; felt in that moment that he would've helped him if he could have, but knew he couldn't. They came from completely different worlds now.

"Let me get you another beer," Bill said, signaling to the bartender. "That one's probably flat."

"No, Billy, thanks. I ought to get home." Rick pushed his glass to the far side of the bar and reached toward his back pocket for his wallet.

"I'll get this," Bill said, reaching for his own wallet. He felt he owed Rick at least these drinks for the story he'd just told. And he paid his own tab as well. Frank and the other men had drifted to a table at the far side of the room. Bill walked past them on the way out, shaking hands, murmuring the glad-to-see-you's he imagined everyone expected of him; answering that he didn't know to the question of how long he'd be in town. Would they be seeing him again? No doubt sometime before he left, and he left it at that. Rick had moved toward the door and Bill joined him just as he stepped outside.

"Are you going to be okay? Want me to drive you home?" Rick began shaking his head. "You can pick the car up tomorrow." Rick held up a hand in answer. He didn't want Bill's help, and he couldn't say the words at that moment because he was trying to hide the fact of his tears.

"Okay," Bill said, shaking the hand Rick held out to him. "Get yourself home safely."

"I will, Billy," Rick said finally, his voice breaking. He took a deep breath. "Thanks for listening."

Bill watched him get in his car and drive away, got in his own car, and sat for a few minutes with the engine off and the windows open. He lit a cigarette, aware of how fresh the air tasted in the instant before he took the first drag, not sorry to have the freshness sullied by the smoke. He started the engine: the car rumbled when it idled, the muffler shook in its clamps; whatever peace this patch of the night had held a minute ago was ruptured now. The way Bill's thinking about Rick was suddenly ruptured by thoughts of Lilly.

Rick hadn't said that much about the girl beyond the suggestion that her presence on the bridge had been the reason Wayne had gone there. She was there, she was in the water, she was pulled out of the water, end of Lilly's part in it. But Bill wondered if Rick had been careful about what he'd said after he saw how surprised Bill was hearing that Lilly was involved, and maybe he hadn't wanted to upset Bill any more so soon after his father's death. Bill couldn't help thinking about it though: shouldn't Lilly have been smart enough to have kept Wayne from jumping? She'd known he was slow, probably knew he couldn't swim. Didn't the fact that she didn't try to stop him make her responsible in some way? And didn't it make sense that questions like these would've occurred to Rick too?

Bill pulled slowly out of the parking lot, his eyelids drooping over his beer-blurred eyes. It was only ten-thirty, but most of the houses were already dark. Bill kept the car at a slow speed: there was no sense risking an accident with that one other car that might be on the road somewhere. And it gave him the chance to think things through before he got back to his mother's house. He flicked his cigarette out the window. Lilly must've been making that jump for years already by the time Wayne jumped with her. She'd been fourteen. Kids had always started when they were ten or eleven, egged on by older siblings and friends. So she knew the serious dangers of the spring freshet, of the eddies formed in a high river. If she'd been thinking at all, she would've made sure Wayne didn't jump, maybe wouldn't have jumped herself. Maybe like any fourteen-year-old she believed she was indestructible. But she knew, she must have known, that that wasn't true of Wayne.

Bill's mother had left the outside light on, but inside the house was dark. He pulled a beer out of the six-pack he'd put in the refrigerator that afternoon, turned the television on and sat in what he remembered to have been his father's chair. His eyes were watching the screen, but they weren't focused. He wasn't thinking about anything now, this last beer turning some switch off in his mind. He waited for his eyes to grow heavy enough and then took himself to bed.

1975

ON A THURSDAY in early October, Alan Gill, a classics professor who had been on Cannen's faculty for twenty years, invited everyone for Friday. Nina had less than twenty-four hours to arrive at a viable excuse for not going. The last thing she wanted was a couple of hours among people who—in spite of the fact that she'd been introduced to some of them at Tony's side—were basically all strangers to her. Diane had said they were thirsty for new blood, and hers was even newer than Tony's. She couldn't bear the idea of being the center of attention—she didn't like it even when she was most at ease—of having to explain herself, especially when what most clearly explained her now was that she felt lost to herself, something she didn't want to talk about to anyone but Chris. She wanted Tony to refuse the invitation for both of them: say it was impossibly short notice, that they had other plans, she was ill, anything that would give them some time alone since they'd had so little of it in the three-plus weeks she'd been there. That's how she presented it to him: as desire, without a note of the anxiety that was ruling her. But Tony thought he should go, it was the politic thing to do, and he wanted her to be there with him. He assured her that Gill had said "an informal gathering," promised they wouldn't stay late, they'd have the whole rest of the night to themselves. She knew that if she objected any more, he'd want to know more about her objections.

When they walked into Alan Gill's house they found themselves staring into a crowd in which most of the men wore jackets, some had ties on as well, at least half a dozen of the women sported variations on the little black dress, and the host was wearing something like an ascot. Tony's black turtleneck and worn jeans gave him an appropriately bohemian, painterly look, but Nina suspected she appeared merely young in her jeans and sweater. She looked like these peoples' students, like their children in some cases, like herself.

"Well, here they are," Alan Gill exclaimed so that his voice was heard above the din. He walked toward them with his hands outstretched, put himself between them, took their arms in his, and led them to a makeshift bar. Nina put her hand back in Tony's as soon as Gill released their arms.

"Now," Gill said after he'd filled glasses of wine for them. He rubbed his hands together and turned to Nina. "To introduce you to the waiting masses. Come."

The masses did not seem to be waiting at all, but Gill steered her directly into their midst. She pulled Tony along behind her, hoping he would think it was just another expression of her desire not to be without him. He stayed close by her side and kept them connected with a hand on her shoulder, at the small of her back, behind her neck. She let her inner attention be drawn toward each touch, the caress in the simple pressure of his fingers, that instant of knowing between them. And gradually, gratefully, she began to feel split: one part of her able to make the requisite sounds of attention and conversation, the other safely removed into Tony's presence.

Professor Gill—as everyone seemed to call him—moved her from person to person, extracting from each whatever information he deemed interesting and necessary for Nina to know, and giving them just enough time to ask her one or two questions in return. Names she was told attached to faces only until she was told the next; the information she was given to know about them—years at Cannen, departments, brief personal anecdotes— she listened to without really hearing. Diane was an unexpectedly welcome sight. She kissed Nina hello and whispered, "Courage," into her ear in an exaggerated French accent, and it was the one encounter that might have put Nina at some ease, but Professor Gill moved her along as if there were a clock to beat.

Diane had been wrong about people's interest in Nina, her new blood notwithstanding. Most of them wanted to know where she'd gone to college, and when they learned she hadn't, and that she also hadn't decided what she was going to do here yet, their attention to her became diffuse and took in Tony as well—how did they like the cottage, how was Tony finding Cannen, what did he think of the caliber of his students—until Professor Gill decided it was time to move on. After about fifteen minutes, the two parts Nina had felt herself separate into began to come together. She was still sharply aware of Tony's touch, but there was a buzz in her head now that she couldn't ignore: the repetition of the same questions asked of her and of her answers—no, I don't know yet, it's fine—all of it more accidental sound than meaning. She felt as if she were speaking a language she hadn't quite mastered, unable to make it express anything more than the simplest facts, and even those might have been interchangeable with others, opposites, falsehoods, for all they mattered. She felt muted by the brief, halting conversations: as if their only purpose were to remind her that if there ever had been any complexity to her thinking, to herself, it was gone now. She could hardly imagine what she might say if she thought anyone would really be interested. Tony's hand grew heavier on her neck, its steadying effect giving way to its simple weight and heft. Her body yearned past it, back out the front door, into the car, onto the road, where she could race out ahead of herself.

"Tony's been telling me about you," said a woman who introduced herself as Andrea Torrance and playfully pushed Professor Gill out of the way, assuming a familiarity that grabbed Nina's attention. She briefly caught Tony's eye and he smoothed his hand back and forth across her shoulder in what she could feel he meant to be a reassuring motion. "I've been anxious to have a chance to talk," Andrea went on. "I've got a proposition for you."

"Well. A proposition," Professor Gill said, taking a few steps backward. "That's my cue to check the hors d'oeuvres."

Tony ran his hand down and up Nina's back. "I'm going to get some more wine. Refills?" Both women declined. He moved his hand across Nina's shoulder and down the length of her arm before he moved off into the crowd. Her arm swung out, just a few fractions of an inch, in his direction.

Tony had told Andrea about Nina being a self-taught mechanic and how in New York she'd worked at a kind of chop shop, the only woman in the garage.

"It wasn't a chop shop," Nina said, cutting into Andrea's words. She would at least declare what she knew with certainty. "Tony always says that, but it's not true."

"Well, I suppose that's not really the point," Andrea went on, shaking her head as if to put her thoughts back into line around Nina's interruption. Her point was that she thought it would be great if Nina would talk about participating in a traditionally male line of work with the students in Andrea's "Feminism: Literature and Reality" class.

"I don't really have all that much to say about it," Nina said, knowing already that she'd never agree to do it. Over Andrea's shoulder she saw Tony talking to a woman—part of the administration? history department? Carol? Lucinda?

"Well, Tony says you're very articulate about it," Andrea said. Nina began to protest, but Andrea jumped back in: "Don't say no yet. Let me just tell you what I'm thinking."

Andrea spoke fast and her eyes roamed the room as she spoke, a habit Nina assumed she'd perfected and now couldn't leave in the classroom; or perhaps she was making sure that there was no one in the room more important to her at that moment. Nina didn't care. Andrea's split attention gave her the chance to do the same with her own. She was listening with the merest part of herself, everything else antennaed to Tony, who had laid his hand on the woman's shoulder so that his fingers spilled over onto her back.

"He uses his behavior with you to get other women's attention," Chris had said to her a few months before. At the time,

Nina had shrugged the comment off as an example of Chris's tendency to complicate.

"You mean he's a flirt," Nina had said. "I know he's a flirt."

"That's one way of putting it," Chris had said, but Nina had known she was only conceding the surface of her words.

Tony's hand lingered on the woman's shoulder, only his fingers moving, in emphasis of something he was, or wasn't, saying. With his other hand he began to gesture toward the bar, and then back at Nina. He was bringing the conversation to a close. Nina didn't avert her gaze; she didn't care if he noticed her watching them. He slid his hand down the woman's arm as he walked away from her. Nina felt herself split into two again. She knew what the woman's arm felt like, as clearly as if the touch had been to her own arm again. But she was also seeing through the other woman's eyes—any other woman's eyes—what Tony's touch appeared to tell about him.

Andrea's voice cracked through her thoughts: "So will you think about it?"

"Sure," Nina said, managing to pull her lips into a smile, but it was unconnected to anything in the rest of her face, to her voice, or the stiff stance her body had assumed, stiffening more when she felt another hand on her back.

Professor Gill handed new glasses of wine to both women and placed their old glasses on the table behind him. "Well, Andrea, may I have my guest back now?" Before Andrea could answer, before Nina could protest, Professor Gill had steered her onto the dark patio in the back.

"I wanted to show you this," he said, sweeping his hand before them. "Since the fire I've been the only inhabitant of this vast estate and I'm able to roam the property at will." He pushed his long gray hair behind his ears. His moves and words all seemed calculated, though Nina doubted that the effect he was having on her was the desired one. "You can see the attraction even in the dark, can't you." A statement rather than a question, his hand on the small of her back again, moving her along the patio, deeper into the dark.

"I'm sure it's great," she said, stepping sideways out of the range of his touch, which felt indelicate and insipid.

"You will absolutely have to come back in the daytime to get the full effect. Late afternoon is the best. The sun setting, the light golden and long . . ." His voice trailed off and he struck a pose so theatrical Nina had to clamp her lips together to keep from laughing.

"So," he said, rousing himself from his contemplative appreciation, or whatever it was. "Tony tells me that you're an automobile mechanic."

"Yeah. I can fix cars."

"Tony says you are a supreme practitioner of the automotive arts."

Nina was certain that Tony had never said "automotive arts" in his life. "Well. I'm pretty good at it."

"Something tells me your modesty runs as deep as your talents," Professor Gill said with a complicated flourish of his right hand. "Tony is such a superb painter. I'm sure his visual sense extends to you as well."

Nina tried to look him in the eyes, but the darkness made holes of them. "I guess. He does like the look of grease under my nails."

A low, bubbly trill escaped from the professor's mouth. "Well, no doubt he does, since a little grease could hardly mar your beauty," he said, placing his hand on her shoulder, pulling himself toward her. "But I meant that Tony is of course capable of seeing beneath someone's physical beauty to her more divine attributes."

Nina stepped out from under his hand. "And that has to do with the fact that I fix cars?"

"Well, my dear," he said, and Nina could hear in those three words the leading edge of annoyance at the fact that she wasn't succumbing to what he might imagine were his considerable charms. "I only mean to say that you are clearly—"

Someone called him from inside. He placed his hand on her shoulder promising they would·finish this conversation later, and he walked quickly into the living room.

She started to follow him inside, but thought better of it. Why not just stay here? She had a full glass of wine and her cigarettes, her sweater was warm, and the patio was protected from the wind. There was no one she wanted to have any more conversation with, and she didn't see Tony anywhere. She pulled one of the wrought-iron chairs out of the light from the living room, lit a cigarette, and took a long drink.

It was a black night: the sky clear and moonless, and though full of stars, their collective light was bright enough only to gray the far background of space. The closer darkness, the one that seemed to exist beneath the stars, was the one Nina had known she wouldn't like. It was there in the bedroom at night just as she had anticipated, and when Tony fell asleep first, taking his perception of her with him, she felt the darkness move in closer, take on weight, begin to immobilize her with its density. She would close her eyes against it, trying to focus on whatever pale play of light there was on the inside of her eyelids.

She tried here too to focus on the available light, picking out one of the brighter stars in the swath of the Milky Way. But almost immediately it seemed to disappear, as if her looking at it somehow used up its light, reaching out of its own past for her eyes, so far in its future. The star popped back into existence when she moved her focus just to the right—an immeasurable stretch of time and space covered in infinitesimal fractions of both—and it entered her close peripheral vision where she could see it again. One star after another, fading and reappearing, endless light-years, time for a star's birth and death, expressed in a flaw in her sight. Or perhaps the fault was in her perception: the star didn't fade, but her mind refused to acknowledge what it knew no longer existed. She moved her gaze back and forth a few more times, losing and then finding one star in particular. Perhaps that's what she needed to do with herself: look obliquely in order to bring whatever was left of herself into view, or to see what there had been before it seemed to have disappeared, to convince herself it hadn't.

She drained her glass and stood, looking into the living room for a minute before going back in. The room was more crowded now, the people more animated—more lubricated, she thought—more relaxed. Their familiarity with each other was clear, the connections as subtle as they were obvious in an unbidden arm around a waist, in the hand that came to rest on a forearm to make a point and lingered to make another unspoken one. She thought that she would never have that kind of connection to these people, didn't want it, didn't need anyone's stone-like, presumptuous touch. She thought about walking around the side of the house to wait for Tony in the car, but then she saw him at the far end of the living room, and the sight of him drew her inside.

He was talking to two men, one of whom Nina remembered was an English professor, and the other she thought might be a German instructor but she wasn't sure, their names gone completely. Her forgetfulness made her hesitate and she stopped at the bar to pour herself more wine. She saw Tony see her, take her in as if remembering what he might have momentarily forgotten, and in the next instant, turn his head, and take his eyes off her. His hands moved in a small, directional gesture which the two men followed, glancing her way. She didn't know them, couldn't know how to read their faces, but she had the distinct impression they were having something about her explained to them, as Tony might explain one of his paintings.

Nina had never imagined that Tony thought of her as "his," but now, watching his mouth move, trying to extrapolate sense from shape, she saw him marking her: his lover, his girl the mechanic, part of his picture, his. Tony was looking at her again: his gaze seemed full of judgment and possession. She turned her back on him and topped off her glass. How much had she had? It didn't feel like enough. She drank half the glass and filled it again. It would be better if she would just stop assuming what she couldn't possibly know, stride across the room, join Tony and his colleagues, and pretend to have thought nothing of the conversation they might be having. But when she turned back toward him, her plan instantly dissolved. Tony was looking at her out of the corner of his eye, as if the conversation she'd imagined had turned away from her, but he hadn't been ready to let her go. She didn't move. His eyes shifted slowly back toward the other men, but Nina felt as if she were still being observed, being kept in his peripheral vision. She waited for him to look her way again, but when he did, nothing seemed to pass between them, and he was quickly moving her back into the periphery. She was sure of it. A look, and then a look away. Just as she had done outside, looking at the stars. Putting them into focus by looking away. Nothing there except her perception of what was no longer there. Maybe nothing here either.

She put her glass down and made her way to the patio door. A hand around her waist—Tony's hand, she knew in the instant before it settled on her—his voice, stopped her short.

"Where're you going?" His lips brushing her ear from behind. His voice soft, amused, curious.

She turned toward him. His eyes were full on her, seeing her there, right there. "I want to go, Tony."

"Are you okay?"

"I'm fine. I'm just tired of this shit." Tony's face broke into a perplexed smile. "First, Gill shuttles me around like something for show and tell." Tony let out a peal of laughter. Nina hadn't meant it to be funny. "Andrea Torrance wants to make an example of me. And you're over there having some leering conversation about me." She could see he was surprised by the anger in her voice. She was too.

His voice was quiet in response. "What are you talking about?"

"What were you telling them, Tony? Regaling them with tales of the girl mechanic, like you did with Andrea?"

"I'm sorry about Andrea. She asked questions about you and I answered them. I wasn't thinking. I'm sorry."

"And what were you telling your pals?"

He looked perplexed again, looking right at her, studying her, for answers, she thought, or maybe for substance. She could be disappearing under his gaze.

"I was telling them about the time you told that critic off, whose name I've happily forgotten, at Jack's show." She had overheard something disparaging the critic had whispered about one of the paintings. She'd tapped him on the shoulder and told him that she thought he was a very fine writer since he so clearly expressed the full range of his arrogance, pretension, and stupidity in his reviews.

"Why were you telling them that?" She struggled to keep her voice angry, but it was laced with curiosity, and concession.

"They were talking about a certain literary critic they can't stand, and I just remembered the look on that guy's face after you got through with him."

Tony was smiling, but she could see he was still perplexed by her anger. Nina turned her head. She wasn't angry at him any longer, but she couldn't look at him. She could hardly breathe.

Tony put his arms around her shoulders. "Are you all right, babe?"

This touch was hers. There was no one looking, no one watching, no one for her to watch but Tony. "I just want to go." He held her face in his hands and kissed her. She believed his touch, the kiss, his words. She believed he was looking at her, seeing her. Or trying to.

*　　*　　*　　*

The temperature dipped sharply in the middle of the month. The cottage had a woodstove, the college provided the wood, and Nina assumed that making a fire wouldn't be a problem.

What could be so difficult? She'd watched her uncle do it in his living room fireplace every Thanksgiving throughout her child-hood, and he was no backwoods type. Fireplace, woodstove, there couldn't be that much difference. She placed a few logs directly on top of balled-up newspapers which she held a match to in several places. But there was no fire: just a few puffs of smoke wafting determinedly out of the stove into the living room as the newspapers quickly and ineffectually turned to ash.

"You were never a Girl Scout, I take it," Diane said to her a little later when she saw the remnants of Nina's attempt. Nina shook her head no. "Never went to camp?" Nina shook her head again. "Never went camping?" Nina laughed out loud.

"I think that's the first time I've heard you laugh like that," Diane said, pulling her hat back down over her ears. "I'll be right back." Nina stayed where she was, staring at the door that Diane closed behind her. She waited to feel annoyed at Diane; to feel that her privacy had been invaded by Diane's scrutiny of her pat-terns of laughter. But it was Diane's pleasure in the moment that Nina was most aware of; that and her undeniably clear and quiet generosity. Nina had felt the same thing from her at Alan Gill's party, but had assumed it was just her own vast need of comfort that night making what it required out of something that would otherwise have felt discomforting.

Diane came back in a few minutes with an armload of various-sized kindling. She showed Nina how to open the flue, how to build what she called the "fire-starter's ziggurat," when to close the door, when to add the logs, when to close down the damper, when to add more logs. Nina was amazed at how illogi-cally she'd approached such a logical process, and after the one demonstration, felt confident she'd have no more trouble.

"But we didn't get any kindling in the delivery," Nina said, admiring the fire behind the glass, beginning to feel the heat rise from the iron. "Do you know who I call about it?" Diane's raised eyebrows and checked smile were enough to answer the question, but she elaborated and Nina was suddenly facing the prospect of frequent forays into the woods. She thought long-ingly of radiators, banging pipes, recalcitrant supers.

"Just watch out for fir trees," Diane said, getting ready to leave again. "The resin can coat the chimney and cause fires."

"I thought I wanted fire."

"Not in the chimney." Diane put her hands on Nina's shoulders. "Don't look so defeated. It's not nearly as painful as paying for heating oil." Easy for you to say, Nina thought, you make your own cakes.

Tony loved the image of Nina with ax and saw—neither of which they actually had, she was quick to remind him—cleaning the forest floor for the greater warmth of a cottage called Sophia.

"You know I'm not the only one who can wield this imagi-nary ax, Tony."

A couple of beats passed before he said, "I wasn't saying you should do it all," and in those few seconds Nina thought she could see that he was considering what to say so she wouldn't feel pressured or condescended to, so he wouldn't upset her fur-ther while he measured the few more aspects of her that proba-bly seemed diminished: energy, physical strength, even daring might be in there. She remembered the admiration he'd expressed for her and Chris when he found out that they had secretly run messages and supplies for the protesters at Columbia in 1968, so it wasn't hard to imagine what he might think of her now: so caught up in some unaccountable fear that she hesitated even to venture into woods that were tame and limited and abutted their backyard. She imagined him feeling cheated of the person she'd seemed to be, the one he thought had come to Vermont with him, the one they both thought had come. She felt inept—her complete lack of intuition about the stove, the stupid questions she'd asked Diane—and as small as Tony might perceive her to be.

When Tony left for his first class the next day, Nina followed him out the door by only a few minutes and walked around to the back of the house. The edge of the woods was fence-like and, she found herself thinking, foreboding. There weren't specific things she feared in the woods, but there was too much she didn't understand, too many signs she wouldn't know how to read. So she armored herself: two sweaters, a jacket, leather gloves, a hat pulled low, the steel-toed boots she'd used at the garage. Her body felt safely separated from the world.

At the edge of the yard, she pushed aside some branches, aware of a boundary being crossed, and stepped into the woods. Behind her, a sunlit, obvious backyard; in front of her, a world defined by light filtered through pine needles and leaded by bare branches; by a geography of height and circumference; by the strange, soft strength of its floor. There was a very thin coating of snow on the ground and though sunlight had melted some of it, Nina could make out animal prints, whole and partial. When she walked through them, her own prints canceled some out, but others distorted hers, leaving evidence of her presence that was more about where she was than who she was. There was no wind, no wave-like sound in the upper branches, she had no sense of being targeted by swaying trees. But the stillness was eerie in its own way. Everything seemed poised, observant, a still life that needed no further illustration to make its dichotomy clear. She took small, slow steps, aware of how each one broke through the stillness, which then redefined itself in repair. She was aware too of other small sounds and motions: an almost imperceptible play of air against needle and bark, a squirrel rushing between the trunks of two trees, a dry leaf drifting to the ground. But even in the noisiest moment—a raucous outburst from crows—she was only made more aware of the silence behind it.

In the city there had been times when the sounds of the street filled her apartment: the windows wide open in the heat, the four stories between her and the ground acting like a funnel for sound, her own sounds and thoughts displaced by engine noise, voices, horns, sirens, music, the large din of the city. Sometimes she didn't mind it, sometimes she thought it would drive her mad, but sometimes she could quiet herself enough to find the silence under the noise, inhabit it for a while before the sounds overwhelmed her again. As she walked deeper into the woods, she quieted herself in that same way, thinking that here the effect would be to allow her to hear more sounds, more evidence of recognizable life. But instead, the stillness seemed to grow even larger, the silence deeper inside it, and she was inside of them both. Her steps became slower, more calculated, stillness being drawn up out of her as well. She was dreading something: didn't calm always precede a storm of some kind? She imagined the storm in herself, but it didn't happen. A little discomfort, the flick of an irrational fear at the back of her head, but that's where it stayed. She felt a seed of calm take hold, so entirely unexpected it felt like another form of irrationality.

Who are you? she thought to and at herself; I do not commune with nature.

She reminded herself that she was here to get kindling. Smell them, Diane had told Nina when she asked how she was supposed to differentiate between fir and deciduous branches, and that's what she did now. She felt ridiculous at first, as though she were doing a bad imitation of an animal: bent over, sniffing along, twisting small sticks to expose the flesh underneath the bark. But the scent of fir was so certain and heady, Nina soon lost that image of herself, everything in her slowly focusing on the richness of the aromas, fir and otherwise now, the textures of the barks, the shifting pools of light. Her eye and hand and nose worked in a more and more perfectly choreographed routine and before long she'd opened the zipper on her jacket, pushed her hat back off her ears, and discovered that she'd already gathered too many twigs and branches to carry back to the cottage in only one trip.

She loaded wood into the crook of her arm, cradling the pieces against her chest, piling them carefully so that they interlocked. She felt them become a shape she was both holding and being supported by. Straightening up, stumbling just a little as the blood rushed from her head, Nina jiggled the wood to keep the bundle together. She thought of an illustration she'd seen of Alice in Wonderland holding the pig which seconds before had been a human baby. Alice, baffled but obstinate, trying to make sense of the transformation. Nina, in her own peculiar wonderland, baffled by the transformation that had just taken place in her own arms: her mind working in some way she wasn't following, making this unruly pile of twigs and branches into something of interest and substance for her. She shook her head and took a deep breath, unsure of where her mind might come to rest next.

She could see the clearing of the backyard in the distance, but without the balance of her arms, she had to keep her eyes on the ground most of the time or risk tripping and dropping the wood. She concentrated on the elements of her own movement, and all other thinking slipped below the surface. She was aware finally only of the way the ground took shape beneath her feet, the way her hip locked as she pulled back from an unsure footstep in order to find another, the subtle adjustments her arms made to keep the bundle of wood secure. And only when she emerged from the woods, the light bleaching out the neat yard and the dark red walls of the cottage, did she realize that her mind had settled in an unexpected place again.

When she went back for the rest of the kindling, she tried to keep track of her thinking so she could see where and why it slipped away from her. But when the cottage came into view this time, it seemed somehow two-dimensional, not nearly as real or accommodating as this spot where she was standing among the trees. This was a different sense of place than she was used to understanding, and she didn't think she was ready to understand it yet. The bundle of kindling suddenly felt cumbersome and scratchy and she pushed herself out of the woods to add it to the pile of kindling she'd already made. She took a quick guess at which pieces would fit the woodstove, was fairly accurate, and following Diane's instructions, built a ziggurat, lit a match, and started a fire. By the time Tony got home, the stove was throwing off a glorious heat.

"What would Chris say if she knew you were becoming an outdoorsman?" Tony asked, rubbing his hands in front of the stove, playing attentive audience to Nina as she added logs to the fire.

Nina closed the doors on the flames and fiddled with the baffle. "Well, first she'd give the offender a small lecture on the evil of gender-identified nouns."

Tony laughed sharply. He pulled a chair up close to the stove and waved Nina into it. He sat on the floor and leaned back between her knees.

"I don't think one day in the woods qualifies me for outdoors-anything." Nina said, running her hand down Tony's arm, which he'd slung over her leg.

"I don't know. Considering the deepest woods you've known till now are in Central Park—"

"That's not true," she said, looking straight down into his face, looking to see if she could tell how serious he was, to see if he was measuring her again.

"Okay, Inwood, right?" he asked. She nodded. "Yeah. But even lost in Inwood," he went on, "you're never too far from a bagel and a subway station. Anyway, why belittle your accomplishment?" He looked back toward the fire, but his words seemed to linger in the air in front of Nina, distorting rather than dissipating, their tone increasingly beyond her grasp.

"What accomplishment, Tony?" she asked, her voice abrupt. "Picking sticks up off the ground? Building a fire? Wow. I guess there's no stopping me, huh?"

He got up on his knees and turned to face her. "Nina, I wasn't being serious."

She could see instantly that he was telling her the truth. The urge to cry rose up right behind her relief; she struggled against it but Tony must have seen something.

"What's up?" He dipped his head so he was looking up into her eyes.

"Nothing, Tony. I'm fine. It's just, you know—"

"No. I don't know. You've hardly said a word about yourself lately."

"Well, there's not that much to say."

"I don't think that's true."

Nina said nothing. He was right, of course. There was so much she'd put aside over the last two months, thinking she had to understand it all herself before she could explain it well enough, safely enough, to him. Like this afternoon: moving in and out of feeling so oddly at ease in the woods; not quite comfortable, but taken far enough out of herself so that she could at least begin to appreciate the feeling.

She leaned forward so their faces were close, and closed her eyes. "Nina, you have to talk to me," Tony said, pressing his forehead to hers. "Am I making it hard? I mean I know I've been busy with my own—"

"It's not that, Tone."

"Then what?"

Nina shook her head slightly from side to side, her skin moving gently against his.

"Don't shut me out, Nina." He pulled back so he was looking into her eyes. "I wanted you to be here because I wanted us to have a life together. Not because I wanted someone to keep the fire going."

"I know that," she said, an almost imperceptible smile crossing, then leaving, her face. "I just have to put things into place." She leaned back in her chair and focused past Tony into the flames. "Maybe I've got to start looking for work," she said, making her voice lighter than it had been a moment before.

Tony sighed, and sat back on his feet. "There's no rush. You should look when you're ready," he said. "The money's no problem now."

She forced herself to smile.

A log settled noisily in the stove. Nina made a move to stand up but Tony kept his hands braced on her thighs. "Promise me, Nina. You won't stop talking."

"I promise," she said, but he didn't move, and he kept his eyes on hers until she'd kissed him, and then maneuvered herself up out of his grasp.

She went back into the woods the next day, and then several times over the next dozen days. The seed of calm she'd been surprised to feel in herself the first time took solid hold, reclaiming her on each excursion once she was busy with the gathering, her mind off herself and on the subtle demands of the chore. She gradually stopped feeling a split in her perception of the woods and of herself in them. This was just the way she felt there, gathering kindling, sensing what was going on around her—the sounds, movements, smells, the changes in temperature and light—without imagining that any of it signified something other than itself. Her mind wandered freely, rarely bogging down with questions and complications. She thought often about Tony, about what it had meant for her to have come here with him, and what it was turning out to mean to be here; but it made sense to her that she came to no conclusions.

She'd taken seriously what Tony had said about feeling shut out from her, and did what she could to change it. She started telling him about some part of each day, and she could see how he appreciated even this slightly stilted effort to bring herself back to him, to them. And stilted or not, the effort quickly led them back to the kind of conversation that had been missing since they came to Cannen: easy and rangy, full of impression and idea. She'd forgotten how his attention to her when she was talking seemed to be a kind of seeing, different than her own, that she could appropriate in those moments, one lens slightly distorting the other, but not blurring it. She'd forgotten how his knowing her was part of the way she defined herself. She'd forgotten the complex pleasures of merely thinking aloud with him. She'd inadvertently let go of all that since they'd moved to Vermont, trying to create a sense of certainty by holding tightly to herself. Now, the certainty presented itself to her in the sound of their voices, in the casual expression of themselves to each other, even in the brief silences that drew the conversations around unexpected corners, pulled them from room to room, hour to hour.

Yet, there were still moments when she couldn't help thinking that Tony was disinterested in what she was saying, or that he was studying her and not really listening; moments when she remembered the sidelong glance that kept her in the periphery of his vision, when she remembered all the ways he might be disappointed by her. So, though she talked with him about being in the woods, she didn't talk about the calm she felt there, the surprise of finding that in herself, the growing sense of being other than what she'd always been. She thought she would keep this to herself for now, at least.

1994

AFTER HALF AN HOUR of packing her supplies into boxes and hauling them upstairs, Nina decided she'd done enough for the time being. The dining room table was clear, and Tony was still in his studio. From the window in her workroom, she had seen that he'd moved from sitting at his table to standing in front of the wall where the canvas he was working on was hanging. She knew that unless she went out there he'd lose himself to the painting, assume she'd gone for a very long walk, or forget to assume anything at all.

Tony's dedication to his work had always been one of the things Nina most admired in him: the single-mindedness that could keep him working with no sense of the passage of time. It had been part of the romantic image of Tony-as-artist that had sucked her in when she first met him, and she knew she was still subject to its pull. But she'd learned that it was also a

profoundly incomplete image and that Tony was good at foster-
ing it during those times when his focus wavered or dimmed.
And right now, one knock on the studio door would tell her if
he'd been waiting for her to come get him—another test for
her, just like the phone call four days ago had been—or if he
really was involved with his work to the unintentional exclusion
of everything else.

She stepped out into the mudroom whose sixteen-paned
window gave her a full view of the studio. The house wasn't
very warm but in this room she might as well have been outside. She grabbed a sweater from the row of hooks and quickly
pulled it over her head. The smell of lanolin filled her nose and
once she had her arms inside the sweater, she pulled the neck
up over the bottom of her face so she could breathe it in again.
She'd gotten the sweater practically off the back of a sheep
when she and Tony had spent time in Scotland fifteen years
before, their first big trip together. The sweet, musky smell of
the lanolin, the waxy tug of it in the wool, still brought back the
more ineffable qualities of that time: whatever it was that had
made it feel more rich, and absorbable than any trip they'd
taken since. She took one last deep breath of the aroma and
slowly exhaled, focusing again on what she could see clearly in
front of her.

But the mudroom's window cut Tony's studio into sixteen
parts, and Nina saw it as if sixteen slides were being projected at
once. Each pane showed a small abstract: studies in shape and
color, darkness and light. Nina moved her eyes quickly from
one to the next, trying to make them cohere, but they remained
sixteen different views, the narrow width of the panes enough
to keep the whole disjointed. The harder she tried to imagine

the slim planes of connection, the more separate the pieces appeared to her. And then, more one-dimensional, as if the only place the studio might exist were on the surface of the window.

The cold had penetrated the sweater and she put on the old leather jacket that hung there as well: Tony's jacket, vintage 1968, the fringe still basically intact, though mostly curled and tangled. She turned from the window, traded her shoes for the pair of boots that Tony insisted made her feet look like loaves of bread, pulled a watchcap down over her ears, low on her forehead, and grabbed the pair of insulated gloves lying on the bench.

Stepping outside, Nina noticed a newly thick thread of smoke rising from the studio's stovepipe: Tony was settling in to paint for the night. She decided then to leave him to whatever it was he was doing, to build a fire for herself. She entered the path she'd taken toward the studio earlier and veered off of it into another one that led in a roundabout way to the woodpile. The studio path was even more roundabout, with a little offshoot that circled back to the pile; and a series of tight short switchbacks led to the garage from where, in the only straight section of the whole network of paths, the bird feeder could be reached. Nina had designed and dug the network: she'd figured that if she had to do this endless shoveling to keep their small compound usable, she would at least amuse herself. With each snowfall the walls along the sides of the paths had grown, the paths becoming increasingly trench-like, their useless complexity increasingly obvious and pleasing to her. Tony invariably made sounds of frustration as he took the long way, the only way, to his studio, and the switchbacks could make him throw up his hands and more or less laughingly curse Nina's name.

The deer, on the other hand, tired of the high step they needed in deep snow, had begun using the paths by the end of January. Making the world an easier place for woman and beast alike and alone, Nina thought, winding her way to the garage, exaggerating every twist of the switchbacks with her hips, enjoying her handiwork.

In the garage were four large piles of different-sized kindling. Nina had collected all of it late in the fall when six inches of snow had already fallen and the local, widely voiced prediction for a bad winter was sounding increasingly convincing. She'd begrudgingly brought in enough for the entire season, knowing it made sense to do the whole job at that time, but knowing, as well, how much she'd miss gathering the wood in the months to come. It was her favorite winter ritual, an unfailing way to disappear from herself at moments like this one: trying to second guess Tony through a haze of her own expectation, anger, and hurt; her process of thinking things through only making those things seem increasingly intractable. The largest pile of kindling on the floor in front of her resembled those thoughts: an unpatterned lace of intertwined branches, no obvious points of stability or strength. But the longer she stared at it, the more it also looked intricate and beautiful, like a treetop that, for some delightfully inexplicable reason, had been lowered gently into the garage and left to hover just a breath above solid ground. Reminding herself that there was still a part of the ritual left to her, Nina lifted a branch from the pile, took the small hand saw off the wall, set up an old folding chair as a work surface, and holding down one end of the branch with her knee, began, easily, to cut the wood to size.

All the knowledge of the task was set in her muscles: she

could feel just how much pressure to apply so the saw wouldn't get bound in the wood; just how far through the branch the blade needed to go before she could crack the wood with her hands. The rhythm of the movement took the place of thinking it through, her body slipped into a smooth mechanics, her thoughts began to quiet. It was just the effect she'd been hoping for.

The fire had been burning in the woodstove for about an hour, and it had taken Nina almost that long to concoct a meal from the depleted contents of the cabinets and refrigerator. She opened the vegetable bin one last time to make sure she hadn't missed a wayward carrot or radish. Nothing. This would be it: the last of the soup she'd made for herself earlier in the week, eggs, a small salad, bread, some cheese if Tony wanted. If he'd missed the 'fuck you' in the mess she'd left, perhaps he would get the one implicit in this meager meal.

She wouldn't wait for him any longer. If this was a battle of nerves between them, maybe to admit defeat was to have the upper hand: she could decide what attitude she'd have when she saw him if she was the one bringing it to him. She lowered the flame under the soup, put on the old leather jacket, and made her way slowly to the studio, keeping her eyes on its lit window, trying to see Tony before he saw her so she might gauge what his reaction would be to her knock on the door. She caught sight of him at the far wall, bent over the table where he kept the paints he was working with. She could see the painting-in-progress hanging behind him: it looked considerably different from what she remembered having seen of it before he'd left

two weeks ago, and there was some satisfaction for her in knowing that he hadn't come out here merely to avoid her, or to make
a point. Of course, she'd been trying to make a point by not
going to the studio sooner, but seeing how involved he was in
the painting, she wasn't sure—

The studio door loomed up all of a sudden—it seemed to
have approached her while she wasn't looking—and without
thinking, Nina threw her hand up as if to protect herself from
it. Coming down, her hand banged hard against the door, and
yelling out in pain, she announced herself in a way she hadn't
intended. She pushed the door open with her unhurt hand,
shaking the other—she didn't have gloves on and in the cold the
pain seemed to reverberate in her bones—and practically
crashed into Tony, who'd obviously leapt across the room when
he heard her shout. He grabbed her shoulders to bring himself
to a stop and the door, closing, smashed against his elbow.

"You okay?" she asked as he grabbed his arm and squeezed
his eyes closed.

"Funny bone," he managed to say through a grimace.

Nina felt as if she were caught at the center of one of her
contraptions gone wrong: some bolt she'd forgotten to tighten,
a miscalculation in timing, a balance of materials off by just an
ounce and here they were, not confronting each other soberly as
she'd imagined, herself in control, but tumbling clumsily into
each other, two stooges in no need of a third. Nina tried to hold
her laughter in—the door had really bashed Tony—but it burst
out of her, doubling her over. All the intent and seriousness
she'd brought to the studio with her seemed to have gone out
with the gust of laughter, and taking their place was a gesture
she was hardly aware of making: her hand reaching up to find

Tony, coming to rest on his chest, all the estrangement she'd felt ten minutes ago undercut in this barest of touches. When Tony began to laugh she felt it in her hand first, the rhythm of it moving down her arm like a second, faster pulse, his and hers alike, the feeling as familiar as the sound of his laughter itself when it reached her ears an instant later: soft and level, observant and appreciative. She felt Tony's eyes on her, on the back of her neck, on the curve of her back through the jacket; she felt him enjoying her amusement at the situation as much as the situation itself, and enjoying her more than either.

"Where have you been?" he said, pulling her out of her crouch and smoothing her arms over his shoulders before he put his own around her waist. Over the past four days, she'd set herself against him—her mind's eye shutting down on his image so it could conjure just what it needed of him to fit her anger—and his face in front of her now was like something new. She was seeing it for the first time again: an instant of surprise at its rough beauty. Everything new as if she didn't know exactly how to read the eyes, hadn't felt the lips everywhere on her body, had not stared at them when anger or remorse made it impossible to look into the eyes. Just for an instant: the memory of her sight, caught and held by this face for the first time, the only source of her knowledge of him, everything else since then stilled inside of her. And, in the next instant, his face settling back into all her knowledge of it, of him, familiar again, though somehow no less surprising for it. He kissed the corners of her mouth while her laughter subsided, as if he were biding his time, and she saw in his eyes, where his own laughter lingered, the endless circular knowing they had of each other. She sensed that he knew she'd planned to appear at the studio door resentful and righteous, and was glad that she'd been figuratively, not to mention almost literally, disarmed. And, surprising herself, she was as glad of it as he might be and moved her mouth into one of his kisses.

"I've been out here for hours," he said. He unzipped her jacket and pulled her toward him as he sat back on the table. "What've you been doing?"

"Stuff," she said, moving in between his open knees, resting her arms on his shoulders. "Anyway, I assumed you were working."

He'd begun to move his hands slowly around her hips, but he stopped, leaned back from her and looked up into her face, his own tilting toward serious. She kept her eyes on him but took her jacket off and draped it on the table, and then dangled her arms over his shoulders again so that her fingers only grazed his back.

"There's something you're not saying to me, right?" he asked.

He was telling her that he would listen, that he wasn't trying to push her beyond what she needed to do or say. But this—this capitulation at this moment—felt more like what she needed. She put her hand on his neck. "Actually," she said, moving her fingers inside the collar of his shirt, "there're several things I'm not saying."

"Tell me." He shook her so that her torso undulated softly.

"If I tell you then I'll be telling you and that'll defeat the purpose of not saying in the first place."

His smile drew up on one side. She pulled her fingers out from his collar and moved them to the tendon that ran from below his ear into his neck, tracing it lightly, and then leaning over to trace it again with her tongue. This spot, her tongue, and a low rumble of pleasure in Tony's throat: it was a guaranteed combination.

She leaned back into his hands and let her arms fall to her sides. "I missed you."

"You sound surprised."

It was true: she hadn't expected to say it. "Yeah. Well—"

He braced his legs around hers, pulled her face toward his. "Promise you'll tell me what you're not telling me eventually," he said before kissing her. She waited a long instant before responding, waited while she felt her desire for him take over, so she wasn't thinking or knowing, wasn't remembering, so that every sensation had a chance to be nothing but new.

Part Two

1978

THE FIRST TIME Nina heard the sound of the pond freezing, she had no idea what she was hearing. It was on the coldest evening up to that point of the first fall she and Tony were in the house they'd bought fifteen miles from campus. The pond was on their property, visible from the back porch, but Nina didn't know to expect that it was capable of such a sound.

It stopped her in her tracks as she made her way from the car to the house: a moan of enormous proportions that seemed to be made of its own wailing echo. It could have been the announcement of the return of the dinosaur, made by one of its larger kin. A time warp gaping wide. Everything she had ever feared might exist in the dark. It was unearthly, ungodly; unless, of course, it was godly. And then it happened again and she realized first that it was coming from the direction of the pond, and, immediately after, that it was the pond. One instant imagining unseen terrors, and in the next, certain knowledge of water turning to ice. As if, between those instants, something in her had solidified, a level of perception reached like a temperature, pushed to the appropriate mark by some combination of age, openness, relief, sensual accumulation, so that information coalesced suddenly into understanding.

There was just enough light left in the evening for Nina to see her way to the edge of the pond. Not long ago, this late-day light would have spooked her, color disappearing into it, and everything, even the air itself, seeming to separate into molecules of white and black which raced in place while darkness took over; everything looking ghostly, shapes losing their edges and becoming one-dimensional. But that had changed now too. In another process she couldn't pinpoint, her uneasiness about the darkness had been pushed to the very darkest corners of night, moonless hours in which the only proof of her hand in front of her face was its pressure against her nose or lips. That's where what she didn't even want to imagine might exist, she imagined might still exist. But not here any longer, in this time of day. Lately, she'd begun to find this light alluring, an easy kind of mysteriousness to enter, as she felt herself doing now, standing at the edge of the pond where she could just make out smooth ice covering almost the whole surface, only inches short of the still-watery edge at her feet. The sound she'd heard was probably made when the ice expanded, she thought, growing out of itself, out of its strongest, deepest point. Or it might be plates of ice expanding against one another, bending into each other and then torquing away before straightening out, the sound made out of the stress of the movement. All of it making possible sense until the unearthly moan burst again into and out of the silence—the embedded echo resounding in the same moment as the sound itself—and Nina felt the ground shake in response. She ran to the house, jumping onto the porch out of the quickly falling dark, just before her thoughts caught up to her.

She stood against the wall of the house, her heart slowing to normal, laughter breaking through her short breaths. Everything in her mind seemed mutable except this core of her most irrational thinking, as if fear of the dark or of eerie sounds might have some evolutionary importance. The pond moaned again. It sounded no less strange to Nina at this distance, but she picked out a plaintive note she hadn't heard before, which made it feel less threatening. And she'd just noticed the light on in Tony's studio. Here was the other irrationality: the presence of another person making the inexplicable endurable. Whether or not she would get most of the grease off her hands today was suddenly enough mystery for the time being.

There were no lights on in the house. Tony had no classes on Fridays and usually spent the whole day in his studio, making his way out there sometimes even before she left for the garage at seven, and not reappearing until after she'd gotten home, until he'd looked away from the canvas, inadvertently glimpsing light in the living room window or from the bedroom upstairs. Windows like semaphores: I'm home; I'm not home; I see you're there; I'm here and staying; I love you but I'm still painting; I'm soaking in the tub and waiting.

She undressed and dropped her grease-smeared clothes in a basket at the top of the basement stairs and quickly put on the thick robe she kept hanging there. Though she and Tony had only been in the house for four months, Nina couldn't remember when she'd started to leave the basket and robe in that spot. It was almost as if the idea had been a product of necessity and logic interpreted by the house itself and offered up as a solution. There were other things like that: the specific place on the kitchen counter where they left the day's mail for the other to see; the bowl where they threw their keys when they came in; or the corner of the picture frame above the desk where they knew to look for notes the other might have left. None of these things had been decided upon; they were customs of the house, as Nina thought of them, as much a quality of home, of being at home, as anything else. She felt that here in a way she hadn't even begun to approach at the cottage on campus, though this was really no more her home than that had been. She'd helped Tony decide on this house rather than another, and he'd had her name put on the deed, but it was his down payment and his mortgage. She might have expected that that would be a constraint for her, keep her from feeling as if she had her own, self-determined part in this picture. But those fears had disappeared once they moved in. Maybe it was because even before they'd moved, she'd begun making a life for herself that would not just fit inside Tony's life, but alongside it, and within the idea of a shared home in all its literal and figurative meanings, for better and for worse.

Nina pushed the thermostat up and waited for the coughing explosion of the furnace kicking over yet another time. She'd build a fire later. Making her way upstairs, she turned on every light: Tony in his studio or not, bright was what she wanted right now, even if she did close the bathroom door behind her. She made the bath as hot as she could stand it and sank into the tub up to her chin. She closed her eyes and felt her muscles gradually giving in to a water-made weightlessness. When she opened her eyes, Tony was sitting on the stool at the foot of the tub. She hadn't heard him come in; she'd been asleep.

"I don't know how you do that without drowning," he said, dipping his hand in the water and stroking her leg.

"But you were going to watch to see how long before I did drown." Nina pushed herself into a more upright position. Tony's eyes shifted to where her breasts broke the surface of the water.

"I was going to jump in at the last minute. You were never in any real danger." He splashed some water toward her face, and handed her a box from the floor. "I left these on the kitchen table for you."

There were three bars of soap inside the box and though the packaging was unfamiliar to her, the smell told Nina that they were the French soap she loved: made with honey, or made to smell like honey, or like what someone imagined honey smelled like. In any case, she loved the smell, and she thought the lather had the feel, if not of honey exactly, then of a softness that honey might have if bees' wings could whip it into a froth. She didn't care about soaps or lotions otherwise, but she'd developed a habit of this soap soon after she'd used it at Tony's just after they'd met. They'd only found a couple of places to get it in the city, and neither of them had made the trip down there in so many months that they'd run out weeks ago.

"Where'd you get them?" Nina held a bar to her nose and inhaled deeply. The normal packaging had been replaced with a hand-drawn illustration wrapped around the bar: a honeycomb in whose chambers could be read the words *"Savon pour toi,"* spelled out in bees.

"I asked Jack to send them." Which explained the wrapping: Jack liked to leave his mark on anything that passed through his hands.

"How sweet of Jack," she said, tearing open one of the soaps, ripping straight through the illustration. "What does he want in return?"

"Talons, Nina," Tony said. He waggled his fingers close to her face, which he cupped finally and kissed. She smiled a big false grin. He stood up. "Diane called. Wants to know if we want to meet them at the Top Hat later."

"Sure. That'd be good. Are you finished working?"

"I need about another hour. I told them we wouldn't be there till eight or eight-thirty. You up for cooking?"

Nina shook her head vehemently. "Why don't we just get something there? I need some grease on the inside to balance what's on the outside." She held up her hands; the hot water hadn't made a dent.

"After all, a little grease could hardly mar your beauty," Tony said in a decent imitation of Alan Gill. He'd decided that Nina had found a perfect foil in the professor. "I'll call Diane and let her know."

When the door was closed, Nina pushed the box with the two wrapped soaps across the room. Now that she knew those were Jack's illustrations, it was as if something more of him, something more solid, had come into the room with the box, had been brought in by Tony. She still found it hard sometimes to believe that Tony didn't know what had happened between her and Jack just after she'd found out about Tony's first infidelity almost a year and a half ago. He hadn't seemed at all curious about why she had, as she'd said, lost her taste for Jack. Instead, he'd begun immediately to try to repair her opinion of his friend, as if Jack had been right at the time when he'd said to her that Tony would understand.

"What would he understand, Jack?" she'd asked, getting dressed as quickly as she could, desperate to get out of his apartment by that point. He was lying on the bed, smoking, but otherwise completely still. Nina felt like a dervish in comparison. "That I fucked his best friend? Or that his best friend managed to convince me to fuck him? Which do you think he would understand better?"

"I just mean that he'd have to understand since he brought it on himself," Jack said.

"That's bullshit," she said, putting on her jacket. "I made the decision. Drunk or not. So did you." Her hand was on the door. "You can't say anything to him."

"Nina—"

"I don't care if you think he'll understand. I'm going to be the one to decide whether or not to tell him."

Jack held up two fingers like a Boy Scout taking an oath. "I won't say anything. I promise." Nina slammed the door behind her.

She'd walked quickly back to Chris's apartment, where she was staying alone—Chris was out of town—and where Jack had unexpectedly shown up earlier in the night. Nina had left Cannen that morning in a terrible state—angry, upset, unwilling to listen. Tony had tried her at the apartment, got no answer, and asked Jack to check on her: he wanted to make sure that she'd even gotten there. She'd suspected it was Tony calling, that's why she hadn't answered, and she hadn't wanted to see anyone, least of all his closest friend. But she'd already had a couple of beers by the time Jack rang the buzzer, and he said he just wanted to come in for a few minutes.

Jack had called Tony then and she heard enough of his side of the conversation to make her feel like a young charge, a runaway, a ward of their two-man state. She agreed to have dinner with Jack so she could make the impression she wanted him to report to Tony: that she did not cry on his shoulder, did not ask for sympathy or advice or insights into Tony's behavior. She wouldn't even talk about what had happened, especially since she assumed Tony had already told Jack all the details: who the girl was, how Nina had found out, what she and Tony had said to each other before she'd stormed out of the house. Jack would see, and hopefully Tony would hear, that all she wanted from dinner was food. But her drinking had far outstripped her eating, and she'd followed Jack's conversation only insofar as it led her to his apartment.

She could hardly remember the moment she'd capitulated, but the moments after were painfully clear. She'd wanted to get it over with almost immediately after it had begun. She didn't want Jack to be generous or inventive. She didn't want to tell him what she liked. She didn't want him. She wanted Tony's full lips and slow kisses, not this thin-lipped rush around her mouth. She wanted the knowledge of Tony's hands, the perfected vocabulary of his touch. She rolled on top of Jack and surprised him by taking him inside herself so quickly. She did what she knew would make him come sooner rather than later and helped his hand make her come: too quickly if he had been Tony, just quickly enough so she was able to sustain the fantasy that it was. She gave only a small part of herself to the orgasm; sobering her up was its most powerful effect. She hadn't known what time it was when she left Jack's apartment, hadn't known how safe she'd be on the street—it was an iffy neighborhood at best—but having extracted the promise of his silence, she'd had no more reason to stay. And she'd already decided to go back to Vermont before Chris returned, before she might try to convince Nina that she should've expected this from Tony. She wasn't interested in Chris's litany of the signs that had been there from the start. It didn't matter. She was hurt and angry without Chris's help.

Nina couldn't believe Tony had done something so typical: sleeping with a student, succumbing to a spark of swooning admiration in freshman eyes. Nina had heard her parents talk about countless affairs between professors and their students. She had even once opened her father's office door on a tableau that convinced her that the student, only a few years older than Nina at the time, was there for more than advice. She couldn't believe Tony had been so susceptible. But she also couldn't dismiss the possibility that he hadn't succumbed to anything but his own impulses: she had never been able to put out of her mind his sidelong, disappointed glances, cast her way at Alan Gill's party that fall. She'd imagined those glances sustained across seven months, and now she wasn't where he could see her at all, and at the moment she probably most needed to be in his sight. She began to think that her reaction to his confession had been histrionic, something acted out rather than felt: expressions of shock, tears, the frantic dash from the house, the numbing drive to the city, one cigarette lit from another, one beer on top of another. Everything the cheated-on was expected to do. Even

Jack fit into the picture that way: the best friend she could fuck for payback. But she wasn't really feeling devastated or humiliated by Tony. She was more worried than anything else: worried that she had left him with the image of her crumbling; worried that she was relying on Jack to assure Tony that that image wasn't accurate without revealing their infidelity. And worried that Tony might have been trying to tell her something else when he told her about being with his student. It was already over with her, it was unlikely that Nina ever would have found out about it if he'd never said anything. She couldn't help wondering why he had.

So she went back to Vermont after only three days, surprising Tony: Jack had told him he thought Nina would stay in New York for a while. Tony apologized again, desperate, he said, to know she'd forgive him. She believed him when he said he needed her to know that it wouldn't happen again, and she wished he hadn't said it.

"I don't want to know if it does."

"That's what I'm saying. It's not going to happen."

"And I'm just saying that I don't want to know."

He'd nodded his head, said nothing for a few minutes, and then asked: "Was it okay that I sent Jack around to check on you?"

"It was okay," she said, determining in that instant that she wouldn't tell Tony what had happened with Jack. But perhaps he already knew—there was something in the question, oddly placed in the conversation and wide open at its end. Now, a year and a half later, the creamy smell of the honey soap slightly soured by her knowledge that Jack had handled it, Nina found

herself wondering, again and still, if Jack had kept his word, if
Tony had known back then that without thinking about what
she was doing she had put them on even footing.

They drove to the Top Hat that night with the Spitfire's top
down. "What's the use of having a '68 Spitfire convertible if
you're not willing to drive it as God intended it to be driven?"
Tony had said the first time Nina balked at the combination of
winter and convertible. Now, fast approaching their third
Vermont winter, they only put the top up when—in an equation of Nina's invention—the snow was coming down quickly
enough to accumulate in the car a solid half an inch in ten
minutes of at least fifty-five-mile-per-hour driving. And her
readiness to be cold was only the smallest indication of how
things had changed in her life over the last almost three years.
She could feel herself holding tight to the notion of old
habits, but the impetus to return to them was growing weaker
and weaker.

Tony was her oldest habit, the most tenacious. She was as
compelled as ever by it, by him, by herself with him, not so
much despite what had happened between them over the three
years but because of it. Her need of him had changed. She felt
that he made it possible for her to prove herself. There was challenge in the mix of feelings that made up her love for him. And
already a kind of nostalgia for the most unsullied moments
between them. Watching him drive now, she was seeing back to
one of those moments, what they had dubbed their ur-moment.
The almost full moon had risen early and was already high overhead, a blue-white light in an otherwise crystalline black sky. It
illuminated Tony's face and spread out onto his shoulders,

gracing them like cloth falling around him and disappearing into the dark as the light reached its limits. This was how she had seen him the night they met. The light then had been incandescent, yellow, illuminating only because it was the sole source of light in that living room full of people, but it had graced him in the same way. When he'd followed her from the hallway back into the living room, she'd watched him move through the crowd, watched other women watch. She had thought: I'm going to have this, thinking only as far as the rest of that night. It was what the look in his face had promised about the rest of him that she'd wanted then, and it was some of what she still wanted, the eye-catching frame for what his eyes reflected back at her: herself at the center of what he saw.

"I'm going to have this tonight," she said, but the wind grabbed her voice. Tony asked what she'd said. "Nothing," she told him, laying her hand on his shoulder. His smile was blue-white.

The Top Hat was just on the border with New York, closer to Greenville, where the garage was, than to Cannen, which was one of its prime attractions for Nina. As small as the college was, it dominated the town, and none of its bars was safe from students or faculty. Not long after she'd started at the garage, she and Tony had run into Alan Gill at the Town Inn, the closest Cannen came to having a dive bar, and the least likely place, usually, to find faculty.

"Look who's slumming," Tony had said quietly as they stepped inside the door. Nina had wanted to turn around before Gill saw them, but he saw them immediately and waved them over, shouting their names just in case they got the hand signals wrong. After a couple of minutes, Tony saw someone he absolutely had to talk to. Nina glared; Tony smiled sweetly and left the table.

"Tony told me you've gotten a job at the garage in Greenville," Gill said, moving into Tony's empty chair.

"That's right," Nina said as pleasantly as she could. She saw Tony at the bar making clearly insignificant conversation with a student and keeping one eye on the proceedings at the table.

"Well," Gill said. "This is just one more manifestation of what a perfect couple of opposites you and Tony are." Nina said nothing: she didn't want to encourage him. But he was already set to go on, moving his right hand in a slow circle in front of his face, conjuring the perfect words. "Eye and hand. Ether and earth. Raiment and . . ." His hand was circling again.

"Sackcloth?" Nina suggested, her voice cheery and false.

He laid his hand on top of hers. "I could never imagine you in sackcloth, Nina."

"Oh, give it a whirl, Alan," she'd said, found an excuse to leave, and vowed to Tony that night that she would go to no other bar but the Top Hat.

At the Top Hat Nina didn't have to worry about running into Alan Gill, or anyone else who might have been even remotely tempted to compare her and Tony to ether and earth. Very few people just stumbled on the bar: it was set back from a small county road, the only building for several miles around, surrounded on three sides by dense stands of pine, and announced only by a small metal sign at the entrance to the parking lot: no neon, no arrows, and, at night, the whole thing poorly lit. You had to be told about it, and people associated with Cannen rarely were. Two of the men Nina worked with, Nick and Gary, had told her about the bar a year ago after she'd been at the garage for only a short time, and giving her the directions they made it clear that she was receiving their stamp of approval. Dispensation for Tony was carried on Nina's acceptance, though Nick had suggested she might want to come by herself sometimes.

Nina had quickly become a regular—with Tony and without—and she'd come to think that it was possible to sense the bar long before it came into view: a cloud of cigarette smoke and the charge of unfettered hormones—the bar's pheromone—carried out into the night on the sound of a vaguely honky-tonk jukebox each time the door was opened. She sensed it tonight, and the building looming up as they rounded a curve in the road—a great dilapidated hulk whose details were turn-of-the-century, and whose deterioration all-the-years-since—was like the sight of a familiar, slightly mad face.

Diane and her husband, George, had arrived before Nina and Tony, and Diane was already deep into a game of pool with a large bearded man called Butch whose monster Harley could be heard coming half a mile away. Diane was more than a match for him, a fact that could be seen cutting a path of realization across his face. Nina had brought Diane here one night when Tony was out of town and George was busy reading student papers. It had been a weekday, the bar hadn't been crowded, but Diane had made such a powerful impression at the pool table that the next time she'd come to the Top Hat, with George in tow, her reputation had preceded her. A few people, like her current opponent, remained incredulous until they were trounced firsthand, and Nina loved watching her do it.

When Diane had finished with Butch, she pulled Nina into a game: the women against the bartender Terry's two cousins visiting from Texas. Beers were on the house for the players and

Nina and Diane quickly slipped into sloppy versions of a Texas drawl. The cousins loved it; a crowd gathered; Nina forgot her hunger. Diane's triumphant laugh had the most surprisingly motherly quality to it: no one could get angry at her pleasure in winning. The door opened and closed frequently, blasts of cold air refreshing the increasingly thick air of the bar. Nina wasn't paying any attention to anything but the game, so she didn't know how long Nick had been sitting with Tony and George when she finally caught sight of him over the length of her cue as she readied a shot.

"You can leave your ass sticking up in the air only so long before you have to expect it'll become a target," Diane said quietly into her ear.

"Sorry. I got lost for a second." She shot and missed.

"That's okay. We're okay," Diane said to the crowd as she and Nina stepped back from the table. Directing her voice to Nina alone, she said: "Are you okay?"

"I'm fine. I'm sorry. I just got distracted."

"I'm not worried about the game, Nina," Diane said, her voice motherly again, but without the laughter. Nina shrugged her concern off, but she stayed distracted—she saw George leave the table, Tony and Nick fall into a more intense conversation, a woman Nina didn't recognize join them, food brought to the table—and she and Diane lost the game.

"You're going to ruin my wife's reputation," George said, handing them drinks he'd brought from the bar. He put his arm around Diane's waist and steered her toward the table. Nina followed slowly behind them.

The conversation at the table was not quite drunken, but not particularly sober either. Nina switched to tequila and refused food, but she felt achingly clear-headed. The woman she hadn't recognized, introduced to her by Nick as Joellen, no last name, was a little shy in the face of everybody's familiarity, but Nina was hardly more talkative. She had to force herself to find something to say once in a while. Tony didn't seem to notice at all, but Diane was watching her closely.

"I'll get the next round," Nina said. She walked slowly to the bar, which was packed and noisy. She told Terry to take his time, she could wait. She wanted to. A few minutes later Nick was at her side.

"I'll give you a hand, chica." She'd told him that that was what the mechanics at Ernie's had called her and he'd adopted it. Sometimes she liked it; tonight it sounded presumptuous.

"I can handle it," she said without looking at him, and then: "What were you and Tony talking about so intently before we all sat down?"

"You, of course. He wanted to know how his girl was doing at her job. He's like a proud papa. It's very sweet. I told him his little girl was doing real good work."

Nina shot him a quick, angry look.

He leaned back from the bar, and put his lips to her ear. "Why are you so pissed at me?"

She pulled away from him just a little, just so he knew she didn't want him that close, without it being obvious to anyone else. She turned her head to look at him and raised her voice: "I thought you were going away this weekend."

"My plans changed, Nina."

"Joellen?"

Nick's lips tightened into a pinched smile. "Tell me you've got a problem with that."

Nina said nothing, but she held his gaze in the grip of her own.

He shook his head and leaned close again. "Here's the deal. You can't be the only one having someone else to fuck when all seven or seventeen different things that have to fall into place for us to see each other don't fall into place."

She turned again to meet his eyes and slid slowly off the bar stool, releasing his gaze only at the last instant before she moved away. She walked as calmly as she could to the bathroom, and shut herself in a stall. All the alcohol she'd drunk caught up to her.

The door opened and Diane's voice filled the room: "Nina. Are you okay?"

Nina took a deep breath and came out of the stall. She fiddled with the elastic holding back her hair. "I'm fine Diane. Thanks."

Diane said nothing but her gaze in the mirror was unrelenting. Finally, Nina turned to face her, leaning back against the sink for balance. "What?" she snapped.

"Nina. If I can see it, Tony can—"

"Maybe that's okay."

Diane let out a long sigh. "Be careful, Nina. You can't even the score. It doesn't work."

"I think it does," she said quickly, as if she'd expected the exact words Diane had used. "It just takes a little diligence."

1967

BILL WAS HUNG OVER the morning after he'd been to the Stoneridge, and the smell of the congealed eggs his mother had waiting for him when he went to the kitchen made him feel sicker.

"I'm not going to have any eggs this morning. Thanks just the same." He sat down at the table as if his body were being lowered, clumsily, by someone else. "But I'd give anything for a cup of coffee."

His mother was standing at the stove holding tightly on to the handle of the coffee pot, but she seemed completely disinclined to pour. She was studying him, and maybe it was the intensity of her stare or maybe it was just the light coming in the window behind her, but Bill felt he had to avert his eyes. Uncountable mornings of his childhood, his father had endured the same scrutiny from her, and Bill had always averted his eyes then too, afraid to get caught in his parents' staring match. Afraid mostly of his mother's stare, so full of damning judgment, while his father's was merely a stubborn refusal to be judged, or to care if he was. As he'd gotten older, Bill had understood that his mother's stare was harmless: his father would get up from the table and grab the coffee pot from her hand, sloshing liquid out of the spout which his mother would have to clean up as he poured his own. Bill's sisters averted their eyes then, but he'd learned he could watch the whole silent exchange and be no worse off when his father had left the room.

He lifted his eyes slowly now until he was staring into his mother's. "I could use some of that coffee." He waited a beat, she didn't move. "But that's okay, I can get it down at the general store too." He pushed his chair back from the table.

"I'll bet you can use some coffee," she said, lifting the pot slowly to the table. "The time you came in last night from that bar." She filled his cup and then stepped back, put the pot on the stove without looking. "It's not as if we have all the time in the world together," she said.

Bill took a sip, watching his mother over the top of the cup. If she'd looked the least bit sad or if her voice had contained a note of softness, he might have felt something for her. As it was, he felt only his annoyance growing at a surprising speed.

"What time did you go to sleep last night?" he asked her as he put the cup down.

"About eight-thirty, I guess." She crossed her arms and brought them down emphatically on her chest. Her breasts seemed flattened beneath them. "What's that got to do with anything?"

"Because that's not long after I went to the bar. And I didn't notice you waiting up for me when I got home. So it's not like we missed any time we would've spent together."

"Well, you know that's the same bar your father used to go to and it never did him any good." She sat opposite from him. He supposed this felt like conversation to her.

"It never really did him much harm either." Bill leaned back in his chair. "Not until he came home," he said, trying to lighten the atmosphere. His mother didn't smile. "Anyway. There were people there I wanted to see."

"Like who?" she asked. She began to play with a napkin she'd left on the table, picking tiny bits off the edges.

"Well, Rick Beecher, for instance. Who told me all about his son's death."

"I wrote you about that."

"Yeah, you did," he said, nodding his head slowly. He took another drink of coffee. "But you never told me that Lilly was involved."

"Well, it wasn't really about Lilly, was it?" His mother tore another tiny piece off the napkin and laid it in the growing pile of small scraps in front of her. "It was about the poor Beecher boy."

"And you don't think Lilly had anything to do with it?" Seeing his mother's eyes fill suddenly with surprise, Bill found himself feeling surprised as well. The question had just seemed to come out of him, out of the conversation he'd been having last night. But the details of that conversation with Rick were blurry. He couldn't exactly remember if Rick had given him reason to believe that Lilly had had more to do with Wayne's death than just being present, or if he had come up with the idea himself. He remembered that Rick had given him lots of details about the event; maybe there'd been something in there about Lilly being responsible. Or not stopping the boy. Or actually pushing him off. Had he heard those possibilities from Rick? He could almost hear them again, but not clearly enough to distinguish between Rick's voice and the voice of his own thoughts.

"I didn't mean it that way, Ma," Bill said, waving his hand as if he could erase the words from inside the silence that had fallen on the kitchen in their aftermath. "I just wondered why you wouldn't even have mentioned that Lilly was there."

"Well, I just told you, didn't I?" his mother said, her voice trying to disguise the fact that she was still shocked by Bill's question, whether he'd retracted it or not.

Bill took a sip of coffee. Their words hadn't really broken the silence and he was aware suddenly of his mother's breathing: shallow but as if a great effort in her lungs were required for each breath. The housedress she had on—sleeveless, shapeless, printed with flowers of too many colors, identical to every one she'd ever worn, and they were the only thing Bill remembered her ever wearing—expanded and collapsed above her chest with every breath, as if it were helping her take them, or hindering her. He'd always heard stories of women who came to life after their husbands died, who didn't even realize how much they had left in themselves, how much they'd been using just to put up with their marriages. He could imagine Rose feeling that way about herself after they split up. But he couldn't imagine it for his mother. He wondered how much life she had left in her at all.

"What do you think of Lilly, Ma?" he asked, straightening out of a slouch and turning toward her.

"I don't really know," she said, her eyes finally beginning to let go their expression of surprise. "We didn't see much of her after the divorce."

"How come?"

"Well, Eva stopped coming around." She pushed herself up from her chair and took the three steps to the stove slowly. "Do you want more coffee, son?"

He'd only ever heard her call Joe "son," and then only after Joe had returned from the war. "Yeah, a little. Thanks." She brought the pot and another cup to the table, poured herself some, and filled his cup. Every movement slow and almost maddeningly deliberate. "Why did Eva stop coming around?"

"When?

"After their divorce. You just said she stopped coming around after they got divorced."

"I don't know. Maybe she didn't feel comfortable around us without Joe."

Bill thought how unlikely that was, how little his mother knew Eva to even imagine that was a possible explanation. "How come you didn't stay in touch with her yourself?" Her face showed him what his tone of voice had been: accusatory and provocative. And maybe that's not what he had consciously intended, but now it was as if he'd been spoken to by his own voice, clued in to what he was really feeling. "I mean," he went on, sliding down a little in his seat, "they are your grandchildren. Didn't you want to see them?"

"There were problems," she said, staring directly into his eyes. Her gaze showed more mettle than Bill thought her capable of. "It happens, Billy. Look at you. Don't you want to see your children more?"

He averted his eyes, and didn't answer her. He wouldn't tell her that he understood what it felt like to not be moved by a blood connection to a child, a blood connection of any kind. That he was here only because there was some level of guilt he was not impervious to. That he understood obligation, but not the feeling that it was supposed to arise from.

"What were these problems, Mom?" This time he filled his voice with condescension, as if he were asking the question merely to demonstrate that it had no valid answer.

His mother didn't flinch. "Your father and Eva never got along," she said. "And I was not about to go behind his back."

I guess you wouldn't, Bill thought. He said: "What didn't my father"—pushing those last two words back at her—"like about Eva?"

"You would've had to ask him," she said, getting up from the table. She lifted the coffee pot back onto the stove, and put her cup on the counter. She turned and leaned on the rim of the sink, her gaze steady and focused on him. "But it's too late now, isn't it?"

Bill wanted to tell her that even if his father had been alive, he couldn't have asked him, since he never made it possible for any of his children except Joe to talk to him. Bill wanted to ask her how she could stand behind a man who treated her like dirt. But he was unnerved by her stare and before he could say anything she spoke again.

"I don't need you coming here after all these years to tell me how I should've lived my life—"

"What do you need me here for?" he asked, breaking in on her words. "Because if there's nothing for me to do around here"—he got out of his seat and started moving toward the door—"I'm going to leave for Texas sooner rather than later."

"I need you to visit your father's grave," she said just as he reached the door. "I need you to show even just that little respect."

He walked out of the kitchen and only responded when he'd started climbing the stairs. "Then let's go now," he yelled over his shoulder. And in a lower voice, unsure whether his mother would hear, or if he wanted her to: "Get this over with already."

He took his time in the shower, and every piece of clothing he put on was followed by a long gaze out the window up through the trees climbing the slope in the backyard. This morning, nothing he looked at evoked any memories and he was glad for it. When he got back downstairs his mother was sitting on the couch, her feet settled square on the floor, her hands folded around the strap of her purse which she held on her lap. She had a small white hat on, an upended bowl with a short veil dropping from the front to the middle of her forehead. She had put on a different housedress: this one was solid aqua blue.

She watched Bill come down the stairs and he could tell she was unhappy with the clothes he was wearing—not special in any way, good or bad—but she said nothing. Instead, she stood, straightened her dress once and then again, and, moving more slowly than Bill thought she needed to, preceded him out of the house and into the car. Watching her from behind, noticing how straight she was holding herself, Bill realized that this stubborn silence may have been the way she was able to hold herself against his father's stubbornness. He thought of saying something else about Lilly, get his mother going again, but he realized in the instant the thought formed that that was exactly what his father would have done.

They drove in silence to the cemetery: a small place cleared out of the woods on a hill overlooking the river. It was surrounded on all sides by Eva and Joe's farm, if it was still theirs, or, more likely, in the hands of one or the other.

"Eva still live at the farm?" Bill asked. They were approaching the house.

"Oh yes," his mother said, moving her head slowly in an exaggerated nod. "And she'd better stay there considering that she fought tooth and nail to get it in the divorce. Robbed your brother of it."

Bill saw the house come and go in his peripheral vision, which is also where he'd tried to keep it in his mind's eye for seventeen years. "He left her, Ma," he said. They turned into the drive down to the cemetery.

"And she gave him good reason."

"How?" Bill asked quickly, and almost immediately regretted that he had. He didn't really want to know the details of Eva's other adulteries, or even just the rumors of them. Until his conversation with Frank at the bar last night, he'd never entertained the idea that she had seduced other men after him. He was convinced that she'd used him, but still, he didn't like to think he could have been anyone. And he certainly didn't want to know it if his mother knew about him and Eva.

Bill stopped the car and his mother was out the door before he could even think of opening it for her. She walked toward the far corner of the yard, the Browning family plot, where a mound of fresh dirt marked his father's grave. Bill hung back, assuming she'd want some time alone, but halfway there, she turned around.

"Are you coming?" she called.

Bill took a deep breath and began walking slowly toward her. "I can see where it is, Mom. I won't get lost."

"It's not just your father. Jean's baby is here." She waited until he had joined her. "And then there's my parents and your uncle Harry, and your great-aunt Livia up in Wellspring. The world didn't come to a standstill while you were gone, you know. You might think about visiting them too." She started walking again.

"Visiting them? I hardly saw them when they were alive. You want me to visit them now they're dead?"

She turned again, so quickly this time that the force of the turn seemed to swing her arm past where she could control it, and her purse thudded heavily against her thigh. "Show some respect Billy. That's all I ask of you. Think of where you are and show some respect." She turned away again and with whatever reserves of energy she had, took purposeful strides to the edge of her husband's grave.

Bill walked up slowly behind her. He needed to get through this the easiest way possible, and if that was going to mean showing respect in the way she wanted him to, then he'd have to do it. She didn't have to know he wouldn't feel any of it. There was no point to make with her, or it had already been made and he was wasting his energy. His willful seventeen-year separation had probably delivered a pretty clear message.

"Sorry." He put his hand lightly on her shoulder, but he hardly let it sit there, certain that he had felt her skin flinch under his touch. She nodded to his apology.

"They have to let the ground settle for a while," she said. A small metal sign was stuck in the ground at the head of the grave site: it told his father's name and the date of his funeral. The smell of the dirt had a pungency that surprised Bill. He imagined his father's body already mixing with the earth. "We got him a nice coffin," his mother said. "Very pretty oak. White satin on the inside." Bill had already heard this from her, and from Maggie, but he said nothing. "It's what he asked for. And he had a funeral policy for it." Her voice trailed off and her body seemed to settle into itself, anchoring her firmly into the little patch of ground she stood on, as if to keep her from toppling into the upturned earth of the grave.

Bill walked to the other graves around his father's. Grand-parents, great-grandparents, cousins who had died before he was born, the pathetically tiny grave of Jean's day-old daughter: "Sherry Blake, born September 12, 1962, died September 13, 1962. Beloved daughter, sister, granddaughter, niece. Beloved of God." All that in a day, he thought.

He lifted his eyes from the ground and found himself looking up through the trees toward Eva's house. He could just make out the edge of the back porch. 'We're going to make love now, little brother,' Eva had said to him there, pulling Joe away from where they'd all been sitting together. Now, with that small patch of the house in his sights all these years later, he felt more akin to the dead he was standing among than the boy—and he had been a boy—who had sat on that porch, thrilling to what his sister-in-law had just said.

The screen of trees broke the piece of the porch he could see into even smaller pieces. He felt his eyes doing the work of keeping the house in focus, and this subtle straining of muscle seemed to be working on the rest of his body as well, making tiny adjustments to his legs to keep him steady as a pit yawned wide in his gut and surprised him with all of what he normally refused to think about and feel. This was exactly why he hadn't wanted to come back, this was it, this feeling right here, this loosing of anger: at Eva, at Joe, at himself for being such a fool. And below that, the thing he most hated to find himself feeling: the unforgivable, girlish sadness about what he had had at that house, even before he had Eva, and no longer had at all. That sense of possibility that had taken over then, and moved into all his thinking, moved through him like breath or blood. That sense that he had killed in himself along with everything else he'd assigned to the pit in his gut, yawning wider now with each passing instant. This was what he had determined never to feel again. And here he was in the throes of it. He pulled his gaze back, away from the house. He would never have driven past it or stood this close to it if it hadn't been for his mother insisting he see the grave, the seeping mess of his father's death and dirt.

He felt as if his feet had sunk into the ground below him and he had to wrench his body around to face his mother, ready to use the voice he had just minutes ago decided not to use with her: to demand that they leave, to wonder why she had needed to bring him here in the first place, to make her know what she was putting him through. But the sight of her stopped him cold: her head bent so far forward that her chin touched her chest and he could see the top of her hat, the circles of dirt where something must have been sitting on it in the closet. She had both hands tightly clasped around the handle of her purse as if it might contain something of real importance. The veins in her hands were blue under the thin skin. Her shoulders sloped down from the base of her neck: they formed no plane, nothing there to carry any weight. She hardly knew anything about him at all, not nearly enough to hurt him, to know how to make him feel like this about Eva, about herself.

He walked to her side. "Are you ready to go?" he asked quietly. She nodded and turned toward the car.

"Maybe you can come back when the gravestone is in place," she said when they were both settled in the car. "It's a very nice one. It has Gabriel carved in above the inscription."

"It's hard to say when I'll be able to come back, Mom," Bill said as gently as he could. He lit a cigarette and started the car up the drive.

His mother said nothing else. Bill thought that maybe he had actually quieted something in himself by not lashing out at her. But then the farmhouse came into view again, and Bill caught sight of a woman sweeping the front steps. Just the back of her and just for an instant before he averted his eyes and stepped on the accelerator, speeding past the property, racing to get away before he could allow himself to know that she was Eva.

But it didn't work. He had barely stepped into his mother's house when he had to leave it again, leave his mother confused—she hadn't seen Eva and that wouldn't have explained his behavior to her in any case—the agitation he was feeling making him move and move until his feet wouldn't do the trick any longer and he had to get back in the car, get on the road, make his way too fast over the rutted dirt track that ran along the river below town until he had come to the old boat landing. He skidded the car into the overgrown parking lot, slammed the door behind him, and marched down to the water. The sun picked out a current of insects mad with motion above the river, but the river itself was moving so slowly it satisfied nothing in Bill, frustrating him even further. He hauled up a handful of rocks from the water's edge and threw each one with enough force and aim so that it hit the boulder protruding out of the middle of the river. The rocks glanced off the boulder at fast, extreme angles, each meeting of stone and stone sharply audible, as was the splash as each rock dropped into the water. Bill gathered up another handful of rocks and threw them one by one at the boulder, but he was mindless now of whether they hit their mark or not. Nothing would soothe this agitation that he refused to name though he knew exactly what to call it.

He paced up and down the small beach. He knew he should leave town now, get in the car and drive, without stopping at his mother's, calling her when he'd gone two hundred miles maybe, or maybe not until he was back in Texas. But instead, not able to stop himself, he was driving back toward the farmhouse, and the sight of Eva in the distance—he could see her in the garden near the road—acted like a lightning rod for him. Everything he'd felt in the last hour, the anger and sadness and agitation, all of it suddenly spiked toward her, and he didn't hesitate for a fraction of a second, even when she looked at the car pulling in the driveway, her face registering confusion and surprise and maybe anger as well. He kept his eyes on her when he got out of the car, as if he could look nowhere else until he'd reached her, made her look at him and see what was there, again or for the first time, or for the only time that would actually matter. But Eva spoke first—"Well, Bill, I wondered if I'd get to see you"—and the sound of her voice stopped him mid-stride, his determination to confront her instantly checked by the surprise of it: so offhand and so intimately familiar it was as if the last words she'd said to him before Joe had burst in on them had sounded in his head for seventeen years, like a ringing in the ear you get used to, not hearing how it changes the quality of all sound.

Eva came out from behind the garden fence, and Bill felt he saw everything about her in the moment it took her to reach him. She'd gotten heavier, though not heavy, just more square, the curves that his eyes and hands had so admired hidden by a more solid flesh. Her hair was still black, but so black he assumed she must be dying it. Her neck was thicker, her jaw not so clearly defined. Her features had hardened a little: her mouth was more set than he remembered, her skin tougher, wrinkles around her lips and at the corners of her eyes. But the eyes themselves hadn't changed: they were as intense as they had been when he first met her, as dark and demanding.

Eva put her hand on his arm, wrapping her fingers around the muscle just above the elbow, bracing herself as she leaned toward him and kissed his cheek. Bill perceived this whole set of quick movements in a kind of slow motion: he felt the tips of her fingers make their very first contact with his skin, and his skin react as if with its own memory: softening around her touch, inviting it to deepen, which it did as she encircled his arm. But his mind shared none of his skin's pleasure. He tightened the muscle under her grip, forcing her fingers to loosen—even a fraction was enough—and just as her lips touched his cheek he shifted his weight back, so that she was forced to right herself, away from him, in order to keep her balance. Her mouth formed a small, knowing smile. Perhaps ten seconds had passed since she'd first touched his arm, but his silence suddenly seemed large to him, revealing in some way he hadn't intended.

"I didn't think I'd be coming to see you," he said, his voice pushed out quickly, almost without modulation. He took another step back, away from her, trying to keep his face and body composed, determined, so that she would believe he meant what he said, though he wasn't sure of it at all. Her smile didn't change. He folded his arms, rubbed at the spot where she had touched him. "But we were coming back from the cemetery—"

"I'm sorry about your father, Bill," she broke in, looking directly at him, her smile shifting subtly from amusement to sympathy. She was pulling the gardening glove off her left hand, the hand that hadn't yet touched him. "Jean says your mother's doing pretty well, though. Considering."

Bill nodded, but said nothing. He felt his focus tighten onto Eva's mouth.

"You look well," it said, and he tried to focus even tighter, to disembody her voice completely, strip it of any association with her, or him. But then her smile resumed its knowing shape, and his gaze was pushed upward by it so he saw her very deliberately look him up and down. "Must be all that oil in your diet."

He wasn't prepared to hear the same flirtatious edge in her voice that he'd known it to have before. He wasn't prepared for her to be so nonchalant with him. Maybe she thought it was funny, what had happened between them; that thing, she might call it. Maybe she thought Bill found it all pretty funny now, assumed he'd left behind that boy who'd had sex with her. Or maybe she gave it no thought.

"You've aged some," he said, making his voice as hard-edged as he could manage.

"Men age, Bill," she said, without missing a beat. "Women ripen." She took two steps past him, turning her head to keep her eyes on him as she moved toward the front door of the house. "How about a cup of coffee? I was just about to have some." She stopped on the steps, raised her eyebrows: was he coming?

The amusement on her lips, the certainty in her eyes, the damn sensuousness that should have changed with age but hadn't, all of it came together in Bill's sight, and he felt the power of the compulsion that had got him there when he probably should have been on his way far out of town, the power of that determination to make Eva see him clearly, on his terms—he could feel it building in himself again, and still, without saying a word, he followed her into the house.

One step through the door and he was looking at the staircase where Eva had pushed him down and straddled him. And at the top of the stairs, the bedroom, the bed, the honey wall. He had never forgotten the sound of the bees, could call it up easily, remembering not merely a sense of it, but the sound itself, as if it were composed of precise measures and colors, and not just tone and vibration.

"Are you coming, Bill?" Eva's voice startled him, his head snapped forward from its bent-back position, his eyes onto Eva's face from where they'd been roaming the contours of the stairs. She'd been watching him.

"Yeah." The word came out on an exhalation of breath he suddenly realized he'd been holding. He took a step toward her and she turned to lead him down the hall.

Down here, he saw now, things had changed: there was dark wood paneling on most of the walls, wall-to-wall carpeting, no furniture that he recognized except for the dining room table, a heavy, ornate family heirloom Joe and Eva had gotten from a

Browning aunt who had no children of her own. Bill breathed easier with so little to recognize but he wished that he didn't have to work so hard trying not to notice how familiar the sight of Eva's body was moving down this hall, changed or not.

The kitchen had been completely redone: there was hardly a remnant of the room where Joe and Eva had made a joke of Eva and Bill, and of Bill alone, and in its unfamiliarity he felt himself take back the momentum the sight of the stairs had momentarily drained from him.

"Does this mean you will have some coffee?" she asked, as he came into the room, an amused smile still in place on her lips. Bill fixed his own lips in imitation of hers, and thought he saw discomfort flicker through her eyes. He took a seat at the table before Eva had a chance to offer it.

"Yeah. Thanks." He turned his chair sideways so he could extend his legs.

In the time it took Eva to prepare the pot and let the coffee percolate, she said nothing, kept her hands busy putting some dishes away, washing others, setting out two cups, a plate of cookies that looked homemade. She met Bill's eyes when some task moved her head his way, but mostly her back was turned to him. He watched her closely, thinking he could read her body language, and imagined that the discomfort he'd seen in her eyes had worked its way into her throat so she couldn't speak, and further, into her hands, so she had to keep them moving to steady them, and still further, into the very core of her confidence so she needed this time to think about how to face him, how to think about him, what to say. But by the time she'd sat down, having met his eyes straight on while she put out the cups and cookies and brought the coffee pot to the table, he realized he'd been wrong. In fact, he thought, she might have been thinking that her silence would make him uneasy, and in retrospect it did.

"So, what do you think of what I've done to the house?" she asked, pouring the coffee, reaching her arm across the table, its strength obvious, its shapeliness still visible under the new flesh.

"It's different," he said, hoping brief sentences would prevent him from acknowledging or conceding anything she might hide in her words. He pulled a pack of cigarettes from his shirt pocket and held it toward her. She shook her head no; he lit one for himself, trying to remember if she had ever smoked.

"I imagine most things around here seem different to you," Eva said, pushing an ashtray toward him.

"Or just the same."

"Seventeen years is a long time to be away from a place for everything to seem the same."

"Unless nothing's changed." Bill rested the cigarette in the ashtray and reached for a cookie. He dipped it in his coffee, obliterating whatever flavor Eva had baked into it.

"You said I changed," Eva said, sipping her coffee, keeping her eyes on Bill.

"I said you aged. I don't know if you changed."

Eva laughed. "I've raised three children, gone through a divorce, run a farm on my own for seven years—"

"I don't mean that kind of change. I mean if you changed inside."

"You really think people change in that way, Bill?" Every time she said his name, he felt as if she'd reached behind him and grabbed at the skin of his neck. "Have you?"

Eva sipped at her coffee. Bill pulled his legs in, sat up in the chair, moved his eyes around the kitchen and out the back window where he could see sheep grazing down by the river. He took a drag on his cigarette and exhaled slowly across the table. He kept his gaze out the window for a full minute while he decided not to answer her, and thought about where he could take the conversation most effectively instead, and then slowly moved his eyes back to Eva's face, which seemed set in a look of patience. She was nibbling at a cookie.

"I met your daughter."

Eva didn't blink. "Did you?" she asked, nodding thoughtfully. "She never mentioned it."

"She didn't know."

"How's that?"

"I didn't know either until later. I was in the general store yesterday talking to Frank Lewis, and she was there at the same time. Then I saw Lewis at the Stoneridge last night and he told me who she was."

"Why didn't he tell you at the store? You could've introduced yourself."

"He thought I knew her. Thought our family was like any other. Uncles knowing their nieces and nephews."

"You knew they'd been born Bill. I never heard a peep from you about any of them."

"Yeah," he said, acknowledging what he wouldn't apologize for. "Anyway. Then I had a long talk with Rick Beecher, who told me the whole story about his son's death." Eva put her cup down and leaned back in her chair, her hands still on the table. Bill put his cigarette out and continued: "See, my mother wrote me about Wayne's death, but for some reason she never told me Lilly was involved. And then Rick told me everything. Including what happened with Lilly."

Eva nodded. "It's some story, isn't it?"

"You could say that," Bill said, trying to hide his surprise at the almost eager tone of Eva's voice. He'd expected to make her uncomfortable by taking the conversation in this direction.

"So he must've told you what went on with the woman who pulled Lilly out of the water."

"He was talking about his son's death, Eva"—would the sound of her name in his voice have an effect on her?—"he wasn't talking about some woman—"

"No, of course not," Eva said, taking a deep breath, placing her hands around her cup. "I'm sorry. I thought that's what you meant when you said he told you about Lilly."

"No," Bill said, making the word cut the air between them. "No, he told me that Lilly had been at the bridge with Wayne."

"You didn't know that?"

"No. I didn't—"

"Yeah. It was awful for her." Eva lowered her eyes. It seemed to Bill that it was the first time she'd let go of his gaze without her back being turned. "Such a terrible waste of that poor boy's life. And for Lilly to have seen it happen—"

"I understand he went to the bridge because of her."

Eva pushed her cup to the side. "What do you mean?" she said, leaning her arms on the table, her body inclining toward Bill.

He was glad to hear some of the calm in her voice replaced by signs of the discomfort he'd hoped to trigger in her. "Well," he said, lighting a cigarette before going on. "What I mean is, it seems he liked her so much he wanted to do what she was doing and she let him—"

"Are you saying you think Lilly had something to do with Wayne's death?"

"No. But it just seems from what Rick said that the kid might still be alive if he hadn't liked your daughter so much, that's all."

"That's all?" Eva said slowly. "Listen to me, Bill. No one, least of all Rick, has ever suggested that Lilly was to blame."

Eva's gaze was intense and relentless; Bill made himself return it. He took a long drag on the cigarette, picked up the matchbook, turned it slowly through his fingers. Finally, Eva looked away. She poured more coffee for herself. She rearranged the cookies so they made a perfect circle on the plate. She folded and unfolded her napkin, took a deep breath, a sip of coffee.

"So," she said, holding the cup in the nest of her hands, looking directly at Bill again. "What about you?"

I'm not ready to end this conversation, he thought. "Let me just ask you one more question about Wayne and Lilly," he said.

Eva's eyebrows pulled together. "I've already told you—"

"I know," he said. "But don't you think it's strange that Wayne would've jumped at all? Unless someone convinced him, someone he really liked?"

She was staring at Bill as if seeing him for the first time since he'd gotten out of his car. "No. I don't think it's strange," she said. "Wayne may have been a simple boy, but he wasn't a vegetable. He had a mind of his own." Her voice was steady and determined now. "What I do think is strange is that after all these years, you're back here for two days or whatever it is, you hear a story for the first time, and you immediately think you have some insight into a tragedy that happened to people you didn't know at a time when you already hadn't been around for a dozen years."

"I knew some of the—"

"And I think it's even stranger," she said, pushing herself up from the table, her eyes beginning to show the anger she wouldn't quite let her voice reveal, "that you come into my house as my guest, but then you think it's all right to show nothing but disrespect for me and my family while you're here." She grabbed her cup and placed it noisily in the sink. "If you're trying to get back at me for what happened between you and me, or what you think happened, then say so and get it over with." Her voice never wavered.

Bill wanted to push his chair over, to take two long strides toward the stove and slap her, leave his handprint on her burning cheek. He was going to have been the one to get them to this point, to have made her twist with discomfort as he eased his way back toward the last time they'd been in this kitchen together. It wasn't supposed to have been Eva, all over again, one step ahead of him. He wanted to hit her so badly his hand was shaking, but he wouldn't let himself: it would just give her one more thing to know about him, one more thing she'd learn how to use against him. He stood slowly.

"It was a mistake to come here," he said.

The back door opened and Lilly stepped into the kitchen, her eyes locking immediately onto Bill. She stopped just inside the threshold.

"Hi Mom," she said, still looking at Bill.

"Hi, honey," Eva said, making subtle adjustments to her posture, draining off anger before Lilly might sense it. She followed

Lilly's gaze to Bill's face. "This is your uncle. Bill. Your father's brother."

"Hi," Lilly said quietly, her face set in concentration, figuring something out. And then with certainty: "Didn't I see you in the general store yesterday?"

"Yeah. You did." Bill tried to smile like he imagined an uncle might, but his mouth felt crooked and stiff. He was trying not to stare, but Lilly had the same effect here in the kitchen as she had had in the general store. And she was dressed more provocatively now: her shorts cut to the middle of her thighs, the material of her tee-shirt thin enough so that what he thought looked like a bathing suit top was visible through it. He pulled his gaze up to her face, but the look in her eyes gave him away.

"You should've told me who you were," Lilly said, the fullness of her voice returned to her. She moved to the table and reached for a cookie. There was something in the way she was looking at Bill, as if she'd known what he'd been thinking when he'd first seen her. He remembered the men at the counter stepping aside just enough to make room for her, knowing they shouldn't want what they wanted, and he was in their shoes now. Without thinking he took a step back, almost stumbling.

"I didn't know who you were," he said, getting the words out quickly. "Till later. Till someone told me last night."

"Frank Lewis, right?" Lilly said, her mouth full of cookie. "I saw him talking to you at the store. He's the biggest gossip in town."

"Lilly," Eva said, warning in her voice.

"Well, he is, Mom." She dug for something in her pocket, moving her hips forward and back to accommodate her hand. After an instant she pulled her hand out empty. She wasn't looking at him, but Bill had a feeling she knew he was watching. The same feeling he'd had at the general store, though her back had been turned to him then. She put her other hand in her other pocket and her hips moved again. Maybe she really was trying to find something, but Bill had the distinct impression that she'd found it in the looking, since this hand came out empty too. "He's as nosy as any of the old ladies who stand around whispering at the grocery," she said, looking for an instant at Eva. Bill followed her eyes there and Eva's locked onto him.

"I should go," he said. "Good to meet you Lilly."

"Yeah," she said, her head bobbing in an exaggerated nod. "Same here." When he said nothing else, she wiggled her fingers in a childish goodbye and sat down at the table, pulling the plate of cookies closer.

"I'll walk you out," Eva said, leading Bill down the hall toward the front door. He noticed how different her stride was from when they'd walked the other way just half an hour ago, everything held in now, her arms crossed so that all he could see of them were her elbows, which looked dangerously sharp. When they'd stepped outside, she turned on her heel to face him. "Don't forget she's your niece, Bill."

"I know she's my niece, Eva."

"Well, don't forget it."

"What are you getting at?"

"I'm getting at the fact that you shouldn't be looking at her the way you were just looking at her."

He could feel the impulse to hit Eva tingling in his hand again. He reached into his pocket for his keys, and jangled them noisily.

"You ought to look to yourself for that one."

"What are *you* getting at?"

"That someone had to teach her to flirt like that, Eva."

Eva's eyes blazed. "Men taught her, Bill."

He said nothing. He got in the car and slammed the door shut. He could feel Eva's eyes on him long after he'd driven out of her sight.

Bill knew the house would be empty, his mother at church, helping prepare for some function on the weekend. She'd mentioned it to him on the way home from the cemetery, but he hadn't heard the details, his mind already full of the sight of Eva. Now, he had more than the sight of her to bring into the dark living room: her voice echoed so loudly in his mind that it seemed to have pushed out of his skull to ring off the walls. Just as it had when Joe had first brought her here, Thanksgiving '48, but now with the opposite effect: not melodic and inviting, but steely and controlled. With Eva's voice seeming to circle both inside and outside his head, he asked himself, for the hundredth time since he'd arrived in Overton, why he'd come.

He walked back and forth between the living room and kitchen, each step pounding out the same thoughts: he'd been an idiot to see Eva, to give in to the sight of her, the ridiculous need of her embedded in the memories of that time. From living room to kitchen and back, and again and again: he felt like a caged animal gone mad with fury. Yet he knew he should probably stay there, hidden from himself if nothing else, and hope the dark emptiness of the house would numb him. Seeing no one at all seemed the only way not to have to see himself acting out of that idiocy. He would do exactly what needed to be done and then get the hell out of Overton for good, hoping his mother would understand, or understand so little that she'd finally write him off. That would be the best outcome. Then he'd never have a reason to come back. He grabbed a beer from the refrigerator and walked into the living room where he sat staring into the dim middle ground until he needed another beer. By the time he'd finished a brief, wordless dinner with his mother, the beers had convinced him that it was all right to venture out again.

1989

WHAT NINA SAW through the open back door of Tony's studio—him and the girl, their arms around each other—could have been innocent or, at least, inconclusive. It wasn't unusual for certain teachers and students to greet each other with a kiss or hug after vacations, or in congratulations. And Tony was one of those teachers, Nina knew that; he was physical in that way with nearly everyone he knew. But he hadn't been away, and Nina hadn't seen the girl before, didn't think she was one of his students. And there was something about their stance, the tilt of their heads next to each other, the way Tony's hand lay on the small of her back, that made Nina think she was probably seeing something more than a simple gesture of affection.

She let herself stand there, her eyes full on the couple's silent exchange, hoping that one of them might catch sight of her so Tony would have the responsibility of convincing her that she hadn't seen what she thought she had. She knew she couldn't do it for herself. But neither of them moved an inch out of their clutch; and if their eyes were open, they weren't looking outward. It wasn't long before Nina's vision began to blur with the strain of seeing them.

She turned and walked quickly toward the end of the building where her car was parked. When she heard her name being called, she realized that an instant before she'd seen someone out of the corner of her eye sitting on the bench that was set in a small grove of young birches not far from the studio building. She hadn't registered who it was, but now the voice told her. When she looked over her shoulder, briefly, purposefully not making eye contact, she saw Alan Gill walking at a brisk pace in her direction. She walked faster: he was the last person she wanted to see, especially if he had also seen what she had.

"Nina." His voice was closer.

She walked as fast as she could, just holding herself back from breaking into a run. She imagined she knew what his voice would sound like in sympathy and consolation—that edge of solicitousness that was always there ratcheted up to a sickly sweetness—and she didn't want to hear it, or have to control herself if she did. She didn't want to hear that it would be okay, or that he knew what she was going through, knew exactly how she felt. She didn't want to be told that she should give Tony a chance to explain before she jumped to conclusions because they were such a perfect couple, and Tony such a wonderful man. She didn't want to know what Alan thought, how sorry he felt, how sorry he was to have seen, but since he had, let him just say this—

She felt his hand on her arm just as she was reaching for the car door, but her name, spoken again, was sounded in a different voice. "Nina." It was pitched low, steady, nothing in it but a statement of his presence by her side. "Are you all right?"

She turned toward him, and she was surprised to see that his gaze was as steady as his voice, as unassuming. "I'm fine, Alan. I'm just . . ." She opened the car door.

"Yes, of course," he said, nodding his head slowly. He squeezed her arm gently and began to walk away. The touch lingered, but Nina didn't feel anxious to shake it off the way she often did when she and Alan talked.

"Alan," she said. He turned, but it took her a moment to find her voice. "Would you like to have a drink?" She wasn't sure how she wanted him to answer.

"Certainly," he said, walking back toward her. "We could go to my house." He reached across her and pulled the car door wide. When she didn't move, he said: "Or someplace else, if you'd prefer. I'm merely thinking that you might not care to run into anyone else at the moment."

"Sounds fine," she said, getting in the car. He shut the door for her.

They drove in silence. Nina could hardly follow her own thoughts. The best she could do was to focus on the route to Alan's house: two miles she knew like a habit, just as she knew all the roads around the campus, around Cannen, Greenville, the connections and shortcuts, what to expect from each in the snow or rain, which were the most and least used. Repetition had taught her to trust this knowledge, but she tended to ignore the same kind of proof in other parts of her life. Which was more strange, she wondered: that she was about to have a drink with Alan Gill at his house, or that she was surprised at what she'd just seen in Tony's studio?

She'd never been at Alan's when it wasn't full of people; she wasn't sure she'd ever been there in the daylight before. It was always an evening in October that she was here, year after year, dutifully accompanying Tony to Alan's annual gathering: the tacitly designated place for the new at Cannen to be introduced to the old, the first ritual of arrival. Her own time in that spotlight was still vivid for all the wrong reasons. And as she stepped over the threshold, she felt as if she were traversing the fourteen years between that moment and this, between her first instance of doubt about Tony, about herself, and this one, a straight path that somehow led back to its beginnings.

The living room was vast, the ceilings high and vaulted. She'd taken note of these things at the parties, but they were nothing more than architectural details when the room was full of people. Now she thought about what it must be like for Alan to inhabit that room alone every day. He had moved past her and was standing in the kitchen doorway.

"Why don't we sit in here?" He extended his arm to her. His voice was still steady and unassuming. "I think you'll find it a warmer room."

The kitchen was off limits at the parties and Nina was surprised, again, at how typically homey it was. Maybe that's why Alan never wanted anyone to see it: the plastic napkin holder, the labeled canisters, the enamel salt box hanging near the stove—his unexceptional self. But he appeared to move more comfortably in these quarters, and Nina felt her body relax a little as well. There was deep, late sunlight coming through a row of windows above the sink, and when she sat at the wooden table in the middle of the room, shrugging off her coat, the warmth of the light seemed to radiate up from the wood to meet its source. Nina felt enveloped by it, comforted, gentled, as she imagined Alan might say, and, suddenly, she was close to tears.

"If I remember correctly," Alan said, holding up one of the bottles he'd brought out of the pantry, "it's bourbon for you, yes?"

Nina was afraid that if she spoke, the words leaving her tongue would somehow unstopper the tears which felt increasingly imminent. She nodded.

"Straight up, water back, right?" he asked, reaching for a glass in the dish drain.

It was the hint of humor in Alan's voice that touched Nina, the offer of it, his willingness to discover that it might be unwelcome. She couldn't remember having treated him well enough to warrant this kindness: she wondered if she'd looked more distressed than she'd realized when he saw her at the studio building. She smiled and nodded again. He poured the bourbon, put the glass in front of her and the bottle within reach. She watched him fill a glass with water, and another from a bottle of sherry. His movements were quiet: there was nothing at all flamboyant or considered in them. He put the glasses on the table and went back into the pantry. Nina was glad for the reprieve; he wouldn't see the tears she quickly wiped away.

He put a bowl of oyster crackers between them when he finally sat down. "In case you need a little something," he said.

"Alan, this is very kind of you," she said, using her voice carefully, afraid of more tears. She lifted her glass to him, and he to her; he put his down and reached for a cracker while she took a first sip. "You'll have to forgive me," she said, unable to find anything else to say. "I feel incredibly awkward." She met his eyes for the first time.

"Please don't. I'm glad to help." He reached across the table and patted her hand: the perfect gesture for that kitchen. "What is it the students say?" He pulled his hand back. "Shit happens?"

A laugh burst out of Nina: in fourteen years she'd never once heard him use profanity. He seemed to relax further and joined her laughter. Nina leaned back in her chair knowing she wouldn't cry now. She rubbed her face, and sighed, "Oh God," into her hands.

"May I tell you something about the young woman you saw with Tony?" Alan was leaning on his elbows, his hands folded on the table. "Do you know her?" Nina shook her head.

"Well, Suzanne Garyle is a freshman, and a very serious, already well-established flirt."

Nina took another drink. Hearing the girl's name was like seeing her with Tony all over again.

"And I want to be certain," Alan went on, "that you understand the profundity I mean to impart to the word flirt. This young woman approaches everyone, man and woman. Flora and fauna for all we know. She has even made a pass at me, if you can imagine such a thing." He took a small sip of sherry. "She's very smart, very spoiled, and she absolutely revels in her ability to attract people."

"From what I could see, she's very pretty."

"Yes. That she is. But I think it's very safe to say that her beauty is severely skin-deep. And from what I have been able to glean, her sexual appetites, for all their advertised fullness, are fairly skin-deep as well. She is apparently much more interested in demonstrating her prowess as a seductress—if you will forgive the feminization of the noun—than she is in satisfying the passions her seductiveness has been known to stir."

"That would be an interesting challenge for the right person," Nina said, turning her eyes to the window.

"Nina. Forgive me if I overstep my bounds by saying this, but I know, of course, that you and Tony have had your share of difficulties."

He'd been looking down at his hands but raised his gaze to meet Nina's now, making sure, she thought, that he could go on without hurting or angering her. She wasn't sure. After fourteen years, she and Tony had a pretty large share of difficulties, as Alan so delicately put it. She didn't know if she was ready to think about how much Alan might know, or about how many other people associated with Cannen could also say that "of course" they knew about her and Tony.

Alan considered her silence and went on. "But I wanted to tell you about a conversation I was privy to at the beginning of last semester between Tony and one of his students."

"Alan, I appreciate what—"

"It's not what you're thinking, my dear. Quite the opposite, I suspect."

At any other time, she would have been quick to tell Alan that he couldn't possibly know what she was thinking, but everything about this moment with him was different and maybe this time he did know. In any case, he was so determined to help, it seemed important somehow to let him try. She reached for the bottle of bourbon. "May I?"

"By all means," he said, leaning back. He waited for her to pour and take a drink before going on. "Tony invited me to sit

with him and his student in the lounge one morning. He introduced her, told me she was a freshman, and then explained that
Rachel, I believe her name was, was having a little trouble adjusting to Cannen, and maybe I could help convince her that it was
not an unusual occurrence."

He took a sip of sherry, his movements slow and naturally
elegant. Tony had told Nina about Rachel, about his talk with
her, but Nina couldn't remember him mentioning that Alan had
been there.

"Well, we talked for a while, and young Rachel seemed wholly
unmoved by what we were saying. Finally, Tony steered the conversation toward you. He told Rachel that when you arrived here
with him, you'd experienced a terrible sense of dislocation. And
then he described how you came to learn to appreciate what you
hadn't even thought considerable before. He spoke about how
you observed the world around you then. How deeply you took
in the details in order to know the whole. And he talked about
the quality of feeling you brought to seeing. Those were his
words. 'The quality of feeling Nina brings to seeing.' "

He paused, his eyebrows raised, waiting for Nina's reaction.
But she knew that phrase well: Tony had begun using it many
years before, sometimes seriously, sometimes sarcastically when
he felt she was looking at one of his paintings cursorily, or making up her mind too quickly about something or someone.

"But he didn't stop there," Alan said quickly, breaking into her
silence. "He began to tell Rachel about your contraptions. A
wonderful word for them, I might add. He described to her how
ingenious they are, and how he loves watching you lose yourself
to the thinking they require. And soon he was hardly talking to
Rachel's quandary at all any longer. I think the poor girl was a bit

baffled, but I was deeply moved to hear him speak about you with such admiration and love."

Nina appreciated Alan's impulse to help her, but she was beginning to feel oddly exposed: as if he thought he was somehow a participant in her life because he'd heard a piece of it described. She pushed back her chair.

"Thanks for telling me that, Alan. I know Tony loves me"—she cringed inside at the sound of the words: whose sake were they for?—"but it's always good to know—"

"The point is Nina," he broke in, and reached across the table to touch her hand again. She felt the urge to pull away this time, though the touch was still gentle. "The point is that Suzanne Garyle, and young women like her, couldn't possibly mean anything to Tony."

Nina stood up. Alan was wrong, but it didn't matter here. "Well, it's lovely of you to say. I mean, it's kind of you to tell me this story. Really. Thank you."

"I have overstepped, haven't I?" he said, putting his hand to his heart. It was the first gesture he'd made in the time they'd been together that seemed at all theatrical.

She pulled on her coat. "No, Alan. Not at all. It's just"—there was so much she didn't want to say to him—"I think I just need to think things through." She pulled her coat tightly around her though she wasn't cold. "On my own."

Alan looked worried, tentative. She could see that her discomfort was making him uncomfortable, and she had the feeling that at any moment he might sweep his hair back from his face dramatically, or flutter his hand in search of the perfect word. "I'm going to go," she said. "But thank you. Really."

He walked her to the door. She noticed again how austere the living room was, how small she felt there, how small Alan looked. "You'll be all right?" he said, stepping outside with her.

It was just getting dark. The blue at the horizon was as deep as space. "I'll be fine," she said. "Thanks again." She smiled at him as she got in the car. She could see him in the rearview mirror watching her down the long driveway.

Nina headed north, the long way home so she wouldn't have to pass the campus. She drove a mile before she realized she needed her headlights, and, once on, they seemed to throw some light back at her as well. She was suddenly aware of the smile still frozen on her lips, and the feeling that if she could just keep it there, she wouldn't have to think about why she'd put it there in the first place. But even as she recognized the feeling, the smile began to fade, and the more distance she got from the conversation—she was driving fast now—the less easy she was with it.

At one of Alan's parties not too long ago, he'd told Nina how jealous he was of what she and Tony had: their longevity, their physical ease with each other, the many levels of their intimacy. She'd had a lot to drink, but it had been possible for her to sense how reluctantly he chose the word jealous, as if it hurt him to admit the truth. Still, even having sensed that, she'd managed to dismiss the remark as one of Alan's theatricalities. Now, she wondered if that jealousy hadn't somehow played a part in the conversation they'd just had, in Alan's desire to help: maybe he saw this as his way inside their lives.

Or maybe it was just Nina's perception of things at the moment that was problematic. Certainly it was less complicated to doubt Alan's good intentions than to begin to doubt Tony again, taking the first step down that familiar, awful path. And yet, there was the feeling of being exposed that she couldn't shake. Of course, she'd understood that people on campus knew some personal things about her and Tony: if nothing else, there had been those two years of living in that fishbowl circle of campus cottages during the time when she and Tony were laying the foundation for what would become their life. But she didn't like to think about what the collective sense might be of the nature of their "difficulties," as Alan had called them, or that there was a collective sense at all.

She was circling south now back into the valley, closer to home than to Cannen. It was almost totally dark and a mist had formed over the snow melting in the fields. If a deer came running out of the mist into the road, Nina would hardly have time to stop; she slowed the car. There was a long, elegant curve in the road: she'd always loved the way the car felt taking it, holding tight to its simple, perfect arc. But now she was working hard to keep the car steady. She could do nothing about it: there were people who would think they knew her because they'd heard what there was to hear, and they would know nothing. Just as Alan had told her Suzanne Garyle's reputation, and it gave Nina nothing real to know about the girl. And wasn't she "knowing" Tony right now through his reputation as well: the one he had with her, the one that she knew distorted her vision of him sometimes? Alan had tried to show Nina the other side of that reputation, the loving, devoted, admiring partner: Tony watching her lose herself to thinking through the workings of a contraption. She thought of how he'd always loved to watch her, for pleasure and painting. How he'd watched her with disinterest in his eyes as well, and, at times, she thought, with disdain. All these years of looking hard for one reason or another, and she still wasn't sure he had found what he was looking for.

When Nina turned into their driveway, she saw mist coming off the pond, meeting the mist rising from the snow. She sat in the car, the headlights catching the movement, eerie and beckoning, the studio and workshop almost completely enveloped, blurring at the edges that were still visible, as if the mist could alter the elemental structure of the building. She hadn't been aware of any buzz from the bourbon, but she wondered now at the hesitation she felt about getting out of the car, the sense she had that the mist could reach her before she could find the lock on the dark porch; that it could start at her feet, touch off her disintegration, or complete it. The mutability of substance, an old irrationality. She was glad to see that a light was on somewhere in the house, promise enough to get her out of the car, onto the porch, her hand easily finding the lock with the key, the door open and then quickly shut behind her.

The lamp by the desk at the foot of the stairs was on and an arm of light reached into the kitchen. Nina dropped her keys in the bowl on the counter and turned the heat on, wondering if Tony had left the light on to let her know there was a note for her stuck in the corner of the picture frame there. But the only note was the one she'd left him that morning saying she might be on campus in the afternoon, reminding her now that he'd known, while his arms were closing around Suzanne Garyle, that she might see them like that.

She felt exhausted suddenly—the bourbon finally hitting its mark—and dropped onto the couch. The deep comfort of the familiar was immediate. Everything inside her felt agitated, but she could make herself breathe deeply here. It was as if the room had waited for her to settle, before settling in around her, reminding her that there was this too: that she and Tony had made this home, together, this life of fourteen years already.

She let her gaze wander across the bookshelves that dominated the room; floor to ceiling along the full length of two walls. Tony had built them in the days just after they'd moved in, and they'd been practically filled by the contents of the boxes they'd brought from the cottage: the favorite books that each of them had carried place to place until they ended up intermingling at the cottage, and the ones they'd acquired together in their first years as a couple, the delight of purchasing something out of mutual interest, discovering the shape and extent of that mutuality. Nina thought of the books on the living room shelves as familiars, constant and attendant in their way. Her eyes moved across their spines like fingers might take to worry beads, finding a rhythm of solace. And on one of the shelves, fitted among the books, there was a box of glass, lit from above and below; a mock museum setting—labeled in embossed tin as "All work and . . ."—for the first contraption Nina had ever made: a simple mechanism that rang a bell, lifted the receiver of a child's toy telephone, played a segment of the voice tape from a Chatty Cathy doll ("I want to play with you") and replaced the receiver with a heaving sigh produced by a toy bellows and a tiny plastic whistle. Nina had made it for Tony, a silly gift that became his gift to her when he led her to think of what she might do with that turn of her mind.

She pulled the throw blanket around her. Tony was built into this place. She came home to him no matter where he was, no matter how much she resisted the feeling.

"I wish it was easier for you," Diane had said some years before, sitting across from Nina in this room. They'd been talking about Nina's decision to leave the garage, to put a last end to her on-and-off involvement with Nick.

Nina had thought about getting up, going to the kitchen for more tea, going to the bathroom, anything not to hear what might come next. Diane had always thought Nick was a problem.

"It doesn't feel so hard," Nina said finally. "I don't think there's any other choice to make."

"I'm not talking about Nick, Nina," Diane said, rubbing her eyes. A wave of exhaustion seemed to wash over her and into her words. "Well, maybe I am in a way. I guess." She dropped her hand heavily to the arm of the chair.

Nina was surprised by the last-effort tone in Diane's voice. "What are you talking about?" she asked, though now she could guess what was coming.

"You and Tony."

Just what Nina had thought, and it wasn't the conversation she wanted to be having. She shifted in her chair. "And?"

Diane leaned forward. "And I wish, for your sake, Nina, that it was easier for you to cope with what goes on between you and Tony."

Nina had the feeling that Diane was trying to draw out of her something Diane herself didn't want to say. But Nina said nothing at all, she didn't know how to react out of the annoyance and discomfort she was beginning to feel.

"It's hard seeing you in such turmoil all the time," Diane said.

"Well, I'm sorry it's so hard for you."

"Nina, that's not—"

"What else would you have expected? That I would've learned to share him happily?"

Diane leaned back. "It seems to me you learned to share each other. And in the worst ways possible."

Nina took her time lighting a cigarette. "I don't think it's been much of a problem for Tony."

"That's ridiculous, Nina." Diane's voice grew impatient—or was it angry?—through the words. "You think it's been easy for him to know you were with Nick?"

"Yeah. I do," Nina said, her voice deliberately quiet. She slowly twirled the cigarette along the edge of the ashtray, keeping her eyes there. "I think Nick made it easier for Tony."

"Nina, you could've left Tony," Diane said, her voice more gentle, but no less pointed. "You could've left any time. If it was bad, you could've walked away. And I know that wouldn't have been easy, and I'm not condoning what he's done, but you stayed. And, forgive me, but you're not blameless."

She'd stopped speaking, but Nina could see she wasn't finished.

Diane took a deep breath. "Maybe this thing with Nick was a reaction to what Tony was doing at first, just like you always say. But it's been going on for, what? Six, seven years? You and Tony have been together only a few years more than that."

Nina found something in Diane's words to grab onto, to pull her thoughts back into the place she wanted them to be. "And now I'm leaving Nick," she said, nodding her head with each word. "Doesn't that count for anything?"

"I don't know. You tell me."

Nina went silent again. There was nothing to tell. Leaving Nick was a meaningless gesture: he'd begun pulling away from her several months before, making it clear he was losing interest, thinking about marriage, wanting to spend his time with women he might turn out to love. Words delivered to Nina nonchalantly, but with the most sustained eye contact he'd been able to maintain outside of the bedroom in almost seven years. Nina was leaving the garage just to get out of the way: his and her own. Tony had hardly figured in the equation. So Nina said nothing to Diane. She'd sat there—just where she was sitting now—unmoving, until the cigarette had burned so far down she could feel the heat in her fingers. She pretended to be burned and left the room. Diane had followed her into the kitchen after a few minutes, made sure she was all right, and left.

Nina had stopped smoking later that year. Left the garage, left Nick, stopped smoking. But she hadn't kicked her habit of certainty about Tony, and five years later it still clung to her. She had to fight with herself now to keep the image of Tony and Suzanne Garyle from solidifying in her mind and leading to the next image: of a kiss; of her hands on his ass pulling him tight against her; of his hand moving down from her shoulder, over her breast, into the curve of her waist and hip, between her legs.

Nina pushed herself out of the chair and went into the kitchen, switching on the overhead light, hoping to dim her thoughts with its brightness. She poured herself more bourbon and, after looking around the kitchen slowly, walked back into the living room. She thought of Alan's living room again, of the way it had dwarfed them not only with its size but its seeming demand to be filled. She thought of the difference in feeling between that and this: the warmth of this room, the ease of it, of the whole house; the way people visiting for the first time sat down in these chairs, or at the kitchen table, as if they'd had the run of the house for years. How welcome people said they felt, how quickly they felt at home. It was no small thing, she thought. It was fourteen years already of no small thing.

· · · ·

Nina saw nothing else to convince her that Tony was having an affair with Suzanne Garyle. She wished she could've kept herself from looking in quite that way, but she was glad, in any case, to come up with nothing. And in a fortunate stroke of timing, Tony's gallery in New York gave him a three-month deadline for a series of paintings they wanted to show in the fall. His focus became so tight on his work that Nina would have had to drill him with the most obvious questions for him to even have begun noticing her suspicion. He went from his studio to campus back to the studio with end-of-the-day forays into the kitchen and their bed: four angles of necessity and desire in which Nina felt comfortably, and for the moment, happily situated. There had been times when Tony had seemed merely selfish during a period of intense work, when his desire seemed little more than self-regard. But this time he seemed more present when they were together. Nina considered the possibility that he only appeared to be so because she needed to believe he was. And for an instant, she considered another possibility: that he was more attentive out of fear that otherwise she would find out about Suzanne Garyle, that there really was something to find out. Still, after two months, she was able to push both thoughts to the more remote reaches of her mind.

But on the first Monday in May, when Nina was given the paperwork for her first intake interview of the day at the

Greenville Women's Center, she saw that the name on the form was Suzanne Garyle, the reason for the visit: possible pregnancy. Nina dropped the file on her desk and leaned back in her chair. This is not happening, she thought.

"This is not happening," she said quietly, and then each word more slowly as if she could make them a barrier against the other thoughts she could already feel gathering: her suspicion being revived, turning toward certainty.

"This could have nothing to do with Tony," she said, hoping that hearing the words would make them seem more substantial. But her voice rang hollow and unconvinced. She stared at the paper on the desk, trying to see it as she saw all the forms that were put into her hands here: someone's situation, a story to hear, a puzzle of need to be figured out. Suzanne Garyle as one more woman among all the women who passed through the center, all the women, hundreds of them, whom Nina had talked to in the almost five years she'd worked there. Suzanne Garyle could be just one more in that long procession. She could just as easily be that as not.

But the suspicion was muscling through and finally it filled Nina like an adrenaline rush, pushing her deeper into her chair, and pushing her back as if the last two months hadn't occurred and she was on campus looking into the open door of Tony's studio. Or further, and the last five years hadn't passed, and she was reaching for Nick, for that numb pleasure. Or she hadn't noticed the last decade, had learned nothing, let nothing of value accumulate in her head or heart. That was the worst of it, she thought, but the thought was fleeting, all the thoughts were, and she was left with a taste of salt and metal on her tongue as if suspicion were a survival instinct.

She got up, walked out from behind her desk and then back again. Cannen students rarely came to the clinic and when they did, they often asked to speak with someone else once they realized who Nina was. That's what would probably happen with Suzanne too. But what if she didn't ask to see someone else? That might mean that she didn't know Nina, but it could also mean that she was ready to flaunt her involvement with Tony. Nina stared at the form again and made herself consider one more possibility: that Suzanne was here because she had no reason not to be. In the same way, for the same reason, that Tony hadn't bothered to close his studio door that day. Nothing to hide. All these gestures hiding nothing, it could be that simple. She would have to believe it was that simple if she was to do for this young woman what she did for any other.

"Suzanne?" Nina said to the only person in the waiting room. The young woman looked up from the book she was reading. She didn't seem to recognize Nina. "That's me," she said, collecting her things, standing up, moving slowly enough so that Nina had a chance to see her beauty more clearly: unstudied and confident. She had on loose jeans and a man's oversized oxford shirt, but it was still possible to see how easily her body moved and that the loose clothing was for comfort, not camouflage. Nina could see how she might have fit well inside Tony's arms.

Nina offered her hand. "I'm Nina Webber," she said, conscious of what she needed her voice to sound like—welcoming and friendly, but not presumptuous—and unable to gauge if she'd managed it. Suzanne showed no sign of recognizing her name. They shook hands. "Come on in." Nina led her down the hallway to the office.

"So. Suzanne," she said when they were both seated, she

behind the small desk where her feet, one tapping nervously against the other, were hidden from view; and Suzanne comfortably draped into the chair opposite, her legs crossed and unmoving, her gaze steady and expectant. She doesn't know me, Nina thought. "I'm curious," she said. "Why did you chose the Center over the facilities at Cannen?" She knew she shouldn't be asking this; it was none of her concern. "I know that Cannen has a very fine clinic for its women students."

"I'm going to be living near here this summer," Suzanne said, her voice steady. "And maybe staying off-campus next fall, so this seemed the logical choice."

Nina nodded, hoping that the interested but neutral look she was attempting to keep on her face was actually there. She knew she should tell Suzanne who she was—she leaned forward onto her elbows and tried to stop her foot from shaking—and she knew she wouldn't. "That makes perfect sense," she said, nodding again, a little too enthusiastically. "So, why don't you tell me what's going on."

"Well"—Suzanne pointed toward the form under Nina's hand—"I think I'm pregnant."

"Have you had a test?" It was the first thing Nina had learned when she was training to do intake: don't start asking until she's finished telling. But Suzanne seemed unperturbed by the question.

"No, but I'm almost sure," Suzanne said. She kept her eyes on Nina's face, but she seemed to disappear for an instant, turn inward, or outward beyond the room, the moment. She won't meet my gaze, Nina thought. Why is that? Maybe she does know me, after all. A good actress, but not quite expert enough to pull it off. "I've been pregnant before," Suzanne said finally, her words rushing out. "So I know what my body feels like when it happens."

Nina was pulled up out of the spiral of her own thinking by the sound of those words: as if Suzanne were anxious to get them out of herself before they might endanger her. Nina had heard the sound before, in the voices of other women who had talked to her from that chair. Young women mostly, determined to be free of the thing that wouldn't let them go after they'd had an abortion. "How is it possible," one of them had asked Nina, "to be so relieved and so upset about it at the same time? I didn't want the baby." Or she hated the guy who got her pregnant; or she would have children someday, but not now, she's too young, didn't want to raise a child herself; or she knew she would never want children. How was it possible then to feel such different things about it at the same time when she'd been so clear about her decision? Every voice trying to avoid asking the question, trying to sound unwavering. Young women's voices mostly, but some older, asking the same question; her own, older, echoes of it still in her thoughts.

Suzanne carefully described the feelings she recognized in her body as pregnancy, her voice becoming quieter and quieter. "So," she said, biting her lower lip, her beauty suddenly more tender than striking. "I'm pretty sure I'm pregnant again."

Nina wanted to tell her to give it a little time, to not put too much faith in those physical comparisons. She'd done it herself; she knew it was a mistake. "And the earlier pregnancy. Did you carry that baby to term?"

Suzanne hesitated again before answering and Nina saw something else happening in her face, this time something being adjusted behind her eyes. She was pulling herself up, leaping away from the moment of girlishness and uncertainty she'd let herself succumb to, reinhabiting her woman's skin. When she finally spoke, her voice was a peal of disbelief: "You mean did I have it? I was still in high school. Of course not."

Nina wanted to ask her if she thought that no high school girl had ever given birth, that everyone had her wherewithal and wealth, that absolutes could govern anything at all. "So you had an abortion?" Nina asked. Suzanne nodded quickly, impatiently. "And were there any complications?"

"No." All tenderness gone from her voice, her face; everything now an absolute. "Should there've been?"

"Of course not. But things do happen. And if there'd been problems, you'd want to be cautious around having another abortion."

"I didn't say I wanted another abortion."

She stared directly into Nina's eyes now, her gaze unwavering.

"You're right. You didn't. I'm sorry about that," Nina said, hoping she sounded apologetic. "I was trying to——"

"I'm thinking of keeping the baby. That's why I'm here."

Nina leaned back in her chair. Alan's description of Suzanne as the consummate flirt came back to her, and here was the consequent other side: chilly and controlled. She doubted that Tony had ever seen this Suzanne. "Well, then there are lots of things to consider——"

"I've given it a lot of thought already," Suzanne said, her hand slicing the air. "What I need to talk about are logistics. I want to find out about midwives, home birth. That kind of thing."

"We can do that," Nina said, thinking of one of the midwives she knew who still liked to encourage the father to partake of the placenta. "And are you going to be doing this on your own?"

"You mean is the father going to be my Lamaze partner or something?" she said, her voice full of sarcasm.

"Well, that's part of it, but—"

"He's fine with me having the baby."

Nina's foot began to shake back and forth again. "But is he going to be involved?"

"He's not going to disappear, if that's what you mean." She looked away from Nina and then quickly back. "He's got other familial commitments. But he'll be part of the child's life. And I'll be around here, so he'll be able to see his child without much trouble. From me anyway."

Nina let Suzanne's words go unanswered, let them take up the air of the office for a long moment, so they could fade while Suzanne was listening, so she might hear their power fading as well, if it would. And in that moment, Nina wanted to see the challenge fade from Suzanne's eyes; she wanted to see some transformation in her again, back to girlishness. She wanted evidence that this was all bravado on Suzanne's part: not certainty, not such clear understanding of Tony that she could know he wouldn't disappear on her, would be happy about a baby. Nina wanted to see something in Suzanne to convince her that it had been Suzanne who had grabbed Tony into an embrace in his studio, that she'd been love-struck, misinterpreting Tony's warmth, not seeing how it extended elsewhere, everywhere, taking her chance to convince him, seduce him if she had to, thinking how she'd managed that countless times, how she could do it again; she'd heard rumors of Tony's infidelities: she could be the next, the best. Except maybe she'd failed: Nina wanted to see something to convince her that Suzanne had failed, that in the instant after Nina had seen them in the studio, Tony had gently pulled Suzanne's grasp apart, pushed her to arm's length and said he was flattered but it couldn't be: he had commitments, a growing stretch of fidelity to lengthen. Nina wanted Suzanne to burst into tears, leap out of her seat in anger, point an accusatory finger across the desk, and then crumble. Admit that she knew who Nina was, that she was angry, hurt, vengeful, that it wasn't Tony's baby, there was no baby, she would leave them alone, she was sorry. Nina wanted something, the smallest thing: that was all she needed to build a fantasy around what she was more and more convinced was their reality.

Instead: a sober, almost severe conversation about midwives, doctors, the sliding-fee scale for prenatal care at the Center. Nina gave Suzanne the appropriate pamphlets: she seemed to take everything in calmly, she wanted to look everything over, she wanted to make another appointment for the following week, to set something in motion then.

"You can see any of the counselors," Nina rushed to tell her. "Your file will be here, so they can see what we've talked about"—except they wouldn't know what we talked about at all—"and take it from there."

Suzanne stood up. "Well, I think I'd rather only see one person. And this time is good for me."

And maybe this isn't finished yet, Nina thought. She walked Suzanne to the waiting room, shook her hand, pushed a smile into place—the waiting room was filling, eyes would be on her—and watched the door close behind Suzanne. The sound of the latch was like a signal to Nina's body. The agitation her foot had managed before to shake off spread through her now. She thought she could feel all her muscles vibrating, a shout forming at the base of her throat, a rush of blood about to turn her face

crimson. For an instant she felt herself following Suzanne outside, out of the Center's stifling premises, declaring who she
was, asking her straight out about Tony, warning her off, making
a fool of herself if it came to that. She had herself outside in the
parking lot, about to say something, resolved and terrified,
before she realized she hadn't left the waiting room, and the
receptionist was saying her name.

Nina got through the day without any serious slip-ups, either
with the women or the paperwork. A few clients she'd seen
before asked if she was all right. She imagined her gaze seeming
both intense and unseeing, easily unsettling to someone in crisis
who'd already decided to trust her. She rallied herself in those
moments, pulling in all the strands of her concentration twitching back toward Suzanne. The women who were seeing her for
the first time couldn't sense that something was off, and whatever Nina did automatically after almost five years on the job—
the right first questions, the right tones of voice, the things
Suzanne had caused her to ignore—sufficed to put the women
at enough ease. She saw no extreme cases that day: nothing that
required a call to social services or the police. She knew to be
grateful for that, for not needing everything in herself, for
enough in reserve to get through the staff dinner-meeting that
night; to discuss lucidly what needed to be discussed; to eat
enough not to draw attention to herself; to say goodnight, pass
some last words as they all got into their cars; to hold everything
together until she could let it all begin to come apart unseen.

Finally alone in her car, she thought she could feel her
thoughts sparking against the underside of her skull, each one
another part of the interview with Suzanne. It didn't matter if
she didn't know who Nina was, Suzanne's unconscious could be

at work—in her voice, her choice of words, the moments of eye contact—revealing the hard core of her story: I'm giving Tony the child he wants.

Nina was back at the house before she was aware of enough time having passed, enough road to have gotten her there. Tony had an evening class, he wouldn't be home for another half hour or so. But the house felt full of him anyway, as if the mirrors were holding his reflection while he was out, the surfaces of tables, counters, furniture, saving the imprint of his last touch. Everything about the house that was normally calm and calming for Nina seemed filled with anticipation of Tony's return. Everything in its place, everything waiting, and Nina there too, in place.

She strode through the house, but with no purpose. Her mind wouldn't stop churning: the same sparking thoughts setting up the same conclusions until they became a dull, unsurprising noise in her head. She could think of nothing to do but get into bed. She didn't want to have to talk to Tony when he came in. She turned off all the lights downstairs—she should've left something on for him—each pool of darkness hiding something of him. She undressed quickly, brushed her teeth quickly, left the hall light on—some light would creep downstairs—got into bed, the lights in the room out, the shades still up.

No position was comfortable; her skin was somehow wrong against the sheets, her muscle and bone incompatible with the mattress. When her body finally folded into a tolerable shape and place, her thoughts began to spark again. What if I'd had the baby, she thought. Things might have turned around just as Tony had hoped. Or at least turned them in a different direction, away from us always at the center, ourselves always under our own microscope. She could have had it for those wrong reasons and it might still have worked out. She could've told him about the pregnancy for all the wrong reasons—I've got what you want and I'm not going to let you have it—and even then it might have worked: he might've convinced her, she might've convinced herself.

She and Tony had had a dozen conversations about children, each of them moving through the same arguments. She wasn't ready, wasn't sure when she would be, he rarely saw the son he already had, what guarantee against that happening again, and where would that leave her, especially if she agreed now because it was what he wanted. And it was what he wanted: this time it would be different, he was different, and Nina wasn't like Cleo, Jay's mother, this would be the child Tony'd decided it was time for him to have, not like Jay, unplanned and unwanted at first, and then unknowable as Cleo kept him at a distance. Conversation after conversation, Nina remained unconvinced, and finally, in what would turn out to be the last of the conversations, she'd found other ways to ask the same questions: Why hadn't he insisted on more time with Jay? Couldn't he have demanded it? Helped more with child support if that had been the only way to bribe Cleo into being more even-handed with their son? One of them might have thought about Jay first, rather than about what portion of injury they still needed to inflict on the other. Why hadn't Tony been the one?

He'd waved his hand as if parting a smoke screen her questions had sent up. "Nina, you know it doesn't matter what I do. Nothing makes a dent in Cleo. And anyway this is about you and me. Not Cleo and me, or Jay and me. This is about whether or not you think it's possible that we could have a child and make it work."

"I guess I don't have the faith you do," she'd answered quietly. They were sitting on the bench outside her shop. Tony had brought lunch down from the house, a bottle of champagne that had been in the refrigerator for months waiting for an occasion. He'd proclaimed the possible onset of the waning of mud season and popped the cork.

"In yourself or me?" He put his glass down on the ground, put his arm around the back of the bench behind her.

"Neither of us," she said, looking off toward the pond.

His hand fell away from her back. "At least you spread it around."

She could have let the conversation end there: it would've been little different than the others. She could have let herself believe that by not saying the words he couldn't misconstrue— she didn't want them to have children, didn't believe they could without making a mess of it—she was sparing Tony some large disappointment that would be easier to take if it came in increments, over time. But in his last words—"at least you spread it around"—she'd heard a note that she thought she hadn't heard before: as if disappointment had already reached a measurable level in him, and there was nothing easy in bearing it. His face was turned from her almost completely, but there was enough of his eye still visible to her so that she thought she could read the look it was casting out across the field.

She put her hand on his back and moved it up to his neck. The skin there would get dark once they started putting the garden in. She turned red in the sun, wore a broad-rimmed hat in the garden so her neck wouldn't burn. But his neck would turn chestnut and chocolate, and then almost black, her hand paler and paler against it. There were more creases in the skin of his neck every year. She was amazed to realize that they were already watching each other age.

"It's not really you I don't have faith in, Tony." He turned to face her. She'd been right about the look in his eye. "I know you've done what you could with Jay. But us. Tony. Look at what we've been doing to each other for ten years."

"We'll stop."

"And what if we don't?"

"We will. We'll have to."

"Because there's a child?"

"We'll stop because we'll want to."

"Because there's a child."

He stood up quickly. "Yes. Okay?" His hands lifted up at his sides and fell back down. "Yes. Because there's a child. Because there'll be a child. Something to keep us from looking so fucking closely at each other all the time. Looking for what's gone wrong now. And then tomorrow. And two days after that. And not being able to get ourselves to do anything about it."

"That's why you want a child."

"Ah Nina," the sigh and her name one forlorn sound. "I want this child because I want a child with you. And yeah, because I want it to make a difference for us." He sat down but didn't look at her for a moment. "I think it can."

For you maybe, she thought; maybe this desire would translate into consistency for you. "What if I screw her up, Tony? What if I end up giving her everything I can't stand in myself?" Everything that keeps me from letting you have her.

He slowly stroked his hand though her hair and let it come to rest on her neck. "I promise I won't let it happen. You won't let it happen." She leaned her head into his hand. "She'd be beautiful, Nina," he said. "Think how beautiful she'd be." He pulled her toward him until their foreheads were touching. "We could make a jewel."

Nina listened for the sound of the world around them but heard only the mirroring sighs of their breathing. "I can't Tony." Her voice was a whisper.

His fingers tightened slightly on her neck. With his other hand he cupped her face. "Imagine this baby, Nina." She could. She tried to pull her head away, but he kept his hands clasped to her.

"I can't," she said. Tony began to rock his forehead gently against hers. "I'm sorry, Tony. I can't. I'm sorry."

His head came to rest. If she opened her eyes she might see into and then out of his. She could feel his breath enter her. "I love you babe," he exhaled, letting go his hands, rising, walking in the direction of his studio.

Four months later, Nina was pregnant. She knew it before she had the test: her period had been late only once before, when she'd gotten pregnant at seventeen. Then, her entire experience had been focused outside the physical boundary of her body, on the logistics of illegal abortion: the connection, the cash, the address; the right word at the door, the effort to believe that the steel tool in her body was sterile. But when she became pregnant the second time, with the strange ease that the legality of abortion afforded her, Nina was aware of every physical sensation. She sensed contours just under her skin, as if the fetus had begun immediately to perceive through her. She felt another rhythm in her body, not quite a heartbeat or pulse, more like a wave with peaks of sensation—though she couldn't describe what that sensation was—and valleys when she could feel herself straining to find the sensation that she knew she couldn't let herself want.

She had the pregnancy test done at the Greenville Women's Center, which had only recently opened then, and when the result came back positive, as she knew it would, she made an arrangement for an abortion the following week. The intake counselor she talked to was careful to determine if her first abortion had been without complications: no hemorrhaging or infection, no psychological wounds that hadn't healed. But she was careful not to pry, especially, Nina thought, since she clearly recognized Nina: they'd seen each other many times at the Top Hat. She might even have wondered who the baby's father was, Nick or Tony, but she never showed even a hint of curiosity. She merely assured Nina that if she wanted to, she could have someone in the room with her during the procedure.

Nina knew it was Tony's baby, she hadn't been with Nick in too many months. She'd even told Tony when she and Nick had broken it off that time—an anchor to the idea of making the break permanent. But she didn't tell Tony about the pregnancy. She didn't want to have that last conversation again, the possibility of the baby now a reality, something Tony could bring to specific life in his mind, extrapolating from a palm to Nina's still-flat belly, holding the idea of the baby as if its birth were just a final detail.

Tony was in New York when Nina had the abortion; she'd chosen that day for just that reason. The counselor who'd talked with her was in the room while the abortion was being performed. She was adept at comfort and support and Nina was glad for her presence. When she got home, she slept for a few hours—she hadn't slept much the night before—and when she woke up she stayed where she was, remembering the first abortion: an experience made of technicalities which she'd put behind her with no trouble, and no regret. It had been the summer she'd moved out of her parents' house and everything that had happened had become part of the larger project of becoming an adult. But this second time: no danger, no difficulty in the process, and no distraction.

Nina came awake gradually, unsure of where she was until she remembered Suzanne Garyle, their interview, her deception, the long dreaming memory of her own abortions. Tony's body was curled against hers. He must have been there for a while already; his breathing was deep and regular and didn't change when she changed her position, turning onto her back and moving his arm so it lay across her stomach.

In the year after the second abortion, Nina's period became irregular; not by much, but some months it was two or three days late, and it never returned to its unwavering twenty-nine-day cycle. There was no physiological connection between the abortion and the onset of the irregularity, she knew that. But that hadn't prevented her from also knowing that they were related. Not a question of mind over matter, but of the two in concert, bringing back to her, each time there were extra days before her period, the specter of pregnancy, the sensations of other bodily contours and rhythms inside her own, flooding her for that day or two before the first sign of blood declared her body's deception: part desire, part remorse, the promise of another loss, however phantom.

Tony's fingers rustled against her skin. The night was light-less, but Nina didn't need light in order to see him. The dark in the bedroom seemed to have become embossed with his defini-tion over time. His fingers moved again and his breath quick-ened: a dream, perhaps his own specter of loss. Or of recovery. A child to take the place of the child he'd lost without being told.

When Suzanne came for her next appointment at the Center, she was less sure about the decision to keep the baby. Nina did the right thing at first: she asked why and listened without inter-rupting. But when she began to ask the questions that arose from Suzanne's explanation, she calmly stepped across the line between following the train of Suzanne's thoughts and directing them. She felt all the skills she'd honed over the years—listening to women, learning how to help them with a well-placed or -phrased question—being dismantled and rearranged in some grotesque reincarnation of purpose: Suzanne would not have this baby.

The following week, Suzanne called a few hours before her appointment. She was canceling because she'd found a doctor in Rutland who would perform an abortion in her office, and she had an appointment with her on the following day. Nina made the appropriate notes in Suzanne Garyle's file and gave it to the receptionist to close. At the end of the day she met Tony at the Top Hat and when they got home, she stopped him in the kitchen and pulled him into a slow kiss that pulled him to her. She kept looking for signs of sadness or anger in him, signs that Suzanne might have told him what had happened, but she noticed nothing out of the ordinary. She thought of Suzanne the next day, prone on her back, her knees up: the steel, the vacuum, the deep emptiness. And the father of her child there or not, one person or another.

At the Center, Nina began to feel that she'd lost the hang of her job, the delicate rhythms of inquiry and empathy in the interviews now completely undone, and beyond repair. She'd gotten used to feeling as though each of the women's stories found a place to settle inside of her, and from that place, tapped into a well of intuition that Nina might otherwise have never discovered in herself. But that process too seemed disrupted: the stories took no hold in her. She made copious notes after each interview to help her remember details she would normally have had no trouble learning and recalling. To all appearances, she was working as well as she ever had, but everything she said and did felt false. There were fewer and fewer reasons she could think of for the women to trust their stories to her, and she no longer trusted herself to hear them.

1967

BILL WANTED TO get out of his mother's house, he wanted to forget what had happened that afternoon with Eva and Lilly, but he didn't want to see anyone he knew, no one who knew Eva or Lilly or his brother, so he crossed the river, drove through Rowman, and, almost without having to remember where it was, turned onto a dirt road that led through county gaming lands toward an out-of-the-way bar he'd gone to as a teenager. They'd called it Anderson's though there'd been no sign and no one there who claimed the name. It had been the place to go drinking if you were under age. An old, decrepit house, the beers served on the sagging glass-enclosed porch; beer only: cheap and from a tap, probably home-brewed and served without a license. But no one had ever seen a cop there, and most of the cops within a thirty-mile radius had probably patronized the place at one time or another. The only uniform Bill had ever seen there was on a woman from the Salvation Army who had moved from table to table with her collection bowl, saying nothing as poachers, renegade teenagers, and regulars too drunk to think much through, dug into their pockets for coins. Bill hadn't thought about that night in years. He hadn't thought about much that had happened in his life before Eva since the moment she'd come into it.

The bar came into sight through a stand of pines, and Bill stopped the car, thinking at first that it must be the beer he'd already had at home making him see what he hardly believed could be there: the building exactly as it had looked years ago, and still functioning as a watering hole. He drove closer, the trees seeming to recede as he rounded a curve, and there it was, clear and believable. It was still run-down, but the porch had been shored up, and there was a Piels neon in one window, Schaeffer in another. He parked the car near a half dozen others, walked slowly across the yard, up the steps of the porch, and through the door. Now he could see that someone had invested some money here since his day: a bar of polished wood ran the whole length of the porch where before there had been only a row of tables; and the bar was backed by a wall of mirror against which were stacked the bottles on which someone had saved some money: cheap whiskeys, gins, vodkas, bourbons, all of which looked slightly richer for being doubled by their reflections. But the clientele might have been sitting there since 1947—the same slant of the heads over their drinks, the same piles of cigarette butts in the ashtrays at their elbows, the same lack of interest when the door opened and a new face came in. It was just what Bill was hoping for. The bartender, who must have been ten years younger than him, didn't care who he was: didn't ask his name, didn't ask what he was doing in this neck of the woods, didn't treat him suspiciously or with any particular courtesy or gruffness. He put a draft and a shot in front of Bill and then went back to the other end of the bar where a baseball game could just be made out on the snowy screen of a television.

Bill drank the whiskey and lit a cigarette, the smoke giving a soft edge to the liquor burn. Exhaling, he lifted his eyes and caught a glimpse of his face among the bottles in the mirror behind the bar. Eva had been mocking him: he didn't look good, or was it "well" that she'd said? The oil in his diet: he remembered that clearly enough. There never would have been oil anywhere in his life if it hadn't been for her. He would have been just as happy to have never seen Venezuela or Saudi Arabia, or even Oklahoma. He could've gone in on the farm with Joe, or gotten his own. Stood in his own doorway looking down the slope to the river, watching evening settle, morning break, the river rise and fall, the ice form and melt. When was the last time he'd seen snow fall? Or leaves turn color? Everything he'd started to notice differently in those last months in Overton, everything he thought Eva was giving him for free—the pit deep inside him opened wide again suddenly to remind him how much was in there, how much he'd forced himself to not want. And still there was something left outside of it. Some shred of wanting—revenge, retribution, or maybe just a simple acknowledgment from Eva announcing itself loud and clear apparently, considering how easily she had seen it or heard it and figured out how to use it against him that afternoon. That's what he saw in the mirror: the face of a man who'd been outsmarted again, twice by the same woman, once when he was a boy and once when he should have known better.

"Refill?" The bartender was holding the bottle of whiskey above Bill's glass.

"Yeah. Thanks," he said, grateful to have been grabbed away from his train of thought. "Another beer too."

"You got it."

Bill's cigarette had burned down almost to the filter. He dropped it in the ashtray and lit another while the bartender filled his glass from the tap. He heard car doors slam, and then a group of voices making its way toward the stairs and up to the door. As it swung open, he looked in the mirror and behind the bottles saw the reflection of Lilly. She was with another girl and two young men, all talking and laughing at once. It had never occurred to him that there was this chance: that she'd know the place and come here while he was here, that he would have to share this place with her, secretive on her side, suddenly embarrassing on his.

"Uncle Bill!" Lilly called, catching his eye in the mirror. She disengaged herself from the arm around her shoulder, and in a gait that showed she'd already been drinking, made her way to Bill. She put her arms around his neck, and kissed him on the cheek, making sure the sound was loud enough for everyone to hear. "Hey!" she shouted, turning toward her friends. "This is my Uncle Bill."

Bill didn't move, didn't let a muscle move anywhere in his body, didn't say anything. Lilly let her hand drop from his shoulder. She was grinning. She took a step back, but kept her eyes on him. "My Uncle Bill doesn't talk very much," she said, backing up more. "He's a very mysterious man." Another step. "He's been away for a very long time." Another step. "But now he's back." She was up against the chest of the man who'd had his

arm around her before. "This is Ron, Uncle Bill," she said, grabbing Ron's hands from behind her and pulling them around her
shoulders. "And that's Patty. And Mark."

Bill nodded his head slowly. Patty and Mark fell onto seats at
the other end of the bar, and ordered in loud voices. Ron had
pulled his hands out of Lilly's and was finding his own route
with them across her chest and shoulders while she walked them
both forward and took the stool next to Bill. Ron pulled another
close up behind her, opening his knees around her when he sat
down. His hands and arms came to rest around her shoulders
again. He ordered himself a whiskey and Lilly a beer.

"How do you know about this place, Uncle Bill?" Her voice
was languid and her words a little sloppy, but she stepped hard
on his name. He knew it was the effect of booze—in her or in
himself?—but with her head tilted back against Ron's chest, her
eyes looked half closed in a kind of swoon, and he found himself thinking about what else besides drinking they'd been doing
before they got here.

"You think you're the only one to drink at seventeen?" He
watched her closely as she drank half the beer in her glass all
at once.

"No," she said. She put the glass down and took one of Bill's
cigarettes. He passed her his lighter. "But I think you're a little
older than seventeen, Uncle Bill."

"Yeah. I'm a little older than seventeen." He drew deep on his
cigarette and the exhale came out like an impatient sigh.

"Well, Ron's twenty-six," she said, her eyes squinting as if she
were trying to figure out the logic of her own segue. "So he's
legal no matter what."

"That's nice for him," Bill said, the two men's eyes meeting for the first time. Ron's mouth moved slowly into a shallow smile, and he moved his hands down Lilly's arms and around her waist. She was wearing the same thing she'd been wearing when Bill had seen her in the kitchen that afternoon. Maybe it was the bar's dim light, the more suggestive setting, maybe it was Ron's hands moving so knowingly over the cloth of her shirt, the tiny fraction of an inch barrier between his touch and her skin—something made Bill imagine he was seeing more of her body than he had before, that Lilly was intent on letting him see it, and, with Ron's help, on making sure that Bill understood how completely out of reach it was to him. He imagined that she expected to see him squirm in reaction. Instead, he leaned into his elbows on the bar so he was no longer facing her, and, as calmly as he could, ordered another round.

"So how do you know about this place?" she asked again, a petulant note sounding in her voice.

"How do you know about it?"

"Everybody knows about it."

"That's how I know about it. That's how I knew about it when I was your age. It's been here for years."

Ron's hands were moving again. They wrapped farther around her waist as he leaned deeper into her back. His arms pressed up against the bottom of her breasts and Bill could see them rounding up out of her bathing suit top into two smooth mounds under her tee-shirt.

"Not like you," Lilly said, bringing the cigarette to her lips, and then holding it to Ron's mouth so he could take a drag.

Bill turned his head so that he saw her out of the corner of his eye, trying not to see what he wanted to look at. "What do you mean?"

"You *haven't* been around for years."

"Not everybody stays in one place," he said quickly, pushing his gaze back behind the bar, at the mirror, taking in his own face, flushed from the booze or from anger.

"Why'd you leave?"

Because your mother seduced me and turned my brother against me. Because she seduced me and I let her and didn't think about my brother for more than a minute. Because I thought I was learning something important from her, but it turned out I had no idea what I was learning. Bill watched his face twisting through these thoughts. He felt as if he were watching someone else's reaction, but then the bitterness in his eyes suddenly caught up to him, and he had to quickly shift his gaze. He saw Lilly glance up at Ron and shrug her shoulders.

"Things happen," Bill said finally, stubbing his cigarette out. He had to get out of here, away from her. There was no telling what she could stir up in him. He pushed himself off the stool.

"So I heard," she said.

Bill hadn't realized before how much she sounded like her mother. He put some money on the bar, and turned to her. "Heard what, Lilly?"

"Heard that things happened." She leaned forward, off of Ron's chest. She smoothed her shirt down.

"What things?"

"Interesting things." She drank the rest of her beer. She leaned back again and rested her hands on Ron's legs, still wrapped around her from behind. Bill stared at her, wondering how much she knew, how she could've found out. Or how much she was bluffing, playing with him. Those searing dark eyes trained on him like her mother's had been day after day years ago. And today, like they'd been today.

"Yeah," Ron said. "We've heard some interesting things."

Steadying himself on the bar, Bill leaned his body toward Lilly so he was face to face with Ron, close enough to smell the booze they were breathing at each other. "I don't give a good goddamn what you've heard," Bill said. "Or what you think you've heard. Or what she's told you you've heard, twenty-six-year-old Ron."

Lilly was pushing against his chest to move him back. He grabbed her wrist and pulled her hand away. He was staring down into her face and it was like looking at Eva, at Joe, at himself. He flipped her hand back at her and walked out of the bar. She was quickly following close behind him. When he got in his car, she grabbed the door so he couldn't close it, or so she could keep herself upright: it was clear that her last beer had put her over the top. Bill suddenly felt way ahead of her in that fall.

"What the hell's wrong with you?" she said, her body rocking side to side. "You act like I'm some kind of evil bitch or something." She did what she could to steady herself. "No wonder my mother never wanted to talk about you."

She pushed herself away from the car. Bill jumped up and grabbed her from behind, one hand clamping down on her breast, the other around her waist. He thought he felt her body relax against his, like Eva's had in the moment before they'd moved into the house away from the swarming bees, in the moment before she would offer him up, a blind, love-struck idiot just asking to be sacrificed.

"What are you doing?" Lilly yelled. Her body hadn't relaxed at all, she was fighting her way out of his arms. She ran a few steps toward the bar and turned back to face him. "What the fuck is your problem?"

"Isn't that what you wanted Lilly? What you were asking for?" Was this his voice? His slurring words?

She took two steps toward him. She was steadier now, her balance regained in anger. Bill felt himself sway back as she came toward him. "I'm your niece, you drunken pervert asshole!"

"Then you should act like a niece."

It was dark around them, but there was just enough light from inside the car so he could see that she was glaring at him, her eyes full of the same anger that Eva's eyes could hold. "Fuck you." She shot the words at him. "Uncle. Bill." And walked quickly toward the bar.

Bill fell back into the car and closed the door, as if he could separate himself that easily from what had just happened. But more of the scene was unfolding through his windshield. He noticed for the first time that Lilly's boyfriend was peering out the bar's window, his hands cupped around his eyes to block out the lights from behind him. He must have been watching the whole time, or trying to: Bill doubted he could have seen much, the car too far away, too completely surrounded by woods and night, the car's interior light too dull to illuminate much. But now Ron's head whipped around, and Bill saw Lilly enter the bar. He watched through the windshield and the bar's windows, and the two barriers made him feel like an observer, as if he weren't the reason that Lilly was gesticulating wildly, her mouth moving quickly around the words that were no doubt describing what had just happened; or the reason why Ron turned his head back toward where he might see Bill's car if he could. He pointed in the direction of the car, his friend got up from his stool, and in the next instant, there were two figures running toward Bill: out from behind the barrier of the bar window, racing toward this last barrier, this breakable glass shield in front of his eyes, running toward him, and not really far from him at all when Bill finally understood he needed to start the engine and get the hell away.

He jammed the car into reverse just as Ron's hand reached out of the darkness toward the hood. Gravel kicked up from all four tires. Bill ran the car backward, leaving Ron and his friend out of the range of the headlights. Trees loomed up in the rearview, and just as Bill got the car into first, pulling it out of its backward roll, the two men appeared at the edge of the headlight's circle of light again. They kept coming, but Bill wheeled the car away from them and only their yelling followed after him, and then that faded too and the only sounds were the tires against the dirt road, the wind making an outdoors of the car's interior. Bill knew Ron and his friend wouldn't be following him: easier for them to go back to the bar and tell the girls they'd chased Bill away, or dragged him from his car and gotten in a few good kicks. He was certain they'd do that—it's what he would have done—and there were no headlights behind him, but he kept the car going fast.

He could see the end of the dirt road in the distance. He'd have to make a sharp right there. I should slow the car down, he thought, but there was no response from his muscles. The back of the car fanned across the road when he took the turn, and for an instant he felt soothed by the movement, as if the car had slowed on its own, his body's tensions and weaknesses taken over by the sway of the machine. This would satisfy them, he thought: glass, metal, skin, and bone strewn across a deserted road. Suicide induced by guilt? Madness? Brilliant recklessness? They'd be wondering forever. Headlights came over a hill in the distance. His car seemed to gain back its speed and it grabbed Bill's body out of its slow sway, his mind suddenly racing: Steer into the skid? Stay off the brake? He couldn't remember. At the last minute—how did that other car get from there to here so quickly?—he managed to keep the car on the right side of the road, the other car passing with its horn blaring. For an instant Bill thought it could be Ron and friend, out already at Lilly's behest, and turned his head to keep his eyes on it, but the tail lights faded quickly. He faced front just in time to see a deer leap from the road into the woods. He jammed on the brakes— there'd be at least one more—and the car came to a skidding halt. And there was another, crossing just behind the car. Watching its slow progress, Bill became aware of the frantic pounding inside his chest. He pulled the car onto the shoulder of the road and leaned his head against the steering wheel, his head spinning like the wheel no longer was. Adrenaline had gotten him to this point, but the alcohol in his system was catching up all of a sudden. He lifted his head to find that the trees in his headlights were twinned and moving with duplicates of themselves. He couldn't focus, and each breath carried the faint outline of nausea in it.

He leaned back against the seat and fumbled in his pocket for a cigarette. The first drag seemed to slow his heart down, and the pounding in his ears lessened, but his thoughts were racing. Lilly would tell Eva what had happened. She might even admit that she'd been drinking in order to give Eva the whole story. But she'd definitely leave out the kiss she'd planted uninvited on his cheek, her arms around his neck, her body pressing into him, or the way she moved inside her boyfriend's arms, the way she placed them strategically around herself so his hands hovered just above her breasts.

Bill threw the cigarette butt out the window and lit another one. All that anger from Lilly: was he supposed to believe it was all because he'd touched her? He lifted his hand to eye level, as if he could see it roughly cupping her breast, the sensation lingering in the skin of his palm. He closed and opened his hand a few times trying to stop the feeling.

He pulled slowly onto the road, his palm tingling against the steering wheel. Lilly would tell Eva for sure. He accelerated slowly. Lilly would tell Eva, and who knew if she wouldn't exaggerate what had happened. Even if he wanted to, Eva wouldn't give him a chance to apologize: she might call the police, or worse still, she might call Joe. There'd be another confrontation between them. But a different outcome, nothing so quiet as being told to leave. Bill would be lucky if Saudi Arabia was far enough away this time. He pressed down on the gas. He needed to get out now, to just keep driving, maybe not even go back through Overton. The road ahead of him came into view as if he'd been blindfolded for the past few minutes. The car was moving fast again. He wasn't sure where he was. Whatever memory had gotten him to the bar had disappeared, and there was nothing to act as a signpost. All he saw were the passing trees, drained of color by his headlights. His eyes settled into a stare and the trees lost their definition as well. He might have been driving through a tunnel now, bright exactly where he was but deadly dark everywhere else. It would spit him out somewhere and then he'd probably have to leave that place in a hurry too, he thought, so what difference did it make if he knew what the place was going to be beforehand? He couldn't get lost here, he'd recognize something here eventually. He couldn't get lost here even if he wanted to.

He tried to read the speedometer, but the numbers were too blurry. He gave the car more gas. The tunnel was straight in any case, he hardly had to steer, no other cars around. He squinted his eyes against the rush of wind. At least there was no one looking for him yet. That would be tomorrow, after Lilly told Eva the story she would tell, leaving out all the self-incriminating parts. Drunken, pervert, asshole: that's how she'd tell the story. What chance did he stand against those words out of the mouth of a seventeen-year-old? And suppose Eva had told Lilly about what had happened between them? Women talked to their daughters didn't they? Suppose Lilly hadn't been bluffing back at the bar? She might have seen this night as the perfect opportunity to get back at Bill on her mother's behalf. Eva certainly would've framed it like that: He seduced me while your father's back was turned. Forget her ear against the honey wall, her hand calling him over; forget the honey wall one day after the next after the next after the next until the swarm of bees announced a more dangerous storm, and Joe strolled out of their midst into the house. Forget the look in Eva's eyes, and the sound of her voice. She'd tell Lilly that it had been him.

The stop sign loomed up without any warning, the color a shriek. Bill stomped on the brake, but the car skidded almost into the middle of the intersection. He turned quickly, not thinking about which way was best, trying not to think about anything now, and raced down the road. He pulled his head up near the windshield, hoping this would help him see. He smoked several cigarettes, lighting one from the other. He drove for a long time.

Finally, he began to recognize what he still couldn't bring into focus: a house here, a configuration of roads there, one tunnel of darkness leading to another and another until the steel filigree of the Overton bridge came into being in his headlights. He let the car roll to a stop near the end of the bridge, turned off the ignition and got out. He took several deep breaths, steadying himself against the hood. He could hear the falls, crickets, a dog barking somewhere behind him. There were no other cars on this road and he knew that across the river most of Overton would be asleep, that anybody still awake was somewhere else.

He walked out to the middle of the bridge, over the deep water, the spot where the kids jumped from, just to the left of the main support. He drew up from his memory the sensation of jumping. It had been twenty years, maybe more, since he'd done it last, but he could still feel it, remembering that if you could think to spread your arms, wing-like, it was like flying. For an instant. And then you were just falling, at a deadly speed, and the water was part of the fall, not its end: you kept falling when you broke the surface. The water darkened through impossible stages of black, the rocks of the bridge's foundation passing dangerously close to your hand or foot. And you would fall and fall, until you remembered to help your body back toward the surface, hoping that you were below the eddy and you could make for the shore and get there before reaching the falls. The water would be cold—it was spring, there was still snowmelt— the current strong, and once you were standing on solid ground, your body shivering with exertion and dregs of adrenaline, the exhilaration was indescribable. The person who'd jumped before you met you on the beach and pounded your back in congratulations. On the bridge, your friends cheered, and you became part of what coaxed the next person to go through with the jump. Best of all: you didn't have to think about doing it for another year.

Bill leaned over the railing, reminding himself of the fear that accompanied the minutes before the jump, before the terror became so immediate that it was no longer something you were feeling, but something you had become. Every face he had seen go over the side of this bridge had been a bad mask of confidence, the eyes giving away the struggle for composure. His own face would have looked that way too. Rick Beecher had shown him a photograph of Wayne, and Bill imagined him here, on this railing, with no one on the river edge but that woman who was hidden from view, unaware of what she was about to see, and only Lilly behind him, her playful shoves turning more insistent as he shrank from them; his footing, unsure to begin with and then gone. Bill couldn't imagine that Wayne had had the wherewithal to make a wing-like arrangement of his arms. Instead, he saw them whirling in panic, even after Wayne broke the surface of the river: moving more slowly, but just as uselessly. Bill gazed deeper into the water, imagining Wayne there: You wouldn't necessarily have known to help yourself back to the surface, Bill said silently. The rocks would have come at you, hitting one of those desperate arms, drawing blood, and then you would have felt a tug on your leg, and then something quick and smooth wrap around your torso, and your other leg, your arms following, your whole body melded into the eye of a watery tornado, the eddy you'd been warned against again and again, where the water was fast and heavy, powerful with its own intent. Did your eyes stay open? Did you see Lilly enter the water and see you? Did you let go and breathe in?

Bill caught his breath suddenly, a wave of nausea knocking him off-balance. He held on to the railing as he walked back to the car. He lit another cigarette and started the engine. Drunken, pervert, asshole is what she would tell Eva.

Bill was almost a hundred miles away by the time his mother read the note he'd written at three that morning. An emergency in Texas? She didn't believe a word of it. There'd been no phone call and she'd heard him come in, stumbling and swearing. Or so she told him when he called her two days later from the road. She pressed him for answers—what emergency? what about the rest of the time she was supposed to have had with him? what about his sister Jean, who he hadn't bothered to visit?—but he stayed vague and apologized as best he could, listening closely to her words for a sign that the story of his run-in with Lilly had already gotten around. There was nothing he could detect. And nothing three weeks later when he did finally call Jean. But he didn't trust his patchy knowledge of their voices to pick up on the subtleties of tone that might tell him more than their words, so he was glad to be shipping out for Saudi Arabia again where a man could pretend to be unfindable as easily as he could make it true.

Part Three

1994

NINA HAD DRIVEN back to Vermont from Pennsylvania only once before, six months ago, and Tony had been with her then. George had died: a heart attack that had arrived with no warning at all. He was sixty-eight years old, but seemed ten years younger, and the suddenness of his death had felt especially cruel. Nina had worried about Diane's state of mind, had wanted to get to her as quickly as possible, so she'd ignored speed limits and pushed Tony to do the same when he took over the driving. This time she wanted the trip to last as long as possible. She wanted each mile to feel substantial, to add slowly to the one behind it, methodically building up the distance between herself and her house. She'd opened a map and connected the dots between towns whose names caught her eye: Swan Lake, Neversink, Curry, Big Indian, Phoenicia, Medusa, Mechanicville; along two-lane roads on which she assumed she'd do no more than forty-five miles per hour. Nina wasn't rushing to Diane's side this time: it was Diane who had convinced Nina to come, and to plan on staying as long as she needed to. Diane had sounded like she always did: welcoming, easy, interested and concerned. She was doing all right. It was Nina who wasn't.

Tony had gone back to New York after only five days at home. He'd been more angry than she'd ever seen him: a banked anger that threatened never to explode, but to simmer endlessly. Her own anger had died back almost immediately after he'd gone. It had nothing to feed on: the house felt airless, desolate, scraped out by the words that had passed between them. Instead, a kind of fear rose in her, foolish and weakening. She was startled by noises she could easily explain; she left a night-light on when she went to sleep; she kept the radio on for the company of voices no matter what they were saying. She hated feeling so uncontrollably diminished. It made her question everything she'd said to Tony, made her wonder if she hadn't taken things too far with him and for what reason. She tried to distract herself: the contraption she'd been working on was still unfinished, and she had two more she'd promised to deliver by May; she needed to start looking for other work; there was a pile of books to start; letters that had gone unanswered for weeks; the pamphlets she'd agreed to rewrite for the Women's Center back in Greenville; the dozens of details a day required her to focus on. But none of it could occupy her for any significant length of time.

She'd called Chris, her mind and fingers working out of habit, but hung up after only a few rings, reminding herself of what was no longer possible with her oldest friend. Chris's reaction to Nina's calls about Tony had slowly become limited to various levels of impatience. "I know it's hard to see when you're inside of it, but this has been happening between the two of you for almost two decades," she would say if she was feeling at all generous. Or, "It's just one of your fucking, endless patterns, for God's sake," if she wasn't.

"I'm always busy," she had said a few months ago. "The job, the boys, who have managed to become full-fledged teenagers before their time. Home. David. I don't have time to fret the minutiae of my inner life, of which there is precious little left anyway. Maybe you should try it." Offhand, jokey, but they both knew it was the sound of her impatience speaking.

"Maybe you should kiss my ass," Nina had said, and they hadn't talked for a couple of weeks after that. Nina apologized eventually, but she'd expected Chris to do the same and she hadn't. Since then, Nina had spoken of Tony only in order to relay information: he'd be in New York for a week, his next show would be in July, he was back in Pennsylvania, he sends his love. Chris didn't delve any further; she'd apparently gotten what she wanted: to no longer hear about what was wrong between Nina and Tony. And, almost unwittingly, Nina complied with Chris's wish far beyond what it had been aimed at, talking with her about fewer and fewer things of importance, until their conversations had thinned out to small talk, both of them aware of it, neither willing to broach the subject of this completely strange distance between them. Nina had been managing to ward off her sadness about it: she trusted they would talk, find their ease with each other again. But hanging up the phone that afternoon, the connection she wanted impossible, the silence of the house moving back in on her, she wasn't so certain.

She'd thought next of calling Diane but had decided she

couldn't ask her to be burdened with this round of problems with George's death still looming so large. It would have been like complaining about an ample but badly prepared meal to someone who hadn't been able to eat much of anything in months. Nina was glad to find that she could still think past herself, but when Diane called a few hours later, as if she'd sensed Nina's need and hesitation, the sound of her voice was enough to undermine any selflessness Nina had thought she'd mustered.

"I may have totally fucked up this time," was all she could say before she was sobbing, unable to catch her breath. Diane talked, calmed her down, and then insisted she tell her the details.

"I can't." Nina imagined her words circling through the handset back into her own head. "I can't talk about it over the phone."

"Then come here and tell me. You need to visit me anyway. I miss you. You miss me. And you need to go to the store and make sure they're not cheating you blind now that they've gotten so big."

"I'll think about it."

"Don't think about it Nina. You'll think yourself into saying no. I'm okay. You don't need to tiptoe around me. Just get in the car and come."

The roads Nina had chosen didn't disappoint her: after an hour she'd covered only forty miles. Swan Lake and Neversink were behind her, she'd just blinked through Curry, and was headed north through the Catskills, Big Indian at the end of the long road through the park's middle. There was hardly another car on the road, the few houses she saw were either abandoned or closed up for the winter—all of it like an extension of the emptiness in her own house when she'd left that morning. The sun was blazing off the snow, the glare so sharp there were moments when it felt solid in her eyes. She pulled over to find her sunglasses, and the car stalled. The timing was completely off. Tony was supposed to have taken it to Ernie in the city so she wouldn't have had to deal with it in their own freezing garage. Now she understood why he'd taken the pickup when he left two days ago even though he hated to drive it in the city. Or maybe he hadn't gone to the city: he could be anywhere, with anyone. She had no way of finding him, at least not without appearing desperate, which she hoped she wasn't. She got the car started and pulled back onto the road. Tony wouldn't even know she was gone unless he tried to call the house, and even then he might think she was just not answering. In any case, the likelihood of him calling anytime soon seemed remote. He'd slept in the guest room the night before he left and Nina had heard him getting out of bed while it was still dark, realizing almost too late that he meant to pack and be gone before she woke up.

Maybe she should have told Diane the details over the phone: she would have had the relief of getting them outside of herself, even if just for a few minutes. Instead, now, this incessant loop playing in her head. She'd hoped the drive would help to shut it off, but the endless stretches of snow, and lousy radio reception, offered it no resistance: She and Tony two nights ago in the living room after dinner. They'd been fine together up to that point, good even, though Nina was aware every so often of what she wasn't talking about, pieces of their late-night phone conversation the week before rising occasionally to the top of her thinking. She did her best to push them down like she had the first night Tony was home, to believe that time had already managed to drain the call of whatever importance she'd thought it had. Maybe he'd been with another woman the night he called, maybe not; she might have been mistaken about what she'd heard. She'd been half asleep, had had that peculiar dinner with Bill only the day before. In any case, she was with Tony now and only for another two weeks until he had to go back to the city.

Cleaning up after dinner, she'd finally told him about the evening with Bill, not really sure why she'd taken so long getting to it. She retold Bill's story, stripped to its essence, and described how she'd sat and listened though she knew she should've told him to stop, or gotten up and left. With the dishes done, she and Tony sat in the living room with what was left in their wine glasses.

"The whole thing was unsettling," she said, thinking she was just restating what she'd already made clear. But Tony's face took on a look of perplexed curiosity.

"Why unsettling?" he asked. "I mean, finally, all he did was tell you a story." He took a drink from his glass. "It's juicy, I'll give you that. But he didn't try to handcuff you to the table or anything."

"No. That's true," Nina said slowly, wondering where Tony's remark had come from, where it was meant to go.

"On the other hand," he said, getting up, "he did make you eat deer meat in a room with a crucifix."

Nina smiled hesitantly. Tony let out a quick, sharp laugh. He turned to the shelves behind him, where CDs were stacked. The echo of his laugh seemed to sustain itself, holding the room still.

Nina kept her eyes on him. His head was bent lower than his shoulders: she saw only the expanse of his back, the sweater smoothed across it, hiding the contours of muscle and bone she knew to be visible there. It was like looking at a wall.

"That story was so intimate," she said. The sound of Thelonious Monk, playing unaccompanied, filled the room, slowly pushing out the last traces of Tony's laugh. When he turned around it was clear to Nina that he hadn't expected the conversation to go on. "You don't think it's strange that he told me?" she went on anyway.

Tony let himself fall back onto the couch and looked at her for a moment without speaking. A smile crept across his lips. "Nina," he said finally, leaning toward her as if that would help her understand. "The guy's lonely. You're a beautiful woman and he may be sick, but he's not dead. You don't think he might want to keep you at his table for as long as he can?"

Nina had started shaking her head slowly back and forth while Tony was still speaking. "It wasn't that," she said the instant he stopped. "It felt like he was trying to pull me into the story." She could tell Tony was trying not to smile too broadly. "It's hard to explain," she said, waving her hand in front of her face. "Especially when you find the whole thing so laughable."

"That's not it, Nina," he said, his voice suggesting that only some fallacy in her thinking could have led to her conclusion. It was a tone she hated: it was the teacher in him, years after the pleasures of the profession had become habit; or the father, barely tolerating Jay in his know-it-all-years—as Tony had called his teens—and assuming he knew nothing much at all.

"Okay," Nina said. "Dismissible, then."

"Nina," Tony said with a long sigh. "You don't remember

when we were working on the barn?" he asked. "Bill was hanging around the whole time, giving advice, gossiping?"

"So he's lonely. That's not what I'm talking about."

"He never took his eyes off of you the whole time." Tony
fixed his eyes on hers: his imitation, she supposed, of Bill's
gaze. And it was eerily accurate. So much so that, for an instant,
Nina imagined his eyes becoming Bill's, their gaze slipping from
her face to her body as Bill, sitting where Tony was now,
accused Tony of cradle-robbing. She'd managed to put out of
her mind the afternoon Bill had surprised her with a visit, but
the discomfort of that moment came back fully now; and it was
compounded by the thought of Tony having enjoyed Bill
watching her.

"I don't remember that," she said finally, rearranging herself
in the chair.

"Well, it's true." Tony finished the wine in his glass as if in
answer to a toast.

"And?"

"And, he finds you attractive. And he knows I'm not around
all the time. And maybe he thinks he can dazzle you with these
tales of his sexual prowess as a young man."

"That's ridiculous," she said. "And, anyway, it wasn't even his
sexual prowess, it was Eva's predatoriness—"

"There, you see?" He got up again. "That's even more to the
point. He wants you to seduce him." He walked behind her
chair, trailed his hand across her shoulders, and disappeared into
the kitchen. Her shoulders had tensed to his touch.

"You're not listening," she called to him.

He came back into the room with the wine bottle, and offered it her way; she declined. He sat across from her and filled his glass, leaned back, and settled his arm heavily on the back of the couch. "I am listening, Nina. But can you even consider that maybe the whole thing's not as complicated as you're making it?"

"No," she said. "And you have no way to judge. You weren't there. And I'm telling you it was like he was literally reliving every moment he was describing. There was an urgency about it. He was making sure I listened hard enough—"

"You'd be surprised what a man would do for sex," Tony said.

Nina stared at him a moment. His smile suddenly seemed as hard-edged as his voice had been slicing into her words. "I really wouldn't be, Tony," she said, standing up. She grabbed her glass and went into the kitchen. He was right behind her.

"Why are you taking this so seriously?" he asked.

She came to a stop in the middle of the room and turned to face him. "Why are you trying to reduce everything I'm telling you to sex?"

"I just don't see what you're so upset about," Tony said, leaning back onto a tall stool that sat just inside the kitchen doorway.

"I wasn't upset, I was just trying to talk about it. If I'm upset now it's because you won't listen—"

"You're trying to figure out what Bill had over you that could *make* you listen, and I'm just suggesting to you that all he was doing was trying his damnedest to seduce you, mentally at least. And maybe it worked a little."

Standing there, the room wide around her, Tony at one end, relaxed and sitting, Nina felt as if she were in a spotlight, interrogated and studied. She turned to the sink and placed her glass in it as gently as she could. She knew she should get off the subject, that would be the wise course. She should tell Tony to stop, now, but she couldn't stop herself. "Why is it so important for you to make this point?"

"Tell me the truth," he said. Nina didn't like the challenge in his words. She still had time to walk away, but no part of her would move. "When Bill was telling you about himself and Eva, didn't you wonder, even just a little, what it might have been like to be with him when he was nineteen or twenty?"

Nina was suddenly aware of the edge of the sink jammed against her back, but she stayed where she was. Tony cocked his head, prodding her for an answer, something like a leer moving quickly across his face. Maybe this was meant to be a little fore-foreplay, she thought. Like that phone call from Jack's might have been: for Tony's benefit with another woman—the phone call: it was at the surface of her thoughts now, and she let it stay, all the suspicions it had aroused intact.

"The truth Nina. Come on," Tony said.

Your truth or mine? she thought, sensing the suspicions taking hold and then, in the next instant, taking off, moving more and more quickly beyond the reach of her reason, connecting one to another: from Tony at Jack's a week ago, to herself there seventeen—or was it eighteen?—years ago, the night after Tony had told her about his affair with the wide-eyed freshman, to herself a few months later, thinking that maybe Tony had put Jack in her way that night, knowing where it might lead, an opportunity to spread the guilt around evenly, to cancel it out eventually. She'd pushed the thought away then, convincing herself it was crazy, impossibly cynical. But in this instant, all these years later, Tony's prodding voice in her ears, the smug look on his face, it didn't seem impossible at all. "No, Tony," she said finally, quietly. "I didn't wonder about Bill." And then, before she could think what she was saying, added: "But wouldn't that be convenient."

He leaned back against the wall, tipping the stool onto two legs. "What does that mean?"

What had Chris called them? Fucking endless patterns? "It means," she said, crossing her arms, "that if you've got something, someone I guess I should say, going in New York—"

The stool thudded back to all four legs. "You think I'm sleeping with someone in New York?"

She nodded, and watched a change move across his face. His features seemed to straighten up, leaving the look in his eyes to determine his expression.

"What makes you think I'm sleeping with someone in New York, Nina?"

She waited a few beats, gripped the counter behind her. "The phone call you made from Jack's."

"What about it?"

"Nothing specific, but—"

"No, Nina. Be specific," he said, his voice hardening "What exactly gave you the idea?"

"There was something about the tone—"

"No. I want to know exactly what I said that makes you think I'm sleeping with someone else, Nina." He said her name as if it had a bad taste on his tongue. "I want to know just how the fuck your mind works."

Her thoughts raced out ahead of her again; it was as if she'd forgotten that she'd determined their path before this argument had begun. "I'll tell you how the fuck my mind works," she said, matching his harshness. "You get something going in New York and it would be easier for you, again, if there was some balance. Balance in something like me being seduced by Bill."

He looked away from her and back very quickly, but in that instant something stone-like had entered his eyes. She'd seen him direct that look at other people, but never at her before.

"Let me get this straight," he said, rising from the stool. "You get it into your head because of nothing more specific than a tone of voice—"

"You didn't let me finish, Tony—"

"A tone and nothing specific, as you said, makes you think I'm sleeping with someone else, and that I want to convince you that you've got something going on with Bill so there'd be parity between us as far as fucking around goes?"

"Why not?" She was remembering how well Tony had taken finding out about Nick: like a penitent, almost unsurprised, understanding. She was remembering the stricken pleasure she'd taken in his reaction. Now she loaded her voice with the same dismissiveness she'd just heard in his, and said what she almost couldn't claim to have decided to say: "It worked with Nick." She watched Tony's face closely. Maybe this is exactly what she'd wanted: to break a pattern, see him stunned by her. To have parity, as he called it, but of a different kind.

"What worked with Nick?" His gaze was lance-like.

"My being with him. It worked for you," Nina said. There was a small voice in her trying to make her stop her words before they arrived at everything they were pointing to. But she only barely heard it and, in any case, it made little sense to her now. "It worked so well for you," she said slowly, knowing that Tony's anger could be pushed to outrage, "that I sometimes wondered if you'd set me up with him."

"I don't fucking believe this," he said, and walked out of the room.

Nina listened as Tony left the house: a coat pulled on, a door yanked open, slammed closed. She could see him through the back window, making his way to the studio, hear him cursing the curving pathway at the top of his lungs. She saw him open the studio door, saw it close, a light go on inside, and framed in the window: Tony throwing something—a cup or an ashtray—against the wall. Nina jumped as if the sound, which she couldn't hear, had startled her, her anger suddenly pocked with fear.

She didn't know what to do with herself. She'd never managed to make him so angry. Her body felt almost electrified, as if the muscles could decide for themselves to move, but wouldn't. She had to will herself into the living room. She collected Tony's wine glass and the bottle, went back into the kitchen, washed the glasses, dried them, put them away. She put a log on the fire, then another, then moved them around with the poker until they seemed placed just right. She was aware of the fear growing at the center of her anger. She went into the kitchen, took out one of the glasses she'd just put away and poured herself more wine. She went back into the living room and sat, first in the chair where she'd been sitting before, and then in a different one, facing the fire more directly. She crossed her legs and a moment later pulled them underneath her. She fidgeted with the wine glass before taking a deep drink. She couldn't extract any clear thoughts from the tumult in her head.

She didn't know how long she'd been sitting there when she heard the back door open. Tony came into the room. She slowly raised her eyes to meet his gaze, which was fierce and disbelieving.

"You know, Nina, I seem to remember that it was you who talked about keeping the score even." She was surprised by the simple steadiness of his voice. "You remember that?"

She did, of course. She remained silent, and still.

"On the other hand, if I was pimping you, then you'd be faultless in all this shit we've put each other through." He was nodding his head gently, as if it were a mechanism for breaking the gaze between them. "That's what I call convenient."

Nina watched him leave the room. She heard him climb the stairs, and then she heard the guest room door close. She watched the fire die down, the embers lose their glow. Upstairs, Tony was separating himself from her.

Nina had been on the road for three hours when she pulled into a gas station in Medusa. She'd been driving too long, the trip was taking too long. She filled the car with gas, paid, and pulled out the map. She could forget Mechanicville, cross the Hudson where the Mass Pike met the Thruway, and make the rest of the trip as directly as possible. She could be with Diane in less than two hours.

The moments of the morning after the fight came back to her now: hearing Tony get up in the guest room; finally realizing he was going to leave without saying anything; his face darkening when she came down the stairs.

"Where are you going?" she'd asked.

"I need to be away from you Nina," he'd said, his eyes firmly on hers, and he kept them there as he put on his parka and searched for his keys in the pockets. It was only after he'd left the house and Nina had heard the pickup drive away that she felt capable of moving again.

She was moving faster than she should now, speeding across a bridge, unaware of the ice on the Hudson below her, undulating in the long tide.

* * * *

Two days later, Diane and Nina drove to the same turnout where Nina had stood a few days after arriving at Cannen twenty years before. She had been there hundreds of times since; it had become a favorite place, the openness a kind of sea with its rhythms of wind and light. But when she closed the car door behind her this time, she could only remember the first time, when she had been agitated, spooked, unsure of her footing, physical and otherwise.

Nina and Diane left the car and walked up the middle of the road, their long strides perfectly matched, their arms looped together the most comforting touch Nina had felt in a long time. They reached the sign that declared the road closed between November and April, and passed around the snowbank created by the plows at the end of their run. The snow was less deep here than in Pennsylvania, which seemed both odd and somehow appropriate to Nina, but it was deep enough to keep them, one behind the other, on the narrow path that Diane had inadvertently groomed in her walks to the rock ledge where she'd scattered George's ashes.

"I knew a month into our marriage that George wanted to be cremated," Diane said over her shoulder, her voice dissipating before all the words could reach Nina, though she knew what they were: Diane had said the same thing to her several times just after George died, as if convincing herself that it was the right thing to have done. If it had been up to her, she'd said, she would have had a regular burial, a grave site to visit, his name on a stone to run her fingers and eyes across. This time she made no mention of what she would have wanted; it was clear she'd accepted what George had given her to have, made a place to visit of the ledge, discovered that she hadn't lost him in giving him up.

Diane stopped and turned around to face Nina fully. She was smiling and shaking her head. "He said to me, 'I hope you won't be needing this information for a while, but just in case.' And I thought to myself, I've married an insanely practical man who's going to drive me out of my mind." She laughed quietly, and the sound rang softly between the trees. Her gaze seemed to follow the sound for an instant, her smile faded, and then she turned slowly and began walking again. Nina moved in close behind her and put her hands on her shoulders.

"I've told you that a dozen times, haven't I?" Diane asked without turning her head or slowing down.

Nina pulled her to a stop, wrapped her arms around her from behind, leaned her chin on Diane's shoulder, and finished her friend's train of thought in a low voice: "Who knew that all that practicality would convince him it wasn't really practical to be too practical?" Nina felt Diane's cheek pull up into a smile. She put her arms over Nina's in a gentle hug and then moved out of it, and along the path.

Nina let Diane get a ways in front of her before she followed.

Diane had wanted her to come but it was clear that this was a pilgrimage she was used to making on her own. Nina knew what that was like: how different the woods seemed when you were alone in them and when you were with someone, however much you thought you wanted the other person there; how it wasn't so much the presence of the other that changed things, but their perception of you, their knowledge, that could act like a screen on which the world outside the boundary of the trees was persistently, intrusively projected.

Nina walked slowly, trying to keep her own part of the outside world at a distance, but it was with her, a kind of rasp beneath the sound of her footsteps, a pattern of sound reminding her of her voice reciting to Diane the details of the fight with Tony. She'd thought that if she stripped the description down—I said, I thought, he said, I was suddenly saying—she could see more clearly where it had left her, and why. But Diane's questions, her thoughts about what Nina told her, had led Nina into the messier, inconclusive layers of interpretation, and sleep had only seemed to thicken her thinking. She'd felt split in two all morning: part of herself in place at the kitchen table, drinking coffee, delighting in something Diane had baked, nodding firmly in answer to Diane's question of whether she'd slept all right after last night's conversation; the other part of her still inside that conversation, inside the story she'd told Diane. She tried now to turn her thinking to Diane, to call up the admiration she felt for her, for the grace and the quality of the strength she brought to her own situation of loss. But it hardly worked to keep Nina's mind off herself: she began to wonder how she would act if she were in Diane's shoes right now, trying to live without Tony, and she could imagine little else besides self-recrimination, and a sense of having begun to disappear. Much like she felt at the moment.

When Nina caught up with Diane, she was sitting on an exposed rock, facing the valley spread out in front of her, but she turned her face to Nina, and held out her hand. "Come. Sit," she said. "I've discovered it takes about twenty minutes for the ass to be fully numbed. But until then, it's perfect."

Nina sat and Diane linked their arms again, turning her gaze back toward the valley. Except for the black lengths of the larger roads, it was a monochromatic scene: shades of white and intensities of glare; little different from the snowscape of Pennsylvania, but Nina could feel herself seeing it differently, missing it though it was there in front of her.

"He never said what he wanted me to do with his ashes," Diane said. "But I think this was okay."

"He loved this place," Nina said.

Diane nodded slowly. "You know, I go along and I think I'm okay." Her voice was low and tentative, as if she were frightened of what she knew she was about to say. "And then I have these moments when the bottom falls out and I'm stunned." She kept her gaze firmly on the far distance. "And then, on top of everything else, I get upset that I'm still stunned."

"It's only been six months, Di."

"Yeah. The longest fucking six months of my life." She'd raised her voice to curse and there was a shallow echo. She closed her eyes and shook her head.

"There's a fine memorial for my dead husband," Diane said, her voice lowered again.

Nina knew what she was thinking: George hadn't like profanity, especially around the kids, not because he was puritanical, but because he thought there were better, more interesting ways to express the same things. The kids, of course, swore like truck drivers, though not around their parents, the only people Nina knew who could make "hell" or "damn" sound threatening.

"I somehow think George would understand." Nina said.

"Do you?"

Nina nodded, wishing she were more like Diane, always sure of what was needed in a given situation: silence, consolation, humor, the perfect layer cake. Nina couldn't be sure if her own brevity now was in response to something she was picking up from Diane, or if it had merely to do with how depleted she felt by her own circumstances, by having spent much of the previous day talking about what had happened between her and Tony. Diane had been as attentive as if she had absolutely nothing else to think about. Nina wished she knew how to reciprocate, but everything she said now sounded slight.

After a few minutes, Diane gently pulled her arm free of Nina's and put her hands in her pockets. "Do you remember the time George dragged you and Tony up here to go snowshoeing?" Her voice was steadier, and when she turned her face toward Nina, there seemed to be an invitation in her expression.

"Of course I remember," Nina said with a soft laugh. "That was our introduction to his relentlessly enthusiastic side."

"Was he relentless?"

"Well, he said he wouldn't take no for an answer and then he really wouldn't. He kept pointing to all of you in the bus—"

"The VW. I forgot we still had that then."

"Just. It hardly stayed on the road when it was idling, much less moving. And he kept pointing to it and saying: Those kids and that dog—"

"Zinc," Diane said, with a childlike look in her eyes. "She was a wonderful dog."

Nina would follow Diane through the conversation: "And that name was so perfect for her somehow," she said.

"George thought it was perfect for everything. He wanted to name every animal in the house Zinc. Cats, hamsters, the gold-fish. Like Thing 1 and Thing 2 in *The Cat in the Hat,* which, of course, we'd been reading by that time for about ten years with-out let-up." Her eyes pulled away to a distant point again.

"More relentless enthusiasm?"

"Yes, I guess so." She pulled her knees up to her chest. "Did you ever tell him you thought he had relentless enthusiasm?" Nina shook her head no. "I think he would've liked that." She rocked a little back and forth, and turned to Nina. Her face was suddenly relaxed again, the smile not straining to fit. "He was such an oddball, don't you think?" she asked.

"He was a wonderful oddball."

"He was brilliant at it, wasn't he?" Nina nodded. Diane looked back at the distance. "He was so fond of you and Tony. Right from the start."

"Probably because we let him take us snowshoeing."

Diane laughed quietly and leaned her shoulder into Nina's.

The sound of a truck in the valley rose in a whining buzz toward them and they followed its progress along the road that hugged the river. The truck looked toy-sized; and the buildings and woods, the length of river that had been part of the con-text of Nina's life for nearly twenty years looked like nothing more than a model set up especially for the toy truck. She would have to go back to Overton soon, but this is where she wanted to be: with Diane, immersed in Diane's life, talking about George. He and Diane were the first people Nina had ever been aware of learning to love. She'd been skeptical about them at first: they were more her parents' age than her own; she found Diane's friendliness and George's welcoming eccentricity suspect, and she was slow to try on other ideas about them. But it was just that slowness, she thought now, that had allowed her to comprehend her affection for them as it took shape. That hadn't been the process with family: she couldn't always tell the difference between what love she might feel and a sense of obligation. And she couldn't remember a time when she hadn't known or loved Chris. And Tony? She'd fallen into him all at once: everything blurred, permanently, it seemed, by the fast, euphoric fall.

Nina watched as the truck finally drove out of sight. The valley regained its quiet and its proper scale. It was the place she knew again. When the sun was filtered through a passing cloud, she noticed that there was almost as much open water as ice in the river.

Diane pulled one of Nina's hands into her lap and held it there between her own. "That was Tony who called last night during dinner," she said.

Nina had suspected it was him at the time: Diane's too-modulated voice while she was on the phone, and her too-nonchalant manner after she'd hung up had been tip-offs. "What did he say?"

"He was hoping you were here or that at least I'd know where you were. He wanted to make sure you were okay."

"What did you tell him?"

"I told him you were okay as far as that goes, but that you're very distressed and struggling with what happened."

"Distressed and struggling?" Her voice was cut with the little sarcasm she was able to muster.

"You think that's an inaccurate description?"

Nina caught Diane's gaze and then turned away, shaking her head slowly. "No, I don't." She said nothing for a moment. "He didn't want to talk to me?"

Diane rubbed Nina's hand as if to warm it before letting it go. "No. He just wanted to know if you were all right. He was very subdued."

"Not distressed and struggling?"

"Nina. Don't be an idiot."

Idiot being a pretty accurate description too, Nina thought. "Sorry," she said quietly.

"Of course he's distressed," Diane said, her voice more stern. "And no doubt he's struggling with the fact that the woman who he's lived with for two decades found a profoundly nasty way to fuck up totally, as I believe you put it."

"Don't you get mad at me too."

"I'm not mad at you. I'm . . . frustrated with you. You seem always to be invested in not trusting him. And when there's not enough to mistrust, you fabricate some craziness. It wasn't bad enough that you used to think Nick gave Tony an excuse—"

"What if I didn't fabricate it?"

"Oh, come on, Nina. You don't really believe he pushed Nick at you. You can't."

"I don't know. I don't know what I really believe about either of us."

"I've never understood the two of you."

"I know. You've told me this a million times."

"Well, it's been true a million times." She stood up, brushed snow off her pants. "I love you both. And I don't get either of you." She put out her hand for Nina to grab and pulled her up. "But at the moment, I get you even less." She held Nina's eyes for an instant, touched her cheek with a gloved hand, and started for the car.

It was hard hearing disapproval in Diane's voice—frustration hadn't been all she was expressing—but Nina had no case to make to change her mind. Diane was probably right that Nina couldn't finally believe what she'd accused Tony of, however possible it still seemed. She followed Diane onto the path.

Diane moved with the same ease and grace Nina still remembered noticing on the day they met. George's death could have shortened her stride, stiffened it, quickened it with fear, but none of that had happened. Nina had never imagined that George had been responsible for the strength and sureness of Diane's step, only that he had known to admire it and what it meant about her. So perhaps it had not been his to take away.

Diane waited for Nina to catch up to her at the road. The only sounds now were their boots in the snow, and the chuff of snow blown from the pine branches. When they got to the turnout, Nina steered them to the edge of the clearing. From here the river looked completely frozen, though she knew now that it was just a trick of the light.

"You know," Nina said, "I've always known exactly what I love about you and George. Every piece of it. From the very beginning. But I can't always recall what I love about Tony."

"Maybe, Nina," Diane said, and then hesitated a moment

before going on. "Maybe it's yourself you've lost sight of. Not Tony."

Nina let out a long sigh. "I suppose that's possible."

They stood there for a few more minutes. Finally, Nina yielded to the gentle pull on her arm and let Diane lead her back to the car.

*   *   *   *

On the morning Nina was leaving Cannen, she woke before Diane, and sat with a cup of coffee in the front room where the first sun would enter the house. She'd been there now five days, and though Diane had insisted she stay as long as she needed, Nina couldn't see how long that might be, and this seemed long enough. Tony hadn't called again, and Nina had forced herself to stop trying to imagine what that first conversation between them might be like, or when it would take place: she didn't know where Tony was—though Jack's was a safe bet; or the woman's, if this one actually existed—or when, or if, he planned to come home.

She moved to the window and leaned her forehead against the glass, which was cold but almost free of frost. Hard to believe that winter might actually be breaking. Strange to find herself longing for signs of spring so avidly, since the transition between these seasons had always been a difficult one for her. The possibility inherent in spring seemed to demand something she was unable to satisfy: a mood to be matched, cheerfulness on demand. Tony enjoyed the dig in waking her with the greeting: "It's a glorious day. You're gonna hate it." But she was always glad for the warning. She needed to come to it in her own time. She wanted this winter's snows to be gone already—their hypnotic blankness was as demanding in its own way as the rich activity of spring—but she wouldn't mind a small pause before spring began in earnest.

The contraption she'd given Diane and George for their thirtieth anniversary sat in a deep windowsill on the other side of the room. It was named "Here. No, there," and it was one of the more complicated ones she'd ever made. She'd gotten the idea for it from a rhyme George and Diane had invented for their three children when they were all under the age of ten: "Here. No, there./ There's no there there./ Or here a here./ Here. No, there./ There's no here here./ Or there a there./ Here. No, there./ No here./ No there."

"Apologies to Gertrude Stein and Dr. Seuss," George had said sheepishly when Nina first heard him reciting it with the kids, their laughter ringing through the constant misplacement of "here" and "there" and the circular maze of words required for correction: "No, here goes there," "That's not a there there," and so on with George looking happily on.

"Forget Tony," George said after his first inspection of the gift, his arm around Nina's shoulder, his eyes fixed on the contraption. "This is a work of art. Absolute genius."

"I told her that too," Tony called from the kitchen where he was helping Diane. "I've been telling her that for years. She never believes me."

"It's okay," she called back. "I don't intend to believe George either."

George had loved "Here. No, there" so much he often turned it on when guests sat down to dinner in the adjoining room. If Tony and Nina were not among the guests, he would regale them with tales of peoples' reactions and of the recitation of the rhyme by the children while the contraption thunked and pinged and rang and rattled in the near distance. If they were at the table he communicated with Nina in a series of winks and nods and signs that would have done a third base coach proud, in order to let her know he was about to reveal her as the creator, which he always did with a profusion of praise.

Nina would have preferred less of that kind of attention but, in fact, "Here. No, there" was the contraption she was most proud of. She hadn't been sure, after she made the first sketchy plans, if she'd actually be able to construct it, much less get it to run. She'd given herself six months to complete it, and she'd needed every minute. But as soon as she'd gotten started on the actual construction, the piece had seemed possible, not in spite of its complexity, but because of it. She walked across the room to where the contraption sat. She wouldn't turn it on now, she didn't want to wake Diane, but she could make it run in her mind, flipping the switch to the small motor, starting the conveyor belt that started the whole thing: six small wooden balls lifted one at a time up out of a holding pen, dropped into a slide she'd divided into four separate chutes—two marked "here," two "there"—which, by elaborate, circuitous, noise-making pathways eventually deposited the balls back into the pen. A continual, random, and, as long as the battery lasted, endless loop.

She'd salvaged the balls from a doll's croquette set she'd found at a garage sale, but all the other materials she'd used came from her shop—some of it worked into the design from the beginning, some finding its way in out of the shop's thick clutter: a guitar neck, a set of tiny bells, bits of wood, metal, and plastic made into small gates, chutes, and slides, a pair of toy cymbals detached from a windup bear, the clutching hand from a plastic doll. Combining everything to make "Here. No, there" had been painstaking, demanding work, but there was also something organic about the construction she'd never felt before: the mechanisms that she hadn't thought all the way through seemed to clarify as she approached the need for them; the materials often seemed to have innate purpose. She'd never before felt so keyed into the processes of visualization and real-ization that the contraptions required of her. And in the end everything had worked perfectly: a precision of mechanics that gave birth to a confusion of movement and sound.

"It's a little like life itself," George said to her after they'd had "Here. No, there" for a few months. When Nina asked what he meant, he held his hands up to the contraption, as if he could calculate its metaphysical measurements. "Things go one way or the other or another in life and what decides it?" He moved his hands to one side. "A precise but unpredictable moment of tim-ing and decision. The force of the wind. The size of the moon. What you had for dinner last night. Anything at all." He cocked his head. "We piece lives together from various sources that can be determined or merely stumbled upon and try to make it all run as smoothly as possible." He moved his hands to the other side. "Sometimes we object to the outcome. We make noise. We bump around uncomfortably. Sometimes it's a smooth passage. Still unpredictable, but smooth. And sometimes the unpre-dictability is dizzying. But if we're lucky, we eventually discern pattern in the lack of it. And that's enough to keep us moving forward." He moved his hands gently back and forth across the length of the contraption—"In our circular ways," he added— and then dropped them to his sides. "But I guess you don't think of that kind of thing while you're making one of these, do you?"

"I will now," Nina had said, half joking, half afraid that she would, and that the process would change for her, deluding her into thinking about mechanism and motion as if they could be used to decipher and explain, and then she'd have no way to see them accurately, to measure their success, or understand how they failed. But, of course, that would be a little like life too.

The drive back to Overton took Nina six hours. Diane had sent her off with her normal salutation, "Safe home," and it rang in Nina's head on and off for the whole trip, not just as a farewell, but as a question: was Nina going toward one or leaving one behind?

Approaching the Overton bridge, she could see in the pale light of the low half moon that the ice on the river had broken up. She pulled the car off to the side of the road and when she opened the door, the sound of the river enveloped her. It was a tumbling roar, water only thickened by ice now, but still a vehicle for it. She leaned over the railing and could just make out the speeding undulation of ice slabs and she imagined the edges steel-sharp from the constant friction of the flow. The longer she stared, the more she could see: the footing of the bridge like the prow of a ship heading upstream against the current; angular edges of ice thrust up out of the pack and then pulled under before riding to the surface again. She was sorry to have missed the actual breakup, the explosion of sound Bill had described. She would've liked to have had the catharsis of that moment, not just the impatient wait for its arrival.

The metal-cold of the railing seeped all at once through her

gloves. She walked back to the car and before starting the engine
rolled down her window. She wanted to stay in the sound, even
as she left it behind.

There were no lights in the house, and Tony's pickup was not
in the driveway.

*   *   *   *

Nina had never felt so solitary as she did being back from Diane's.
The house could have been anyone's: she hardly felt familiar to
herself in it, and though everything of Tony's was still there, he
seemed absent in a fundamental way. She tried to work on the
contraption she had in progress, but her fingers felt clumsy and
her mind no more agile. And maybe it was unrealistic to think she
could concentrate on anything demanding when she felt as if she
were using all her concentration, all her physical strength, simply
to come to rest: in a chair, at her worktable, at the kitchen counter;
to stop needing to move without any other purpose than to stay
one step ahead of her fear, which itself was only one step ahead
of panic. She slept, more or less, on the couch the first night—all
her clothes on, a quilt pulled out of the guest room. The next
night she forced herself into her own bed, where she tossed and
turned for hours before returning to the couch.

In the early afternoon of the second day Nina was woken
from a shallow nap—part sleep, part retreat from herself—by
someone knocking on the front door. She was on the couch and
she thought if she just didn't move, the person wouldn't see her,
might assume she wasn't there, and leave. But the knocking
came again, and now a voice accompanied it: a man's voice trying to be polite as it bellowed: "Anybody home?"

Nina didn't recognize the voice and peeking over the arm of the couch she could see through the windows in the door a man in his sixties or seventies whose face she didn't recognize either. She lowered her head, curled her body more tightly, held her breath.

"Anybody home here?" The voice again, more insistent this time.

Nina sprang up and yanked the front door open. "Can I help you?" she snapped.

"Sorry to bother you, Nina," he said, a genuinely apologetic look on his face, which began to seem familiar to her even as she wondered how he knew her name.

"What can I do for you?" she said, searching her mind for him. She saw him realize that she didn't know who he was.

"Bill's friend Rick," he said, leaning his head forward, holding out his hand. "I take him to the grocery every week."

"Of course. I'm sorry." She'd been introduced to him not long after they'd moved in, but had rarely seen him since. She'd forgotten that Bill didn't feel safe driving with all his 'illments,' as he called them. "I'm sorry," she said again, finally shaking his hand. "It's just . . ." but she didn't need to explain herself. "Come on in." She moved back from the door, and he took his hat off as he stepped inside.

"Can I give you a cup of coffee or—"

"No no," he said, holding his hand up. "I'm not going to take up too much of your time." He rocked from one foot to the other as if securing himself to that spot, not wanting to take up too much space either. "I just have a small favor to ask."

He wondered if Nina would stop by Bill's the next morning to see if he needed anything from the grocery: "My daughter's about to give birth to my first grandson, and I want to see that little guy as soon as he's with us." He paused a second, letting the importance of the event sink in. "She lives halfway to the other side of the state, so I need to get on the road and Bill doesn't seem to be home." He turned and cast a glance toward Bill's cabin. "Could be Mike took him to the doctor or something." He turned back to Nina. "Anyway, I won't be home for a few days, but I'm sure he won't mind seeing you at his door instead of me."

Rick's smile was as innocent as his grandson's would be, but Nina couldn't help cringing at his words. She really didn't want to do this. "I'll stop by tomorrow. Sure."

"That's just great," Rick said, his hand on the door. "Anytime in the morning'll be fine. He knew I'd be going when the baby was born. We just didn't know when it would be. And then my son-in-law calls just half an hour ago." A huge grin spread across his face, the kind of grin, Nina knew, most people would have found infectious.

"Well, I hope everything goes okay," Nina said, working to make her voice sound bright.

Rick thanked her, patted his hat back onto his head, and as he got his car out onto the road, tapped his horn quickly, sending a small blast of sound into the otherwise quiet afternoon. Nina supposed the horn sounded cheerful to Rick, but in her ears it was a tinny sound, and somehow mocking. Like Bill's voice had sounded the afternoon he'd come to her house with the kale. She closed the front door and braced her shoulders against it. She hated the idea of putting herself in Bill's way again, of feeling inspected, as she had that afternoon. She hated thinking about going back to that cabin: she'd been trying not to remember herself there that night almost three weeks ago, listening to his stories, his past offered in exchange for her mesmerized attention in the present.

Her coat was hanging on a hook behind the door where she was standing. She leaned into it and took a deep breath. She could still smell the cabin on the cloth: old cooking, cigarette smoke, old man, all of it adding up to an acrid, metallic odor, metal dampened by sweat, the last remnant of memory better left untold but told anyway. Tony was probably right: it had been a kind of seduction.

Nina called Jack that night and got the number of the apartment where Tony was staying. She didn't ask whose it was and Jack didn't volunteer the information. She didn't care, she needed to talk to Tony, to hear his voice no matter what he might say. But she hesitated a number of times before calling him. He hadn't wanted to talk to her when he'd called Diane's, and she knew that if he'd changed his mind he would already have acted on it. She had caused this rift, she told herself, caused him to need to be away from her; she needed to let him decide when that was no longer true. But in the end she couldn't.

She had believed for a long time that whatever she and Tony didn't know about each other's behavior was insignificant. But this last argument had undermined that belief: not only had Tony been shocked at what was thrown at him, Nina had been almost as shocked to realize later what her words had done, and what they might yet do. And the belief was further undermined when Tony answered the phone at the number Jack gave her. His voice was completely indifferent, and though Nina

suspected that it was feigned, at least in part—and for the benefit of them both—the indifference was unexpected, new, and
awful.

"I'm sorry Tony," Nina said after a painful silence. "I am so
sorry about what happened. The things I said."

Another silence. Nina listened for hints of where Tony was,
but there was no sound behind him, and the effort to hear
something there was like memory rising from muscle: she was
acting out of the same, worn suspicion that had caused her to
say the things she was apologizing for.

"I know you're sorry," Tony said finally. His voice had broken
down a little. "We're always sorry." It broke a little more, but
weariness seemed to be all it was revealing. She had heard that
before. "It's always the same. With variations."

"I know." Nina hardly heard her own words.

"But this one was a motherfucker." The weariness topped by
anger.

"I know. I'm sorry." She was having trouble holding back
tears. She felt more frightened than before she'd called. "We
have to talk Tony." There was no response. "Please."

"We will," he said, the two small words large with resignation.
"But not now, not on the phone." Nina heard a door open
behind him. "I'll come home soon. I'll call you in a few days."

She closed her eyes and held on to his voice saying "home."

"Nina. Are you all right?"

She couldn't find her voice. And what would she say with it?

"Nina?"

"I'm okay," she said. She needed to get off the phone. "So, I'll
speak to you in a few days." She needed to hang up first, to not

hear him go. "'Bye Tony." She stood up from the table, the phone in her hand. She held it away from her, wondering if he was still on the line, and then hung it up.

*   *   *   *

"I saw you coming across the road," Bill hollered out the open door as Nina approached the cabin. It had just begun to pour; she ran the last few yards.

"Come on in here. Get out of that rain." He grabbed her arm and pulled her inside; there was more demand than invitation in the tug of his hand, but the demand felt somehow halfhearted. She'd been trying hard all morning not to anticipate feeling discomfort, but when she heard the cabin door close behind her and found that nothing had changed since she'd been there three weeks ago—the same clutter in the same places, the same odors, maybe even the same indentation in the seat cushion her body had made—she felt little else.

"Couldn't keep away from me, now could you?" Bill said, a cough breaking into the last words.

"Actually, Rick asked me—"

"Sit down," he said, taking a deep breath and lowering himself into a chair at the table. "Take your coat off."

"I'm not staying long," she said quickly.

"Okay. But you're not going to stand there, are you? Sit down at least."

Nina unzipped her coat but kept it on. She sat opposite Bill, just where she'd sat three weeks before. Nothing had changed from this angle either.

"Rick came by yesterday—"

"Did he?" Bill raised his eyebrows and leaned back. "What for?"

He was staring at her but she didn't sense any real curiosity behind the question. It was much more like she was being observed again. "His son-in-law called. His daughter's about to give birth—"

"Ah." Bill nodded his head gravely.

"And he was leaving to see her and asked if I'd shop for you today," Nina said, rushing to finish the sentence, hoping she sounded less provoked than she was feeling.

"And he's not coming back today?"

He must know where Rick's daughter lives, Nina thought. "No, Bill," she said. "He'll be there for a few days—"

"And what happened next?" Bill crossed his arms and furrowed his brow in mock concern.

Nina stared at him for an instant. "What do you mean, what happened next?" Her voice came out quiet but sharp.

"Well, did you invite him in? Offer him some coffee?"

Nina zipped her coat up. "What do you need at the store Bill?"

"Ah, come on, Nina," Bill said. "Don't stop now. I was finally getting you to tell me a story." He crossed his arms and winked.

Nina's face flushed with a wave of anger she didn't even try to disguise. She stood up. "Well, maybe you can get your story and your groceries somewhere else." She turned toward the door.

Bill reached out and his touch was almost gentle this time. "I'm sorry, Nina. Don't go away mad. I was just having a little fun with you." His voice was gentler too, almost conciliatory. "Come on. Forgive an old man. Sit right down there again."

Nina hesitated. She didn't understand Bill at all, and suddenly

she didn't know how to refuse what she couldn't understand.
She repositioned the chair and sat.

"Good," Bill said. "There's something I want to show you."
He climbed the narrow flight of stairs to the second floor, moving slowly from step to step, his breath audible and labored. As
were his movements once he got upstairs. When he came back
down—two feet on each step, the railing grasped tightly—he
was carrying only a small paper bag. When he was sitting again,
he opened the bag—the slowness of his step transferred to his
hands—and pulled out what looked like a chapbook.

"Someone put this together about ten years ago. Eva must
have put it upstairs. I just stumbled across it last week." Bill
turned the book over in his hands. "I've been thinking you
might like to take a look at it." He handed it to Nina. "Might tell
you a little about this place you're calling home now."

It was more pamphlet than book, its faux-gothic lettering
smudged and faded: *A Local History: Overton and Environs*. Nina
looked up, but Bill's gaze had settled on the book itself, or on a
middle distance that the book was only part of. She flipped the
pages: poorly reproduced photographs of buildings and homes,
gatherings of people, crossroads, the river, the town in the early
years of the century, the bridge under construction. She read a
bit of the text:

In early 1906, William Wells finished his house atop the west-
ern bank of the Overton narrows which was destroyed by fire
in 1917. A year later, he began construction on the steel bridge
we still use today. From the bridge's completion in 1909 until
the youngest Wells daughter was sent to the Sherman State
Mental Hospital in 1923, the Wells family collected a 5 cent toll

from vehicles coming and going. No one ever knew how much they made from it.

"This is wonderful," Nina said, laughing quietly, surprised to feel herself laughing, to feel relieved because of it.

"Why don't you take it home with you?"

"Thanks. I will," she said, flipping the pages again.

Bill lit a cigarette and the inhalation seemed to scrape his lungs. "There's even something about Rick's boy's death in there," he said, his voice raspy with the smoke.

Nina felt her brain finally putting a few things together. "Your friend Rick. He's Rick Beecher, isn't he?"

Bill nodded and took a long drag off the cigarette, but when he started to cough again, he crushed it out. "That's him," he barked between coughs, his eyes tearing before he could stop. "The one and only. And a true friend to me too," he said, wiping the tears from his cheeks. "Better than I deserve, probably." He got up slowly from the table. Nina didn't remember him moving with so much difficulty last time she saw him. "How about a cup of coffee?"

"No. Thanks, Bill. I'm not going to stay long."

"That's what you keep saying, but there's evidence that you're still here." He caught Nina's eye for an instant.

"Okay," she said. "Some coffee would be nice."

Bill nodded, smiling, and turned to the task.

Nina took off her coat and hung it over the back of her chair. Bill would see it as evidence of her willingness to stay. But she wasn't sure. Maybe it was only evidence of her unwillingness to go back to her house, where she would go over and over last night's phone call with Tony, trying to hear something in his voice, some evidence of what she needed to believe: that when he'd said he would be coming home, he'd meant it.

"They're going to call Rick's grandbaby Wayne," Bill said, filling a kettle with water. "They've been waiting all these years for another boy to come along in that family and take the name."

"Rick did seem very happy this morning."

"Well, he deserves it."

Bill's back was turned to Nina and she watched him closely: the tenuous work of his hands as he made two mugs of coffee; the effort it took him to get the refrigerator open; the way he smelled the carton of milk before putting it on the table. He seemed so harmless.

"You never told me whether you still think Lilly had something to do with Wayne's death," Nina said quietly.

Bill began to shake his head. "No," he said. "I never did." He lowered himself carefully into the chair. "You know what I think about that, Nina?" He pushed one of the mugs across the table to her. "I think I was so mad at Eva, I got mad at her daughter too. That girl was no worse than anybody else."

Nina made little attempt to hide her surprise. "It sure didn't sound that way when you told me the story."

"No, I guess it didn't."

"Why?"

"I don't know. Maybe because what I think now didn't come to me till many years later. Almost doesn't seem like part of the same story."

And you don't seem like the same man who told it, Nina thought.

"Same thing with my living here. Like a different story altogether."

Another story. Nina found herself plainly wanting to hear this one. "How did that happen?" she asked, lifting her cup halfway to her mouth. "You and Eva hated each other, didn't you?" She sipped the coffee: it was lukewarm, weak.

"Well, we did and we didn't, I guess, and after I left the second time I didn't come back till about six years ago, so there were a lot of years for us to cool off toward each other." He began to reach for another cigarette, but stopped short of the pack.

"Why did you come back?"

"Joe died." He nodded his head, his gaze cast down. "He'd been living in my mother's house, and someone had to take care of things. My sisters were useless, so I had to do it myself."

"And your mother?"

"She was dead already," he said, and then anticipated her next question: "I missed her funeral. I missed Joe's too." He took the cigarette and lit it, blowing the smoke out slowly, as if that might prevent a cough, which it did until the last moment. "It always seems to be death gets me back here," he said after he caught his breath. He spooned some coffee into his mouth. Nina wondered if she was asking too many questions.

"What was I talking about?" he said suddenly.

"Coming back here after Joe's death."

"Right. Right." He waved his hand in front of his face, the cigarette leaving trails of smoke and ash. He nodded a few times, and Nina was just about to say she should probably be going when he started to talk again. There was immediately some of the same determination in his voice that she had heard three weeks before—he would tell this story, he would get through it to the end—but it seemed focused inward now rather than at her, making it possible for her to listen rather than demanding that she did.

He told her how Eva had showed up at his mother's house one afternoon: just knocked on the door and walked in. And then stopped in her tracks when she saw him. He knew he'd aged a lot—the back injury five years before that had made it impossible for him to work on the rigs, the emphysema getting worse and worse—but the look on Eva's face had almost frightened him. She looked a little worse for the wear herself, and somehow that silent exchange had allowed them to settle in with each other without having to drag up the past.

They sat at the dining room table, one of the few surfaces not piled high with papers and magazines, pieces of hardware, empty cigarette packs—"Your brother always was a slob," Eva said—things that had just kept piling up as Joe got sicker, weaker, more obstinate about not letting anyone come in to help him. It was so bad, Bill found he was longing for the fastidious grime of the house under his mother's care, though he hadn't done anything about it in the few days he'd already been back.

It took Bill and Eva a long time to catch each other up. Bill insisted he had little to tell, but he told it slowly, testing with every sentence how much he actually wanted to reveal and then going a step further. He told Eva about the long stretches of work, in Venezuela mostly in the last years, and the layoff periods, living well off the wages he'd pulled in, saving nothing. He never remarried after Rose, and never saw her. His kids, all in their thirties now, wanted little to do with him—he'd never met any of his six grandchildren, if that was still the count. His kids hadn't wanted anything to do with him when he asked for their help after the injury either. He'd been angry then, but now he didn't blame them. He'd hardly been a father to them. What did they really owe him? He'd worked in a bar for a while in Seadrift, the small Gulf coast town in Texas where he'd settled after getting out of the hospital, but the injury made it hard for him to stand for long periods of time. So he collected SSI and his pension. Went fishing once in a while on the Gulf, though it was nothing to taking a bass or shad out of the river in Overton. He'd decided it was time for some education and started reading histories: the Durants, first volume to last, American history, biographies of presidents. He'd always known he didn't know much, but he'd never realized before how much he didn't know. He just figured it was a case of better late than never, especially since the emphysema was getting worse more quickly now. He was scheduled to see the doctor again when he got back to Texas, though there wasn't much to be done—"You might stop smoking," Eva said—and it meant he had to drive all the way to Houston from Seadrift, a good two hours.

Eva talked about her sons and their families; about her second, current, problematic marriage; the closing up of the farm, the apple trees she'd finally planted on her husband's place thirty miles south. She told stories about people Bill knew: who had died, married, had children, grandchildren, who had suffered from what misfortune. But she never talked about Lilly. Bill was glad at first: he'd be just as happy to never revisit that moment in his life. But it seemed odd that Eva would maneuver so completely around her daughter, and eventually his curiosity overwhelmed his reticence.

"You haven't mentioned Lilly," he said. "How come?"

Eva's gaze traveled around the room as if it were looking for a way out. Finally, she let herself look at Bill. "Things went bad between us. I kicked her out of the house when she was eighteen. Well, she was already on her way out, really." She looked down at her hands, folded on the table. "I just moved things along a little."

"What happened?"

"She wanted me to take in the boy she was seeing. Except he wasn't a boy. He was in his twenties"—that guy with her at the bar, Bill remembered, running after the car, following me even after I'd lost him—"but he acted like a kid. Couldn't keep a job. Couldn't keep his hands off my daughter. Even with me in the room. Ate like a pig. Never cleaned up after himself, and I was supposed to take him in." She leaned onto her elbows and let out a breath laden with old anger. "Lilly wasn't happy with my decision and some things got said that you don't expect to hear between a mother and daughter." She moved her gaze out the window. "We stopped talking for a good five years. But then she had her babies and I guess that softened her a little."

"Where's she living?"

"In Rowman. But all these years later we still don't see each other much. Some things never got back to normal between us. But she keeps in touch with her brothers pretty good and they tell me what's going on with her." She moved her hand over the surface of the table. "I don't see her kids as much as I'd like though."

She stopped talking for a minute and Bill didn't interrupt the silence. "She wasn't as bad as I thought she was then," Eva went on. "I think she was always looking for a man to take care of her to make up for the fact that she had no father to speak of." Eva rubbed her hand hard against her forehead. "I mean, it may

not be an excuse but it's a reason. At least there was some reason for the way she behaved. Which is more than I can say for
myself."

"That was as close as she came to saying anything about what
happened between us," Bill said. "But by that time I'd pretty
much stopped thinking she was all to blame. I wasn't expecting
an apology."

"And nothing more about Lilly?" Nina asked.

"Not a word. I don't think Lilly ever said anything to Eva
about what happened at the bar," Bill said. "It's more than I
would've expected of her. Though the truth is I didn't know her
well enough to expect anything. Good or bad."

"Does she still live in Rowman?"

"Yeah. I see her sometimes in the grocery store. She looks
right through me." He lit a cigarette. The cabin had filled with
smoke. "On the other hand, maybe she doesn't know it's me. I
didn't always look like this," he said, leaning back so Nina could
more easily see his sunken chest, and perhaps the greenish yellow cast to his skin, and below it, to where his organs were fail-
ing in a wash of weakening blood.

Bill began to cough and crushed out the cigarette. "Anyway,
Eva offered me the cabin because I had no place to be really. I
didn't want my mother's house and Eva could tell I had no heart
for going back to Texas. Said she needed a caretaker for the farm."
He shifted in his chair and turned to look at the photograph hanging above the table of himself, Eva, and Joe. "I knew she was just
taking pity on me, with me being so sick. But everything that happened in the past finally seemed too long ago to matter." He

turned back to face Nina. "Or we were all so different. Or dead." He laughed quietly to himself. "It couldn't matter anymore." He looked around the cabin. "Anyway, Eva did right by me. Not that I really deserved it. And here I am, someone's pity my livelihood, and me bothering my only close neighbor with all the gory details." He let his gaze come to rest slowly on Nina.

"I don't think bother is the right word," she said, though she couldn't think of what the right word would be. Bill's story had certainly gotten into her, but she'd begun to think it had only very little to do with him. "So what can I get you at the store?"

"Well, I'm thinking," Bill said. He gently pulled the book out of Nina's hand and put it back inside the paper bag. "I'm thinking I really don't need anything." He pushed the bag back toward her.

"Are you sure?"

"Yeah. I think I'm set."

"Well, if you think of anything, you should let me know."

"Will do."

They sat for a moment without speaking. Nina began to gather her coat around her.

"You and Tony have been away a lot lately."

"Yeah, we have."

Bill nodded slowly. "So you missed the breakup on the river?"

"Yeah, I did. Was it dramatic?"

"Not really," he said, his voice pitched low. "I was surprised, considering how long the river was frozen. But it was almost gentle. There was nothing more than some cracking I heard in the distance early in the afternoon that first day it got into the forties. But then a couple hours later I saw all the ice riding the water." He pushed himself up from the table. "I guess I was hoping for something with a little more punch this year."

When Bill opened the cabin door for Nina a few minutes later, they could hear the river in the distance—a steady ribbon of sound—and when she looked toward it, she could see light breaking up and scattering along the riverbed.

•   •   •   •

Bill died two months later, early in June. Up until a few days before his funeral, it looked as if he would be buried in a cardboard casket: his children wouldn't spring for anything else. Eva was so appalled that she went house to house along Riveredge Road to collect money for a pine box. Nina gave her forty dollars but couldn't tell from Eva's reaction whether she thought Nina was being generous or stingy. Eva's expression seemed to accuse Nina of not feeling sad enough, but, of course, Eva's expression could have meant many things at that moment.

Nina had visited Bill in the hospital once before he died. He'd been breathing through an oxygen mask, which didn't appear to make the process much easier for him. His skull seemed just barely sheathed by skin; his hands especially long and fragile, every knuckle a knot. The sheet revealed the frailty of the rest of his body. Nina could hardly look at it. She could see that Bill knew he wouldn't be leaving the hospital. It was the clearest thing she'd ever been able to read in his face.

She said she had a story to tell. He nodded and closed his eyes. Nina thought she could see through the lids to the dark irises, which she imagined watching her as she began to speak.

Three days after he went into the hospital, she told him, she'd seen the bees swarm from the hive in Eva's wall. It had been about eleven in the morning, and she was in the vegetable garden, the one he'd seen her dig and fence in a few weeks back. "Fixing to feed the deer?" he'd said, walking across the road to sit on her stone wall, smoking, watching.

On the afternoon she saw the bees, she'd been turning manure into the garden. It was hot, she was working mindlessly, focused on the mechanics of her arms and back, and on the way the ground seemed to resist being helped. The air was still, there were no cars passing, the birds were quiet in the heat, but it took her a while anyway to hear the hum: insistent and pulsing, and once she was listening, amazingly loud. She knew immediately what it was though she'd never heard it before. Bill had left that sound in her head and it was only a matter of the impression finding its like in reality to let her know what she wasn't aware of knowing: that the bees were swarming, coming out from behind the loose clapboard on Eva's house, out of the hive, the honey wall, by the tens and hundreds.

She'd walked along the edge of the stone wall toward the sound. The two maples in Eva's yard hid the chimney from her view, but Nina kept her eyes on the spot where she knew she would see the swarm eventually. The sound grew louder with every step she took, but no less hidden, until, suddenly, the trees seemed to move out of her way, and she could see the bees, her eyes drawn up along the length of the funnel they formed—Bill had called it a tornado—impossibly high and dense.

The clapboard outside the entry to the hive was just as he'd described it: so solidly black and moving that the bees might have consumed the clapboard and replaced it with themselves, the way she could imagine they had replaced the framework of the inner wall with the honeycomb, as if they had the power to make something inanimate come alive. She remembered Bill telling her what one beekeeper had told Eva: that she shouldn't try to have the colony moved, because once the bees were gone, and the honey was no longer cooled by the action of their wings, it would begin to ooze out of the comb and could take the wall with it. There were so many bees out of the hive at the moment Nina was watching, it seemed possible that the honey might begin to ooze just then anyway, some remnant of it from Bill's days helping to soften the wall, the wall that he'd said seemed to soften behind Eva's back when he leaned against her there.

While Nina watched, the funnel started to break down, more and more of the bees making erratic patterns between points she couldn't decipher. Bill had described that behavior as anger or desperation, but Nina thought she saw perfect instinct in it. Like she saw in Bill, pressing Eva against the wall, imagining the honey around them as if it were part of them. Nina thought of him then: young, handsome, and for those moments, living only through his senses, amazed to feel how they could all be satisfied at once. How could anyone have resisted that?

She kept watching the bees, but their flight was just vague patterns finally and her mind had filled with precise images: she'd appropriated Bill's story and leaned herself into the honey wall, moving her leg up the side of his until it rested on his hip, so he could do nothing but follow her deeper into the wall. His eyes were twenty years old and she held their gaze, making sure he didn't close them. She wanted him to watch her, to see what he was there for. And then it wasn't him so much as someone else. Which didn't matter. Being there at all, with anyone, was unthinkable, and perfect.

Bill hadn't heard the end of the story. He'd fallen asleep. Nina supposed that was why she'd been able to tell it, even to herself.

A nurse had come in to tell Nina that visiting hours were over. She put the magazines she'd brought on the bedside table, touched Bill's hand—the skin was so cool—and left the room. On her way home she'd thought that she should have told him about the few thin ice slabs that were still lining the river: covered in dirt, insulated from the sun, holding out endlessly against the reality of the season, like the honey wall in the heat, fanned by thousands of delicate wings.

Tony didn't know yet that Bill had died. Nina would tell him when he came home again on Saturday.

Acknowledgments

For time and place in which to write, my thanks to the New York Foundation for the Arts, the MacDowell Colony, the Writer's Room, and especially the Blue Mountain Center (Harriet Barlow, Sis Eldridge, Sheila Kinney, Elise Kyllo, Diane McCane, Peggy Morrill, Ben Strader, and Sara Zimmerman). Thanks to my parents for their loving support; to my family of friends for all manner of sustenance; to Joe Connelly and Jenny Minton for invaluable early support; to Janice Goldklang for her wonderful generosity toward the book; to Jill Bialosky, for her belief in the book, and the gentle incisiveness she brought to bear on it; to my fabulous agent, Sarah Burnes, for everything she's done, and for the unfaltering intelligence, enthusiasm, and warmth with which she's done it all; and finally, to L.R. Berger, for her sustaining presence in the life of my work and in my life.